MAZUKI

EMI YUSA

# IS LIFE BEAUTIFUL?

McRonald's

THE DEVIL IS A PRISONER TO THE
HOURLY WAGE SYSTEM!

SHIRO ASHIYA

SUZUNO KAM

ALAS RAMUS

Life is beautiful.

CHIHO SASAKI

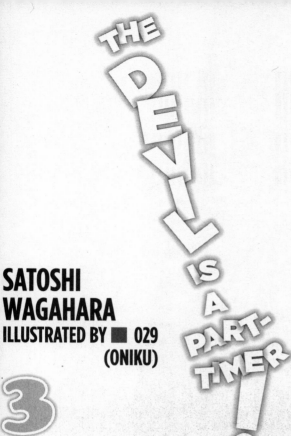

# THE DEVIL IS A PART-TIMER!

**SATOSHI WAGAHARA**

ILLUSTRATED BY  029
(ONIKU)

YEN ON

NEW YORK

THE DEVIL IS A PART-TIMER!, Volume 3
SATOSHI WAGAHARA, ILLUSTRATION BY 029 (ONIKU)

Translation by Kevin Gifford

HATARAKU MAOUSAMA!, Volume 3
©SATOSHI WAGAHARA 2011
All rights reserved.
Edited by ASCII MEDIA WORKS
First published in 2011 by KADOKAWA
CORPORATION, Tokyo.

English translation rights arranged with
KADOKAWA CORPORATION, Tokyo,
through Tuttle-Mori Agency, Inc., Tokyo.
English translation © 2015 Hachette Book
Group, Inc.

Yen On
Hachette Book Group
1290 Avenue of the Americas
New York, NY 10104

www.hachettebookgroup.com
www.yenpress.com

Yen On is an imprint of Hachette
Book Group, Inc.
The Yen On name and logo are
trademarks of Hachette Book
Group, Inc.

First Yen On edition:
December 2015

ISBN: 978-0-316-38502-2

10 9 8 7 6 5 4 3 2 1

RRD-C

Printed in the United
States of America

# INTRODUCTION

The western sun had sunk below the edge of the horizon, its light even now overrun by the faint purple of early evening.

Out in the prairieland a distance away from what was once a well-kept road, a diminutive shadow moved through the waist-high grass.

"Geez... I'd be there in a snap if I could fly."

The hazy shape griping to itself within the grass was a woman.

"Fly, and they'd find me. Walk, and they'd find me. Life can be a pain like that sometimes, huh?"

She proceeded warily, feeling out the way ahead while keeping her profile as low as possible.

Soon, she spied a wide wall made of roughly cut wooden planks, extending seemingly forever in either direction.

"My, someone's been working fast. It's only been just a little over a year, no?"

The woman arrived at a piece of that wall and spied crosses, made of five distinct parts fitted together, nailed to it haphazardly.

That was the emblem of the Federated Order of the Five Continents, modeled after a bird's-eye view of the world in which she lived: a large, central continent paired with a set of four satellite islands, each extending in a cardinal direction.

At one point, the Federated Order boasted the combined power of the entire human race, led by the Hero Emilia as she attempted to resist the Devil King and his force of marauding demons.

Now, though, the Order had been reinvented as an organization aiding the Central Continent's provisional government, as it struggled to rebuild in the wake of the demon hordes that had laid waste to the land.

The wall that spread before her, festooned with the crosses that served as the Order's symbol, was built to prevent entry to a certain location.

Even now, as the darkness gathered and descended upon the sky, the arcane presence of that "location" spread its black miasma to every corner of the island, despite remaining out of sight behind the wall.

Devil's Castle.

It was the domain and primary stronghold of Satan, the Devil King, ruler of the demonic forces that had once stormed across Ente Isla. The stories held that only three people had ever set eyes upon the castle and lived to tell the tale: Emeralda Etuva, Albert Ende, and Olba Meiyer—the three companions the Hero had taken on her quest.

After Emilia and Satan met their apparent demise battling each other, the Federated Order engaged in a large-scale mop-up operation to eradicate the remaining demonic armies from the Central Continent.

With both Satan and his lone surviving general, Alciel, defeated, the forces that once plunged mankind into untold misery were suddenly nothing more than a ragtag, rudderless rabble. It took a little over a year for the Order to eradicate the majority of them.

But there were still enough survivors in the Central Continent that small raids and other incidents were common occurrences.

The Federated Order of the Five Continents had decided that their final mission was the complete dismantling of Devil's Castle.

The Castle had been constructed on the site of Isla Centurum, once the land's largest trade hub. It had been a gleaming city that served as the central core of human civilization.

It appeared in a single night atop the shattered, conquered metropolis, and yet it projected a vast, majestic presence, far grander than the holy sanctuary of Sankt Ignoreido on the Western Continent or the ancient castle of Sohtengai that silently watched over the capital of the Eastern Continent.

Its inner construction was as vast as it was convoluted. Tongues wagged continent-wide about what could be found inside—the mountains of bones in the dungeons below, of the poor Centurumni offered as demonic sacrifice; the tainted souls that wandered the grounds nightly; the surviving demons that continued to inhabit its dark corridors...

Having such a frightening, eerie castle remain standing in the middle of the world was both a thought too ominous to consider and a serious blow to morale during the continent's recovery efforts. A sizable platoon of knights had broken into the castle relatively early on, keen to proceed with the demolition job as soon as possible.

But thanks to the continual rash of bizarre disasters and disfiguring plagues that befell these forces—not to mention the dogged resistance from the besieged demons that remained inside—the project faced interminable delays. The power vacuum that prevailed in the Central Continent post–Devil King also led to debate among Ente Isla's four islands over who should take the lead in reconstruction. Ultimately, the Order built the aforementioned wall around the castle to prevent entry, stationing knights around the perimeter and delaying demolition indefinitely until a political solution could be reached.

"Guess it's a blessing in disguise, though. If they just up and tore it down, I would've been screwed right about now."

The woman stood before the wall.

Double-checking to ensure no sentries were nearby, she leaped up. Without a moment's hesitation, she cleared the three-story wall in a single bound.

Her body glowed faintly as it arced through the air, providing much-needed light to the murky darkness.

Beyond the wall, she was greeted with an unbroken landscape of half-razed grasslands and half-scorched forests, making the hardscrabble path she took this far seem like a dutifully maintained high road. It was a world frozen in death, one without a single nocturnal bird or insect stirring.

She ran as quickly as she could through this surreal landscape, toward the center of the world.

Before long, a large, dark shadow grew visible in the air beyond.

A vast spire towered higher than any other castle in the world, as if daring to reach the heavens themselves, a spear at the forefront of the lair of demonic darkness that overshadowed the night ahead. But the woman seemed almost bored as she looked upward.

"Boy, talk about 'seen it all before.' Not a single bit of originality to it."

Soon, she was at the eastern gate of Devil's Castle, facing an entry-way large enough for a frost giant to step through without hitting his head. She glanced at the enormous gate's carvings, depicting large, eaglelike birds in a frozen state of blind rage, before briskly striding into the castle.

From the vast, abandoned corridor, pathways branched out like an ant's nest, linking to every nook and cranny of the castle. Without a moment's hesitation, she chose a single path and plunged forward.

The purple stone embedded into the ring on her left hand shone.

Once, the Hero Emilia and her companions followed the guidance of her holy sword to reach their ultimate destination, the topmost floor where their nemesis dwelled: the Devil King's throne room.

She wound through a long succession of corridors and terraces, so twisted that a typical explorer would lose all sense of up and down, left and right, along the way.

Soon, a full moon hung high in the air, illuminating Devil's Castle and the woman running through it.

There was no telling how much time had passed by the time she reached the masterless throne room.

It was decorated surprisingly sparsely, the scars from the Hero's battle still fresh against the walls and floor. She headed straight for the throne that used to strike fear into the hearts of thousands.

Behind it, a curtain hung silently.

"Ah..."

Behind that was a room.

It was just what she expected.

There was an enormous chest, likely meant for wardrobe pur-poses, its grotesque carvings worthy for the eye of the Devil King of another era. A tall bookshelf, one far too high for a person of normal height to fully access, stood against a wall. A single quill from some great, overgrown bird stuck out above a towering partner's desk that stood higher than the woman herself.

"There's nothing...here..."

There was not a single volume on the shelves. The chest, its lid wide open, eagerly collected dust, and no ink was available for the Devil King's favored quill pen.

But this was not the work of raiders or souvenir seekers. There was never anything here in the first place.

"...I wonder where you went wrong."

She whispered it somberly to herself, then walked across the empty room, opening a large courtyard window to let the moonlight inside.

A terrace lay beyond the paneless window frame, facing southward.

"Found you!"

The terrace housed something resembling a home garden, albeit much larger. Several potted trees were lined in careful rows, dignified in the moonlight.

Branches from two of them had grown entangled over time, creating a single, odd-looking growth.

"Wish they could've been a little more careful, though. This stands out far too much."

The woman smiled wistfully and brought her left hand up, facing the strange, tangled tree.

The purple gem on her ring glowed as it absorbed the moonlight. Then, the tree began emitting a dim light.

Soon, a glowing ball emerged between her hand and the tree. The ring's light fizzled, and the tree, so vividly alive and basked in light a moment ago, crumbled apart like a pile of ash.

"You raised her well. *Very* good."

She smiled at the floating ball of light, paying the ruined tree no further mind. Suddenly, her sharp gaze turned toward the eastern sky.

"!!"

In the moonlit air, five twinkling points of light floated above, arranged in a neat row.

"Noticed already, huh? That was fast. You must be getting desperate. I should've guessed."

Embracing the ball of light, she quickly returned to the room.

"Oh, well. If worse comes to worst, I've got a general idea of where he is. It's his job to raise it. It's time he kept his side of the bargain."

The ball pulsated warmly, as if responding to her words.

"So the chase begins anew, does it? Hopefully you've been polishing your skills a little over the past few centuries, Gabriel."

There was a twinge of excitement in her voice as she disappeared into the Devil's Castle darkness.

The second moon that governed the skies of Ente Isla had only just appeared in the eastern sky, behind the five twinkles looming over the terrace.

By the time the five meteors reached the castle, the moons—one blue, one red—were lined up together.

And by then, the faint light that enveloped the woman as she crept through the castle was a distant memory.

THE
DEVIL
KING
AND
THE
HERO
UNEXPECTEDLY
BECOME
PARENTS

Well-polished gears groaned to life in a room that smelled of machine oil and metal.

The power was enough to spring the connected drive-train system to full initial power, its state-of-the-art gear control allowing for flexible drive operation.

Its performance was aided by the buffed, sparkling framework that formed the body. It was lightweight, but remarkably sturdy.

It was also outfitted with a full line of safety features. The front safety flashers were automatically activated by optical sensors, and an audio warning device allowed the operator to immediately inform others of the vehicle's position. The reflector plates facing all sides were also standard equipment, providing vital support for unexpected enemy ambushes.

Yet despite all of this hands-on functionality, the vehicle lost nothing in terms of transport capacity and driver comfort.

The seat was upholstered in leather. In addition to the large-capacity container on the front, several optional freight-storage units were bolted on to the sides, ready for use.

"Whaddaya think? That's everything on your list, right there."

A man in a greasy workman's jumpsuit pointed at the vehicle, his voice full of confidence.

"...Lemme try it out before I say anything."

Another man, younger, shook his head, his face stern. The machine oil mechanic fired back.

"Yeah, I thought you'd say that. It's fully machined and ready to go—I did all the fine-tuning myself. It'll put up with whatever you put it through for at least the next hundred years, yeah?"

He crossed his arms, as if challenging his partner to defy him.

"I'll be holding you to that." The young man grinned as he climbed onto the pilot's seat. "Whoa... Dang."

The workman flashed a grin of his own as the young man voiced his approval.

Toward the side, someone muttered to herself sullenly:

"...How longer must we perpetuate this charade?"

The young man paid the commentary no mind as he brought both hands to the steering wheel and stomped down on one of the two pedals.

As he did, he let out a whoop of pleasure.

"Whooaaahh! Wow! It's so light! I can't believe how light it is with this gearshift!"

The young man, pumping the gearshift to and fro as he navigated out of the maintenance garage, gleefully shouted to no one in particular.

"This is *awesome!*"

"Thank ya much, Maou! And I'll cut you a deal, too. How does 29,800 yen sound?"

"Sweet, Mr. Hirose! She's got the money for you. You got it ready, Suzuno?"

The young man called Maou tilted his head toward the woman sitting on a folding chair near the wall of the garage, her puffed-cheek insolence ill-befitting her traditional Japanese kimono.

The oil-stained man raised his eyebrows as he turned toward her.

The girl Maou called Suzuno took a crepe-fabric purse out from the goldfish print tote bag in her hand, a look of utter chagrin on her face.

"Mr. Shopkeeper, was there any manner of meaning behind your conversation just now?"

Hirose, owner of the Hirose Cycle Shop in a shopping arcade on Bosatsu Street—just five minutes' walk from the Keio Sasazuka station in Tokyo's Shibuya ward—removed the towel wrapped around his head and laughed heartily as he wiped the sweat off his brow.

"Hey, it's just part of the package, ya know? Part of the package. You really gonna pay the tab this time, though? Ya seeing Maou right now or something?"

The girl's facial muscles visibly tensed at the question.

"I would like you to refrain from such jests. Circumstances beyond my control are forcing me to pay this bill. Sadao, would you stop cavorting like a child? Return here at once so we can complete whatever antitheft paperwork we need."

"All right, all right."

Sadao Maou returned to the garage, grinning from ear to ear, riding his mint-condition, gleaming, high-end urban bicycle.

It was a Stonebridge citybike with six gears, perfectly attuned to Maou's needs. Reflector panels had been installed in all directions over its aluminum frame, and the front light was programmed to flash automatically in the dark.

"Twenty-nine thousand, eight hundred yen for the bicycle, three hundred yen for the antitheft registration... Ah, you don't have to worry about the last hundred. Thirty thousand works for me."

"I appreciate the gesture."

Suzuno unfurled three neatly folded ten-thousand-yen bills and presented them to Hirose.

"Thank you much! Say, while you're here, are you in the market for a bike at all, ma'am?"

Suzuno shook her head at the suggestion.

"I will pass for now, thank you. I have yet to undergo the relevant drilling."

"The rele-what?"

She continued in a wholly deadpan manner to the confused Hirose.

"I understand that although no licensing procedure is required, one must undergo a process of education that involves the use of a support device known as 'training wheels.'"

Maou pictured the compact, kimono-wearing Suzuno pumping away at a child-sized bike with training wheels attached. Perhaps some pony decals and handlebar streamers would be involved. He had to resist busting out in laughter. "That could be pretty cute, actually, huh?"

Suzuno glared a bit at Maou. "Honestly... Mr. Shopkeeper, I would have the receipt, please."

"Oh? Uh, sure. I'm gonna have to handwrite one, if that works for ya. Hang on while I find my receipt pad."

"If you could make it out to 'Sankt Ignoreido Co., Ltd.,' I would appreciate it."

Maou was the only one of them who expressed clear surprise.

"Whoa, is that...?"

But Hirose paid it no special mind as he filled out the receipt and ripped it off of the pad.

"And there you go. Thanks again! Take good care of that thing for me, Maou. It's a gift, I guess, yeah?"

"Um, yeah..."

Waving at Hirose as they put the bicycle shop behind them, Maou and Suzuno walked side by side as they headed toward the apartment building they each called home.

Maou almost skipped as he giddily walked along, shiny new ride in hand. In Suzuno's was a summer parasol, protecting her face against the pounding summer heat.

"Hey, like, what're you even gonna *do* with that receipt, anyway?"

"If I retain a full account of my monetary resources here, I may be able to receive the equivalent amount back in the future, once I am finished with slaying you."

"Oh, you're gonna report to the Church that the Devil King you were sent to kill bummed a bike off you instead?"

Suzuno glared from underneath her parasol.

"I would be happy to spread the word far and wide across the Church that the Devil King is a vile, conniving demon, one not even beneath begging a Church official for a bicycle."

"Hey, you know how politicians and stuff like to pretend they're all 'of the people' and like that, right? I don't see what's so wrong about *me* doing that. Gotta prove that I got my finger on the pulse of the common man, you know? Plus, for me, it's not even some fake act I'm putting on."

As the Devil King of the People bragged about his environmentally conscious (if dirt-poor and, indeed, conniving) lifestyle, he turned around to peer into a shop he almost walked right by.

"Hang on, Suzuno. I wanna hit the stationery store."

Hitching his new bike at the side of the road and locking it up tight, Maou went into the small shop. The retail space was devoted more to cheap candy and kids' trinkets than pens and paper, but Maou's purchase was purely stationery, although still enough to make Suzuno tilt her head in confusion.

"What do you need glue for?"

"Hee-hee! How nice of you to ask. Behold!"

With a greasy grin, he fished a small, red plastic plate from his pocket.

"This is a reflector plate from my beloved Dullahan. The one you crushed into a pulp, if you recall. I pried it off after the cops called me over to haul it away. Kind of a memento, you know?"

As he spoke, he used the glue to attach the piece to the shining metal bike basket.

"With this, the soul of Dullahan, the noble steed who gallantly abandoned his life to protect his master, shall survive into the next generation! From this moment forward, you shall be named Dullahan...*II*!"

"...How exciting."

Having an affinity for one's accoutrements was hardly unusual, but a grown man giving a name to his mode of transport—his bicycle, no less—in this day and age was a pitiable occasion for anyone unlucky enough to witness it.

"Are you quite ready then, Devil King? We should go."

That went double when the man in question was Satan, the Devil King, mortal foe of all mankind.

The girl who went by the name Suzuno Kamazuki in Japan sighed a deep sigh as she proceeded on, not bothering to wait for Maou's response.

The clean, clear-glass hairpin stabbed into her hair shone a bright white in the afternoon summer sun as she dejectedly walked ahead.

✳

Satan, the Devil King. That was the name awarded the demon who mounted an attempt to conquer the faraway world of Ente Isla.

Sadao Maou. That was the name of the young man living a shade away from downtown Tokyo, working an hourly fast-food job to keep himself fed.

No one, neither man nor god, could ever have conceived of the bloodthirsty, ambitious Devil King going from world domination to eking out a part-time living in the Sasazuka neighborhood of Shibuya ward, Tokyo.

It had been just over a year since he was defeated by the Hero Emilia Justina, and thrown into the alien world of "Japan."

He lived in Room 201 of Villa Rosa Sasazuka, a wooden apartment complex built sixty years ago in this neighborhood. The hundred-square-foot, single-room rental served as his temporary Devil's Castle as Satan attempted to achieve independence through low-wage labor, even though the past few months had proven rather frantic for him.

The first year was a constant battle with poverty and disaster, but he nonetheless devoted himself wholeheartedly to his work on a daily basis.

Then, nine months ago, he found a long-term gig at the MgRonald restaurant situated in front of Hatagaya station, a single stop from Sasazuka. After that—in no small part thanks to being blessed by a talented, fast-track manager—he finally began to find some sem-blance of stability in his life.

This humdrum routine began to rip at the seams the moment the Hero Emilia, still chasing after the escaped Devil King, appeared before him under the guise of "Emi Yusa."

Whether Maou's completely lawful, high-fructose-corn-syrup-heavy lifestyle could really be described as a "humdrum routine" for a bloodthirsty space alien demon was a matter for debate, but that can be discussed later.

Regardless, there was no doubt that "rip at the seams" is an apt way to describe what happened next, what with one of his ex-generals attempting to assassinate him and the Hero herself being double-crossed by the humans allegedly supporting her.

But once it all passed and normalcy returned to his life, it was back to his old Joe Shmoe job, back to three meals a day and a warm floor to sleep on. Maou devoted all the strength he had to keeping this status quo…well, the status quo.

Even when the Hero took the train three stops down in order to gripe at him on his doorstep, even when a chief cleric from the Church on Ente Isla moved in next door in an attempt to poison him with her allegedly demon-poisoning sacrosanct food, the Devil King stuck to his daily routine, doing what he believed necessary to jump-start his goals of world domination.

Living a sound personal life, and faithfully building up his rep-utation in hopes of climbing the MgRonald corporate ladder, was what Maou believed would propel him once again to the throne of overlord.

✳

After Suzuno Kamazuki—known on another world as Crestia Bell, chief of the Church's Reconciliation Panel and a girl currently attempting to poison the Devil King by being his private chef, to little effect—destroyed his bicycle, Maou made her pay restitution for it, exaggerating a great deal of its feature set in the process.

She still looked peeved as they walked along, not entirely convinced Maou was dealing fairly with her.

"...Did that, uh, cost more than you were expecting?"

Maou tried to get back on Suzuno's good side, even though the woman had pulverized his bike and attempted to kill him not long ago. Suzuno opted against returning the gaze, sighing listlessly under the parasol.

"I think I am beginning to understand why Emilia allows you such leeway in this world."

"Oh?"

"Are you on friendly terms with the owner of that bicycle shop?"

"Yeah. ...Well, not really at first. We both met when we kept volunteering for neighborhood cleanup duty. But his wife liked taking their kid over to MgRonald a lot. We've kinda come to know each other a lot more since."

The friendship, as Maou described it, couldn't have been more run-of-the-mill. Turning a street corner to duck into the shade, Suzuno sighed—partly in relief that she escaped the sun, partly due to a sinking sense of disillusionment.

"I had resigned myself to my fate once you said we were traveling to the bicycle shop today."

"What d'you mean by that?"

Suzuno removed a thick booklet from her tote bag and handed it to Maou.

"I am referring to the monetary figure that you, the Devil King, would attempt to extort from me. It sent shivers up my spine, to be frank, wondering what exorbitant sum you would ask for. I appreciated, after all, that I did owe you a substantial debt.".

Maou thumbed through the pamphlet with one hand. It was a bicycle catalog.

"'Mountain bike,' 'road'—no, 'load cycle'? Or even one of those wilderness galloping BM-whatevers! I was perfectly expecting one of those to come my way!"

"...You don't have to pretend you know anything about bikes, Suzuno."

"Diligent study is the key to life itself! My point is that, even with the antitheft registration, it was...*disarming* to be asked for only thirty thousand. I had withdrawn two hundred thousand yen from the bank earlier."

"Look, did you seriously think someone living in abject poverty like I do would ask for a top-of-the-line bike model? The Dullahan you destroyed goes for 6,980 yen brand-new at the Donkey Hottie Discount Store over in Hounancho."

Maou tossed the brochure back as he boasted of his cheap spending habits. It only served to make Suzuno further disconsolate.

"The barbarous Devil King is given the chance to make a purchase with a human being's money. I would have expected anything and everything from you!"

"You could *try* trusting me a little, man. Or are you just that dead set on the Devil King being a total prick all the time? Besides, no offense to Mr. Hirose or anything, but he doesn't really deal in, like, Tour de France stuff."

Maou inserted an indifferent laugh midway. Suzuno looked up, a woeful expression on her face. She quickly turned back down, though, as Maou realized something and dared a look at her.

"But you withdrew two hundred thousand yen? You only just came here, you haven't worked a single day, and you got that much in your account? 'Cause, like, I've been working this hard and I don't think my balance has *ever* gotten past two hundred thousand."

"Well, unlike yourself and Emilia, I had the time to make ample preparations." Suzuno shrugged. She did not go into further detail.

Not long ago, she had ventured into Shinjuku for the first time with the Hero Emilia, known as Emi Yusa to most here. The precious gems and other relics she brought into Mugi-hyo, a well-known pawn shop in the neighborhood, fetched a price that would have made Maou's eyeballs pop out of their sockets.

She had zero intention, naturally, of informing the personification of evil living next door of the exact number, but it offered Suzuno enough freedom that she could enjoy several months of modest living going forward without having to find work.

"Huh. Well, neat. Better keep my pinkies up around you, I guess."

He pouted a bit as he spoke, but Maou's attention was still more focused on his bike. He rang the bell on it, like a child with a new toy.

"Anyway, though, thanks. I appreciate this."

"......"

Suzuno looked up at Maou and his unexpected words of gratitude. This time around, their eyes successfully met. She hurriedly used her parasol to shield her face.

The idea of evil incarnate so easily, guilelessly smiling and thanking people was nothing short of outrageous. In fact, when was the last time someone had offered *her* such meek and unadorned gratitude?

"I-it was restitution. And only that. It is now yours, and you may use it as you wish."

"Sure thing."

They walked silently for a few moments.

"D-Devil King?"

"Yeah?"

Suzuno, unable to remain silent for reasons she couldn't verbalize, stopped and pointed to her side.

"Wh-what is that? It seems that a great number of establishments have suddenly begun dealing in flowers."

She was pointing at the front door of a flower shop.

Bundles of unadorned white tree branches were lined up in the middle of the shop space by the dozen, pushing away the colorfully blooming flowers to the side.

"Oh, those? Those are *ogara* sticks."

"Ah, I see. So is that a dried version of the remnants you're left with after preparing tofu?"

"...What?"

Maou had difficulty understanding what Suzuno was talking about before realizing that they had just passed by a tofu and natto shop.

"Oh, uh... No, that's called *okara*. I'm talking about *ogara*. O-Ga-Ra. *Ogara* sticks, all right?"

Suzuno, a veteran officer serving the church's Department of Diplomatic and Missionary Operations, was pretty well acquainted with Japanese culture and customs for an Ente Islan.

In some ways, however, it often backfired. She had a habit of patching up holes in her knowledge with things she already knew about, which occasionally led to stumbles like her obsession over training wheels a few moments ago.

"Ah, right! Perhaps we could have some *okara* croquettes for dinner tonight."

"Jeez, Suzuno, what are you, some kind of housewife?"

"I have to hand it to the chefs and cooking experts of Japan. Croquettes are a wonderful cuisine indeed, but using the *okara* usually disposed of during the tofu-making process to create a lovely low-cost, low-calorie foodstuff was a stroke of genius!"

As Suzuno reflected on the origins of her upcoming dinner menu, a housewife stopped by the flower shop to pick up a bundle of *ogara* sticks.

"Look, the Obon holiday is coming up, yeah? Those *ogara* are used to light the *mukaebi* and *okuribi*, the fires that're meant to welcome in and see off the spirits of the dead that visit during the holiday."

Maou pointed at another bundle as he spoke.

"Obon... Ah, yes, the festival when families offer their respects to their ancestors, yes? But that begins in the month of August, does it not?"

When it came to religious customs, at least, Suzuno had done her homework.

"Yep. It used to be celebrated in the seventh month of the old Japanese calendar, which is August nowadays. But in the Tokyo area, people light those *mukaebi* fires to bring in the spirits in July. That's what those sticks are for."

"Hohh! I had thought this nation was rather secular by nature. Perhaps these traditions are more a part of the culture's fabric than I anticipated."

"But, why does the Tokyo holiday come sooner, then?"

"Well, there's a few different theories, but back when Japan switched to the Western calendar and the shogunate moved their ceremonies to the same dates in the new calendar, it was really just the Tokyo area that followed suit. The rest of the country didn't so much. Kinda weird to do things the same time for hundreds of years and then get told you have to start doing it some other time from now on, after all."

"I see. Interesting."

"Wowww..."

"Most people in Japan get time off of work around the middle of August for Obon, you know? But the government at the time had the strongest grip on power in Tokyo and part of the Kanagawa area, so only those parts switched over to the seventh month of the new calendar. Everyone else celebrated Obon the same time as before—the seventh month of the old calendar, or August."

"...You've done your research, I see."

"You sure know a lot for being Devil King and all, Maou!"

"Yeah, I kinda read up on that stuff last year. Not that it's much more than trivia these days, but...um?"

"Hmm?"

"Yes?"

Suzuno and Maou slowly turned around, both realizing their conversation had gained a stowaway passenger at some point.

"Aghh!! J-jeez, Chi, when did you show up?!"

"Chiho! Since when were you there?!"

Chiho Sasaki, Maou's coworker and the only Japanese person to know the truth about Maou, Suzuno, and the world of Ente Isla, was there in her prim school uniform. There was no way of telling how long she had been standing there.

She was carrying a silver-colored portable cooler instead of her school-issue bookbag.

"Did I surprise you?"

She smiled in triumph.

"I got you back for what you did to *me* before, Suzuno! ...Of course, all I got to hear was about how you were going to make *okara* croquettes for dinner, but…"

"Ohhh… Ha-ha! Neat. But you're out of school already? That's kind of early."

Chiho answered cheerfully: "It's all half-days 'til summer break. All our final exams are over, so…"

Come to think of it, it wasn't that long ago when Chiho was going on about this or that examination, although she never whined about her test scores or took special time off her scheduled shifts. The fact that her involvement in the vast conspiracy that seemed to be unfolding between Ente Isla and Earth didn't seem to affect her test performance at all made Maou wonder if she had nerves of galvanized steel.

As Maou pondered over this, Chiho's eyes turned downward.

"Ooh, new bike?"

"Yep. Suzuno kind of trash-compacted my old one."

He lovingly patted Dullahan II's saddle.

"The Devil King said he had found a worthy bicycle. I have merely paid for it." Suzuno spat out each word, trying to cover up her surprise at Chiho's sudden appearance. "But enough of me. What brings you here, Miss Sasaki?"

"Oh, I was about to buy just what you were talking about."

Chiho pointed between the two, toward the same flower shop as before.

"*Ogara*?"

"Yep! My mom asked me to. And I was planning to visit your apartment after that, so…"

She raised a shoulder upward to point out the portable cooler hanging from it.

"One of my dad's relatives gave us some ice cream, but neither of my parents have much of a sweet tooth. But we have a ton of it, so I thought maybe I'd give some of it to you guys."

"Ice cream?! Seriously?! Are you sure?!"

Maou's eyes gleamed. Something cold and sweet, tumbling down like manna from heaven!

"Man, that's awesome! We'll take it, we'll take it! Thank you so much!"

Chiho smiled, watching Maou all but leap into the air in joy.

"Oh, good! So give me just one second, all right? I need to buy that *ogara.*"

From the side, Suzuno watched the Devil King see the high schooler off.

"...Should I just leave him as he is? Would that hurt anyone?"

The doubts she had begun to feel recently slipped from her lips.

Shouts of glee soon echoed across the steaming Devil's Castle, a groaning fan stirring the acrid, spirit-draining midsummer air inside.

"Ice cream?"

"Ice cream?!"

Alciel and Lucifer, fellow Devil's Castle denizens and two of the Devil King Satan's former Great Demon Generals, gasped in excited surprise as Maou stepped in with Chiho.

"And...and, and it's a premium gift pack from Haggen-Boss?! Are—are you truly sure about this?!"

Chiho removed her shoulder-bag cooler and pointed it in Ashiya's direction. "Don't worry about it, Ashiya. We still have more than enough back at home."

Alciel, the resident accountant and housekeeper at Devil's Castle and a man who went by Shirou Ashiya more often than not these days, fell to his knees, the sight of the cooler seemingly framed by rays of brilliant sunshine.

"I...I could hardly begin to thank you and your parents enough, Ms. Sasaki..."

Ashiya bowed his head deeply, his tall frame almost kowtowing before Chiho. The sight was enough to fluster her.

"Ooh, wow, look at all the flavors in there! C'mon, Ashiya, let's do this! Get the spoons out!"

"Urushihara... You know there's something you need to say to Chi first."

To the scandalous youth whose eyes were already filled with nothing but the sight of frozen treats, Maoh spoke with scorn.

Hanzou Urushihara was the name adopted by Lucifer, the former general who now lived a leechlike lifestyle in Devil's Castle. As such, he paid his former master no mind.

"Oh, it's fine, Maou. I know how Urushihara acts by now."

Chiho's unhesitant castigation was delivered with a smile.

Thanks to her awareness of the truth behind Maou, and his cohorts, she had few good words for Urushihara, who had still been Maou's enemy when she first met him.

Even now, with him more or less back in Maou's demonic army, he rarely moved an inch from his computer, day after day, not even bothering to help with housework. The classic unemployed freeloader lifestyle, in other words, and Chiho was less than warm to it.

Maou smiled bitterly to himself and gave Chiho a light pat on the shoulder, diverting her attention.

"Yeah... Well, anyway, thanks. Really."

"...! Um...uh, yeah. Yeah. You're welcome."

The redness to Chiho's cheeks at that moment had nothing to do with the heat.

She had already publicly acknowledged her feelings for Maou. But since she didn't frame them in a way that demanded a response, the true nature of their relationship remained unclear, dangling in the air like flypaper.

This was something Chiho had made peace with. She understood, after all, that Maou wasn't the sort of man to give a response without applying serious thought to it first.

Little moves like these on Maou's part, however, were still enough to throw her off guard, sending her pulse skyrocketing at unpredictable times.

"Um... Oh! Oh! Suzuno, we should let Suzuno have some... Huh?"

Chiho attempted to call the presumably present Suzuno in order to cover up her blushing. But, even after sticking her head out the door and scoping out the hallway, she was nowhere to be found.

"You looking for her? She went right back out once we got here."

"Oh... Really?"

"Wow, strawberry, green tea, mint... Daaaaang, dude, is this pumpkin? Whoa!"

"Whoa whoa whoa! Save some for Suzuno, Urushihara!"

Chiho had to hurriedly rush back inside to keep Urushihara from claiming the goods for himself.

"Aww! Who cares about Bell, dude? Finders keepers, losers weepers!"

Urushihara was clearly peeved. Chiho puffed up her cheeks in anger as she plucked one of the several half-pint tubs of ice cream nestled in his arms.

"Either *she* gets some, or *you* don't get any! How many of these were you planning to eat, anyway? You're gonna get brain freeze!"

"Dude, I'm not a child, okay?! I'm, like, several million years older than you!"

"Years don't matter with you, Urushihara! You're still a child! Even a grade-schooler would be a lot nicer than you!"

"Guys, can you keep it down? It's too hot to be yapping at each other." Maou gently stepped in, picking up the cooler and handing it to Ashiya. "Let's just take one each and leave the rest for later, okay? Nobody's gonna mind if we give the vanilla to Suzuno, right?"

"Absolutely, Your Demonic Highness." Ashiya deferentially accepted the cooler, giving Chiho another respectful bow as he methodically stacked the cups in the freezer compartment.

"Oh, come *onnnn*. Just one?"

Urushihara pitifully mewled in protest, strawberry half pint still in hand.

"Why do we hafta leave any for Suzuno? She's our mortal enemy and stuff."

"U. Ru. Shi. *Haaaa.* Ra?!"

"Wh-what, Chiho Sasaki?! She's kinda *your* rival, too, dude! In a lot of different ways!"

The mostly dissipated warmth resurrected itself within Chiho's cheeks.

"Well...yes! She, she is! She's my rival, *and* my friend!"

She put as much firmness as she could into it.

"Huhh? What's *that* s'posed to mean?"

"I mean the rival thing's *one* thing, but the ice cream's *another*! That's why you're a child, Urushihara! You don't even understand *that!*"

"Oh, yeah, yeah, *I'm* the child and *that's* why it's all my fault, huh? No way I'd ever understand some crazy girl acting all jealous of—*oww!*"

Urushihara groaned at the sudden impact thudding upon his temple as he attempted to give Chiho his most finely honed, well-polished sass.

"That's enough, Urushihara! If you dare to pelt our kind and generous guest with any more verbal abuse, I'm confiscating that strawberry cup and canceling our Internet!"

Urushihara, teary-eyed, looked up at the goblin face of Ashiya from below.

"A demon like you, eating all our food, wasting all our money, not lifting a finger to help out around the Castle...I would put Crestia and the Church-anointed food she's poisoning us with over you any day of the week! And now you berate Ms. Sasaki, a walking saint who's provided nothing but support to His Demonic Highness and sincerely cares about the state of our Castle! The gods above may forgive you, but never shall I!"

The chief househusband of Devil's Castle kept Chiho behind her as he rained lightning downward.

Ashiya had been less than welcoming of Chiho's advances toward his demonic superior at first, but his suspicions had been thoroughly quelled by the cooking Chiho and her mother provided. Now he saw the Sasaki family as nothing less than the savior of their monthly budget.

Urushihara's face twitched beneath Ashiya's withering rage. He took a step backward.

"A-all right, all right... Man, that teenage girl's got you whipped. Maou, too."

One hand was to his head, the other still gently cradling the strawberry ice cream cup as he retreated back to his default position in front of the computer.

"Now then, Ms. Sasaki... Please, come over here. There's a bit more of a breeze closer in. I have some barley tea to drink."

Sitting Chiho down on the low table at the center of the room, Ashiya presented a Haggen-Boss cup and a glass of tea, adjusting the fan behind him to provide more relief.

The Villa Rosa Sasazuka apartments the Devil's Castle was currently situated within did not offer air-conditioning as a standard option.

It was possible for tenants to obtain permission from Miki Shiba, the building's landlord, to install a unit. Theoretically possible, at least. But Shiba was still out in the tropics somewhere, declining to offer any kind of return date.

Maou was motivated enough to investigate, given how (unlike last summer) he had a regular income to fund some AC with. He contacted the property management firm Shiba had left contact information for, but apparently she had never contracted this outfit for matters related to individual building maintenance.

In other words, the so-called property management guys could change the fluorescent lights that lined the hallway, but anything involving private tenant spaces had to go through the landlord first.

She had done so in the past. Take two months ago, when Shiba herself stopped by to discuss the earthquake-proofing work she had scheduled.

However, installing AC in Devil's Castle involved cutting a hole in the wall to connect the outdoor condenser with the indoor fan. That counted as making "major adjustments" to the building, apparently.

It was especially galling because, while Shiba was overseas somewhere, she was hardly in hiding. On regular occasions, she sent Maou letters describing where she was and what she was up to.

Said letters, though, were usually dated several weeks prior to when they finally reached Maou's mailbox. By the time a dispatch from one tropical paradise or the other arrived, she would already have moved on to her next idyllic retreat. Making contact was all but impossible.

And more to the point, neither Maou, nor Ashiya, nor Urushihara were willing to open her mail in the first place. They gathered dust deep inside the Devil's Castle's prefab shelving. The scars from the "landlord cheesecake pin-up massacre" that befell the trio not long after Urushihara arrived still remained embedded in their hearts.

Thus, the ex-demons had diligently ignored every piece of mail from Shiba until Suzuno moved in next door. Their new neighbor had given them a mouthful about this habit, bringing up the specter of Shiba sending them some sort of important notice and them remaining blissfully unaware. So, not too long ago, the gang decided to open up the most recent letter.

It was the same envelope as always, the gold-lined border giving it the air of contrived luxury. The address was written in an elegant hand using some sort of fountain or quill pen—a sight they were used to by now.

This time around, Maou's landlord was over in Indonesia. The cheesecake pin-up massacre had taken place in Hawaii, but she wasn't soaking up the rays on Bali or anything—instead, for motives and purposes that only Shiba could ever truly understand, she had traveled to the island of Borneo to join some spiritual ceremony held by the local indigenous people.

Swallowing nervously, Maou dared a peek at the photograph included. There was his landlord, wearing a highly conspicuous gold-and-silver-spangled dress and a broad-rimmed hat with several dozen colorful feathers jabbed into it like a mutant peacock's rear end. The inch-thick makeup, meanwhile, was a much more familiar sight.

At that moment, Maou instinctively knew there was no point trying to make contact with her. What happens, happens.

They survived the summer heat last year AC free, after all. Besides, they now had Urushihara, a walking, talking package of bad debt, pushing upon their budget.

Maou decided this was God's way of telling him that just because they had some monetary wiggle room didn't mean they could bust out the caviar. He did not ask himself why the revelations of an Earth-based deity should take precedence over the Devil King of a wholly unrelated planet.

"You know, I thought it would be hotter in here, but this apartment gets a pretty good breeze, doesn't it?"

"Yeah, I guess that kind of saves all our hides, huh? We got the corner room, so there's a few more windows than normal."

To keep the sun from directly beating down on their room, he had placed bamboo blinds (purchased at the Donkey Hottie shop in Hounancho, the birthplace of Dullahan I). All the windows were wide open, the fan deftly positioned to encourage proper airflow. This rewarded them with a draft, albeit a dank and muggy one. The fact that Villa Rosa Sasazuka wasn't adjacent to any nearby buildings, but was separated from them by a tiny, bare-earth front yard, no doubt helped.

"Maouuuu, are we really not gonna buy an AC unit this year?"

Urushihara, in contrast to Chiho as she enjoyed the summer breeze, had fallen into the depths of hell.

"I told you, man. We can't contact the landlord, and we can't afford to install it anyway. Besides, if we bought some cheapo AC, the electric bill next month would kill me."

"Barrrrfffff..."

"I'm not really a fan of air-conditioning myself."

Chiho chimed in as she methodically pecked at her rum-raisin.

"They have AC in the classrooms at school, but whenever we're done with gym class or whatever, someone always turns it, like, all the way down. It's freezing!"

"Indeed, the greatest achievements of civilization wield the power to destroy all of us. The mere thought of the electricity bill is enough in and of itself to send shivers up my spine!"

Ashiya voiced his agreement in a way only he could as he enjoyed his green tea ice cream.

"Yeah, I can totally picture the guy, too. Probably never shuts up, I bet, huh? Then, if you turn up the thermostat at all, he's probably like 'Ohhh, it's so hot, it's so hot!' and turns it back down the moment no one's paying attention."

Maou grimaced as he stabbed away at his Cookie Crunch.

"Yes! Exactly!"

Chiho nodded eagerly.

"I'm pretty familiar with guys like that. It's like their mind's always short-circuiting on them. They just want to satisfy their urges *right now* without thinking of the consequences. And they're *always* the biggest loudmouths, too."

"Right, right! Wait…"

"Hmm?"

Chiho suddenly realized something as she smiled in agreement.

"How do you know all that, Maou? You didn't actually go to school in Japan or anything, right?"

"Nope."

"It always seems like we've had a lot of the same experiences, but… you know, that's kinda strange when you think about it, right?"

"Yeah… I guess, so, maybe."

Maou scarfed down the last mouthful of Cookie Crunch. Standing up, he tossed the plastic lid and clear vinyl cover into the bin for burnable garbage, washed out the paper cup, flung it into the bag for recyclable papers, leaned against the sink, and sighed.

"I guess you could say demons have more…forceful ways of solving their problems. But stuff like that… I guess it's not much different between humans and us."

"……"

Ashiya listened on silently as Maou spoke.

"…Ugghh, one of those little cups isn't enough…"

Urushihara, oblivious to the conversation, placed his strawberry cup on the computer desk, his eyes greedily swiveling toward the refrigerator.

Just then, Maou's eyes pricked up.

"Oh? Hey, Suzuno, where'd you go? Chi wanted you to have some ice cream, too."

Maou spied Suzuno passing by the open kitchen window, carrying a set of large objects in front of her.

"Ah, my thanks to you. I will gladly partake of it once I am finished with this task."

They spoke between the iron bars that covered the window. Suzuno appeared to have something resembling a set of small, square logs in hand.

"...Hey, what's that?"

"Hmm? Logs. Why do you ask?"

"I can see that. I was asking what you're gonna do with it."

The reason why Maou was so insistently asking about his neighbor's possessions was that, in her opposite hand, she held far more *ogara* sticks than she had any business needing.

"As a member of the Church's Missionary Office, I have an interest in this Obon holiday. I decided it would be best to experience it for myself."

"...And?"

"And to begin with, I have to light the *mukaebi*, yes? And then the smoke from this fire will attract the spirits of one's ancestors back down to earth?"

Maou hung his head, his suspicions proven correct, before beckoning Suzuno inside through the bars.

Suzuno, brows knitted, nonetheless opened the door to the Devil's Castle.

"What? They say it is best to do the task while the sun is in the air, so I wanted to handle it as soon as—*ow!*"

Maou cut off Suzuno with a karate chop to her head.

"Wh-what are you doing?!"

"Are you trying to burn this apartment down?! 'Cause you've got *way* too much fuel for the job!"

Suzuno's eyes welled up as she fought back verbally, attempting to invent new and colorful words to criticize him with.

"I was hardly going to burn all of this! The logs are so that I can build a fire pit in the back garden! I am only going to burn this *set* of *ogara*, and... Ow! H-how dare you strike me while my hands are full!"

Maou unleashed his second karate chop.

"That's even worse! You *saw* Chi buy just one little bundle of them! And now you're building a fire pit in our yard?! How many ancestors're you trying to get over here?! You're not making a campfire!"

The parcel of land occupied by Villa Rosa Sasazuka was surrounded by a concrete-block wall. The yard, if it was large enough to call it that, was little more than a bare strip of earth.

Only a single hardwood tree dared to set root inside. Every year, an entire metropolis of cicadas set up shop amid its leaves, seeking refuge from the city's asphalt jungle and reciting their incomprehensible, screeching cacophony summer after summer.

"Hey, let's just calm down a sec, okay? I've got some vanilla ice cream for you, Suzuno."

"It shall be mine!"

If the Devil's Castle lacked AC, it was a given that Suzuno's room was no less scorching. That might at least partially explain why Suzuno leaped at the ice cream offered to her, topping it with some *kuromitsu* syrup and roasted soy flower from her room. She spent a moment to savor it before attempting to defend herself again.

"Well, how are you supposed to light a *mukaebi,* then?! As far as I saw in my research, there are monks that build these enormous fires! Vast pyres of flame, set ablaze in pits lined with straw from the *makomo* rice plant!"

There was no way to tell what kind of research Suzuno could have done in the short time after she returned from purchasing the bike. But, as always, it was off-kilter. She was describing far more elaborate Obon ceremonies, the type carried out at Buddhist temples and large-scale festivals.

"Ashiya."

"Yes! Right here."

With the snap of Maou's fingers, Ashiya went into motion, bringing out a clay dish, a lighter, and some twisted bits of newspaper.

"You can buy all this stuff at the hundred-yen store, by the way.

They throw in the newspaper for free to pack the dish in. This is a *horoku*, by the way, a clay pan you roast tea in."

Maou took a single bundle out of the pile Suzuno brought in and stepped outside the room.

"And the *ogara* here is ninety yen a bundle at the place Chi bought it from. So we're talking no more than two hundred yen for the whole thing."

Chiho and the crestfallen Suzuno followed Maou outside as he climbed down the outdoor stairway and placed the clay dish on the ground, near the front gate that faced the road.

Then, removing the bit of plastic that kept the bundle of *ogara* sticks together, he broke the longer sticks into smaller, more manageable sizes.

It took around two-thirds of the bundle to fill up the dish. Maou passed the rest to Suzuno, then lit a twisted bit of newspaper with the lighter.

Pointing it down toward the bottom, with several other paper bits nestled in to serve as kindling, he instantly set the *ogara* ablaze. Smoke lazily wafted above.

"...Ta-dah! That's the easiest way to light a *mukaebi*."

"...What?"

"By the way, if you live in a housing complex like this, make sure you do it outside, all right? Otherwise it might set off the smoke detector. Any questions?"

Suzuno's stare flip-flopped between Maou and the small fire on the dish, her eyes dubious.

"...Simply ridiculous. The *mukaebi* is a cherished family ceremony, meant to attract the souls of one's revered ancestors. You dare to call this simple, plain affair a ceremony?"

"Well, like, what do you want? I mean, this is kind of *it*, you know? Right?"

Maou looked to Suzuno and Chiho for support. Suzuno turned toward Chiho, hoping for a voice of reason to come to her side.

"It *was* kind of plain, yes, but there's nothing wrong with what he did. It's best if you can use a flame from one of the lanterns they put out for Obon, or from a temple dedicated to revering the dead, but that's easier said than done here in the city. Oh, also..."

Chiho hunched over the dish.

"You put your hands together like this, and then you pray for your ancestors to return home without getting lost."

"And…is that all?"

"That, and if you have a *butsudan*, those little shrines people have in their homes sometimes, you can make a little horse out of a cucumber and put it there."

"Oh, yeah, we make that every year at my place."

"Out…out of a cucumber? Wh-what in Heaven's name is *that*?"

Suzuno's eyes darted to and fro in confusion. Maou gave Chiho a glance, then chuckled a little.

"So when Obon is over, you have to build an *okuribi*, a fire to lead your ancestors' souls back to the afterlife. But one thing you do for the *mukaebi* is take a cucumber, stick some toothpick legs on it so it looks like a horse, and stick it in your shrine. That encourages your ancestors to ride it, so they'll come to the fire more quickly. Then when it's over, you make a cow for them out of an eggplant, and that way they'll ride that and go back a lot more slowly."

Maou explained this all as matter-of-factly as he could, Chiho nodding her agreement on every major point. Suzuno looked at one, then the other, then brought a hand to her temple and groaned.

"…I have encountered a vast range of religions in my time, but a ceremony like this one is rare. Never has something so simple seemed so complex to me…or vice versa."

"Well, if you wanted to get *real* with it, you'd do stuff like line up a bunch of candles down the road, or build a really big fire like you were trying to do. But here in the middle of the city, this is about all you're gonna get. Some Buddhist sects don't even do any of this, and besides, there aren't too many places around here we can go lighting fires. If you wanna see the whole shebang, you could always hit up one of the countryside festivals somewhere in August."

"Wow. You sure know your stuff, Maou."

Chiho's eyes were wide with surprise.

"Yeah, well, you should've seen some of the other crap I tried last year while I was trying to regain my demonic force. I was hoping maybe some demon would catch my *mukaebi* and come on down, for example."

Aha! *This* was the sacrilegious, ritual-defiling Maou Suzuno was more familiar with!

"But it's not like any of my ancestors are here on Earth anyway. Kind of a waste of a fire, you know?"

"You speak as if your ancestors would be awaiting you in your realm."

Maou winced at Suzuno's remark.

"Pft. D'you think the stork delivers demon babies to the underworld or something? I've got parents and family lines just like everyone else."

"Parents...? You?"

Chiho might have been aware of Maou's past, but it was tough for her to picture the concept of a Devil King having a Queen Mother.

"'Course, they're both gone now. So...like, if you're asking whether I wanna light a *mukaebi* and get 'em over here, honestly, I don't really care."

But there was something about the way he blurted out the words that made pangs of sadness blaze across Chiho's mind.

"Oh... Kind of a sad thing to say, though, just like that."

"Well, what, you think we're the kind of goody-goody demons who leave flowers on their family grave or something? Even if they *had* one, I'd have no idea where it is. I hardly even remember anything about my parents."

"R-really...? Um, I'm sorry. Maybe I shouldn't have asked."

"Nah, nah. *I'm* the one going on about it. Anyway."

Maou leaned down toward Chiho and the dish, fanning the flickering flame.

"Don't forget to take care of the fire once it's out. In the real ceremony, you're supposed to put it out with water droplets collected from lotus leaves, but you should still have a bucket of tap water handy just in case. You can toss the ashes into a potted plant or in the burnable garbage."

"...Hardly one iota of emotion to it, I see. I feel I've gained an insight into the spiritual contradictions that drive modern Japan."

"Hey, when in Rome. Think of it as me keeping an open mind, huh? Hey, you mind filling a bucket with water for me?"

Just as Maou gave the order:

"Hey! Maou!"

Urushihara stuck his face out the Devil's Castle door.

"We got trouble comin' on your six!"

"Trouble?"

Maou looked upstairs quizzically, only to hear:

"What kind of *trouble*, exactly?"

At the voice directly behind him, the lord of Devil's Castle convulsed in a full-body shudder.

It rang out loud and clear as Maou slowly, reluctantly turned around.

And there—

"Oh, good day, Yusa!"

"Ah, Emilia! Oh, is it that time already?"

There he saw the owlish face of Emi Yusa, better known in certain otherworldly circles as Emilia Justina, the Hero and savior of Ente Isla.

An unopened solar umbrella was in her right hand, her left holding up a paper bag with something heavy inside.

She leveled the tip of her umbrella at Maou, brushing him away as he looked up at Urushihara from downstairs.

"Lucifer! How did you know I was coming?! You didn't stick another one of your GPS transmitters somewhere, did you?!"

"N-no! Nothing like that! I just saw you in the camera I installed outside! Dude, chill out a bit, okay? We got ice cream!"

"I am as 'chill' as the coolest, freeze-dried, most ice-covered cucumber in the universe! And I'll be even 'chiller' once I've finally slain you all!"

"N-no, really! I'm not lying! Look!"

Urushihara darted back into the apartment, brought out a cup of ice cream and the hacked webcam he installed between the window bars, and waved both of them in the air.

"……"

Emi's eyes were attracted to the Haggen-Boss mint ice cream cup before the camera, but snapped out of it and turned sharply toward Chiho and Suzuno.

"Hey there, Chiho. Is that your ice cream?"

"Oh, uh, yeah. We got this huge gift set, but my mom and dad aren't into sweets at all."

"…Makes sense. Not like these vagrants would ever be ahead of the game enough to buy Haggen-Boss."

"Do you even realize how small that makes you look? Rating how successful a guy is by whether he buys dessert or not?"

Maou, to the side, complained loudly at this brutal treatment. Emi paid him no heed, taking out a handkerchief and dabbing her face with it.

"The mint-flavor Haggen-Boss is only sold as part of those gift boxes. You're never gonna see them individually. Boy, I can just *imagine* the tears of joy you all must've shed the moment Chiho gave that to you. I'm sure the demon realms would be shocked and horrified to see *that*, hmm? Whether you're Devil King or not, I wouldn't really call that 'ahead of the game.'"

"…I'm sorry, Maou. I can't really defend against that."

Chiho bowed her apology to him.

"…So are you just here to gawk at our abject poverty, or what? Sitting in your stupid air-conditioned office all day, your stupid air-conditioned apartment all night… You've got the biggest carbon footprint for a Hero ever!"

"Well, sorr-*ee*. The AC came preinstalled, so it'd be a waste not to use it, right? It's a pretty new energy-saving model, too, and I got it set to eighty-two degrees, no matter how hot it gets outside. I don't think *you've* got any right to complain."

"Ugh! Dammit! You're so obviously trying to lord it over me with your middle-class-ness!"

Maou stamped his feet, frustrated. Emi refused to engage him, turning toward Suzuno instead.

"Are you all set? Sorry I'm a little early."

"Ah, my apologies. Give me just one moment. I will make my preparations shortly."

Suzuno scurried off toward the stairway.

"Oh, wait. Before that…"

Stopped by Emi, Suzuno watched as she handed over her paper bag.

From the lip, she could see a box of energy drinks, a familiar logo stamped on top. Maou and Chiho had no way of being aware, but the boxes naturally contained the 5-Holy Energy β sent previously by a friend of Emi's from Ente Isla.

"Ah, yes… Is this the supply we discussed?"

"Yep. Two bottles per day, okay? These are valuable, so don't lose 'em."

"…What kind of secret smuggling operation *is* this?"

Maou dove into their hushed conversation over the paper bag. The two women both glared at him.

"Be *especially* careful with him."

"There is no need to remind me."

"Hey!"

Maou gritted his teeth at them.

"I don't remember doing anything that'd make you think I was gonna rummage through her stuff!"

"I think that would be one of the *least* despicable things you've ever done."

Emi's reaction was frigid. It had the intended effect on Maou.

"Despicable? How could you call me that? I made it up to assistant manager in less than a year!"

"I don't think that's what she's talking about, Maou."

Chiho's aside was just as cold.

"Are you going out somewhere with Suzuno, Yusa?"

"Mm-hmm. We're gonna look at some appliances and phones."

"Appliances and phones?"

"Indeed. It seems I am destined for an extended stay here, so I need to shore up the necessities of daily life, but it seems my pretrip research was a tad behind the times. I thought it best to have Emilia accompany me in case I should find myself at sea midway."

"Ohh, I get it."

On the one hand, Chiho was happy to discover her new friend wouldn't be leaving soon. On the other, the thought of a woman—the nemesis of her crush, in fact—living right next door to Maou indefinitely somewhat tempered her joy.

"Not that she'd have to stay if I could ever get around to slicing that destitute Devil King in two."

Emi, as if reading Chiho's mind, laughed impishly as she sized up Maou.

Maou erupted in a cold sweat, unable to discern how to respond. Chiho, looking on, was unsure whether Emi was joking or not.

"...Of course, I guess I already said I wouldn't be doing that anytime soon. And since I'm not the kind of Hero to break a promise, I'll just have to station her here until I figure out a Plan B, you know?"

"Uh...yes."

She wasn't joking at all. Chiho's response seemed drained of emotion.

"Ha-ha-ha! Oh, I'm sorry. It's all right. I'm not gonna do it right in front of you or anything, Chiho."

"...I'm a bit concerned about what you'll do when I'm *not* there, but..."

Chiho finally felt it safe to chuckle.

"Well, I suppose that depends on how the Devil King acts, hmm?"

"Gah! There...there isn't a Devil King out there as meek and diligent and environmentally conscious as I am! And I don't even care a little bit about whatever kind of illegal drug handoff you just did right in front of me! So rest easy and get the hell out of here!"

Maou put his hands forward as he pouted like a child, shooing Emi away with both arms.

"You don't find that embarrassing at all? Trying to convince your mortal enemy that you're a meek, diligent, environmentally conscious Devil King?"

"My aim is to be a Devil King I don't have to be embarrassed about, man!"

"Huh. If anything, maybe the people of Ente Isla should be embarrassed about how much trouble they had finishing you off."

Emi shrugged an exaggerated, what-are-we-ever-going-to-do-with-you shrug. Then she questioningly looked down at the nearly extinguished dish of *ogara* at her feet.

"...That, and what're you doing, starting a fire in this heat? I noticed the smoke on the way here. I thought maybe you were burning something."

"Uh..."

"About that..."

"You weren't aware, Emilia?"

Now Maou, Chiho, and Suzuno all exchanged glances.

"...You really don't know? Man, way to give ammo to all the old folks living around here. I can just hear 'em now: 'Kids these days! So ungrateful!'"

"...I'm sorry, Yusa. I can't defend against *that*."

"So be it. I will explain to her later."

"Uh? ...Uhhhh?"

Emi panicked slightly. She had no idea what triggered this indelicate response from Chiho and Suzuno—though she expected that sass from Maou—and began wondering what land mine she had inadvertently stepped on.

"Regardless, Emilia, I thank you for this donation. I will be ready in just one moment."

Bag in hand, Suzuno bowed at Emi and turned to climb the stairwell.

Still unsure where she went wrong, Emi looked at Suzuno, then the nearly dead ashes at her feet. Chiho smiled distractedly, attempting to put the awkward moment behind her. The final piece of *ogara* fizzled out, bringing the smoke to a halt.

The stage was set for the next moment.

"Oh?"

"Huh?"

"Wha?!"

"Yaghh!"

"Whoa whoa whoa whoa!"

Maou, Chiho, Suzuno, Emi—even Urushihara, still spying on the scene through the front door—all reacted in shock when they saw the light.

It wasn't the kind of sharp, blinding light thrust downward in salvos by the sun. This was a dazzling explosion, something with real weight behind it, and it suddenly materialized right above the burned-out *ogara*.

"Oh, crap!"

Maou was the first to take nimble action.

"Agh!"

He held Chiho close, shielding her from the nearby clay dish, before dragging her toward the apartment's sole tree a safe distance away.

Maou groaned out a shout amid the torrent of light, now so bright that it was impossible to keep one's eyes open.

"Grab on to something! It's a Gate!"

"!!"

"What?!"

Emi and Suzuno reacted quickly, all but dropping everything in their hands as they held on to the stairway guardrail with both hands.

The paper bag in Suzuno's grasp fell down the stairs with a loud, heavy thud.

The behavior of a Gate between two worlds depended greatly on the goals of the mage who created it, as well as the nature of the power used to summon it.

But one thing all Gates had in common was that anything that touched it, assuming it was transportable, was immediately sucked inside with no chance of escape.

And with an unexpected crisis like this, Chiho, unprotected by any sort of holy or demonic power, was the one exposed to the most danger.

"Which way's it going? In, or out?!" Maou shouted, his hands full attempting to keep Chiho away.

"Something's coming out!"

He could no longer see her, but Suzuno provided the response.

An "out" Gate. In other words, someone was going through a Gate from somewhere to reach Japan.

Realizing the Gate didn't have the power to suck in everything nearby after all, Maou released Chiho from his grasp, keeping her behind him as he turned toward the light.

"...What *is* that?"

A large spherical shadow could be seen within.

"It...it's not a human or a demon!"

Emi must have caught sight of it, too.

Once the silhouette appeared, the light quickly began to dwindle away.

The Gate's magnificence was still extremely bright, even given that this was the middle of a summer afternoon, but with the initial torrent of energy ebbing away, color and detail gradually became clear across the sphere that appeared within the Gate.

"Some kind of fruit...? No, that couldn't..."

"It's pretty big..."

Suzuno and Emi, closer to the Gate than Maou, carefully drew near the hovering shape.

In a moment, the brilliance of the Gate collapsed, like a flow of water cut off by a closing tap.

Color returned to the world, the summer sun reintroducing itself to the Villa Rosa Sasazuka front yard.

The object they were entranced by, which had just appeared without any advance warning, landed on the *ogara* ashes with a plunk.

"Man oh man..."

"Whoa whoa whoa."

"Ah! Ah...ah..."

It wasn't that the object was unrecognizable. It was its presence on top of the burned ashes that made the three of them spring into action.

Maou picked it up, Emi gingerly moved the dish to the corner to keep from breaking it, and Suzuno nimbly wiped the remaining ash off it with a handkerchief she had on her person.

Luckily, the *ogara* had fully burned out, and the object didn't appear to be singed at all.

The trio breathed a quick sigh of relief, before:

"My eyes! My eyes!"

The groaning voice of Urushihara, who apparently had stared right into the intense light, rang out from upstairs. Maou, Emi, and Suzuno were startled back to attention.

Exchanging glances with one another, the trio looked at the object picked up by Maou and polished off by Suzuno.

"What are you yelling about, Urushihara?!"

"Dude, my eyes! ...Agh!"

"Q-quit squirming around on the floor! I may wind up kicking you!"

"You already *did* kick me!"

"And that's what you get for lying around by the front door! ... Your Demonic Highness, what is that enormous fruit in your hands?"

Until Ashiya's casual query, the three acquaintances in the yard below had trouble coolly analyzing the situation.

It was a hilariously oversized fruit of some sort, large enough that a grown man like Maou needed two hands to carry it.

It was yellow, apple-shaped, and tremendously heavy.

No one could drum up the courage to eat it. Not this. This was something the Guinness folks would hold champagne parties over.

"Is that...really an apple?"

"I guess it could be a pear, depending on how you look at it...but..."

"...They don't grow 'em this big. Not even back in the demon realm. Don't tell me this is a demon shaped like an apple or something. Someone could've at least stuck a shipping label on this thing for us..."

There were, it had to be said, demons that could imitate plant life in Maou's kingdom. Most were humanoid, though, their bodies gnarled and wooden like ancient, sentient trees. He had never heard of one of his minions transforming into some prize-winning pickin's from the county fair.

Gates weren't something that popped up naturally. There had to be some mage or alchemist deliberately sending this apple over to them.

There was no way to tell who quite yet, though. That answer would arrive once they figured out whether it was sent here on purpose, or it was just a coincidence.

"Ugh. Give me a break."

Emi's mind was the first to wander off the present subject.

"How many times *is* this now? Something incredibly weird happening whenever the Devil King and Hero are in the same place? It's barely been a week since the whole thing with Sariel! I swear, nothing good ever happens around you!"

"I could echo that right back at you, lady."

Maou refused to remain silent as Emi accused him of assorted bad-seed behavior.

"Besides, most of this recent crap was kinda set off by you humans, wasn't it?!"

"Ngh…"

"Yes…well, my apologies."

Suzuno turned her gaze away toward the sky as Emi fell silent.

"I mean, did you even think there's a demon out there right now who can open a Gate as blinding as that one?! It's probably some troublemaker from the heavens again, no doubt! So here! Take it! Why don't you stick it in the fridge for a few hours so it's nice and cold before you dig in?!"

Maou brought the apple closer to Emi. Emi took a confused step back.

"What are you, stupid?! We're about to go shopping downtown! How're we gonna carry *that* thing around?!"

"I don't care! That's *your* problem! You're the one skulking around me and getting all up in my business all the time! You weirdo stalker Hero!"

"How… How *dare* you call me a stalker! If you weren't a demon, do you think I'd even *dream* of hanging around *you*, you Devil Welfare King?!"

"Ngh… Just shut up! Look at you, dressed up like you're CEO of the world or something! Stupid Business Casual Hero!"

"Pfft! It beats having to go around in faded, threadbare UniClo junk all day, you Beefy-T King!"

As the words flew to and fro, resembling less an argument and more a very incompetently performed rap battle, Maou finally made the mistake of going one step too far.

"Well, a lady like you, you'd need to wear a kid-sized UniClo sports bra! Flattest Hero Ever, am I right?!"

Emi, fatigued by the sizzling heat and killer slams, shot her eyes wide open, flames of aggression suddenly burning behind her.

"That's *it*! I'm gonna hack you apart right where you stand!"

"Uh—ah—whoa, wait a second, Emi! People're gonna notice! C'mon, no holy sword! Please, we can talk this out!"

"Silence, fool!! My power shall smite all demonic perversions!!"

A burst of holy force shimmered a golden hue in the air, shooting across Emi's right arm as she summoned her Better Half to her hand.

It was the only holy sword on Earth, a weapon wieldable only by a Hero imbued with the Holy Silver, which was guarded by the Ente Isla Church since time immemorial. Its purpose: demon slaying, and nothing else.

"Agh! Ahhh, ahh, ah, are you serious, Emi?!"

"My liege!"

Emi had summoned her most powerful of weapons, a development that went far past their usual unfriendly bickering. Ashiya, unable to stand by idly, took two steps down the stairway.

"Ah, ah, aahhhhhhhhh?!"

Still wearing his indoor slippers, Ashiya's feet found no traction whatsoever on the half-rotted steps. With a clatter and a scream, he fell downward.

"Oh, good job, twinkletoes."

Urushihara, meanwhile, eyesight finally recovered from the blinding light, watched on from behind, still lying haphazardly on the floor.

"Hmm? Where's Chiho Sasaki?"

He looked around the scene, realizing that Chiho was oddly absent in this furor so far.

He noticed Chiho staring a distance away from under the cicada-laden tree, then shrugged quizzically, quite a feat to perform while on one's stomach.

"You have my full permission. Slay him." For some reason, Suzuno was engorged with rage as she glared at Maou.

"Hey! Don't add gas to the fire! Stop her for me! ...Oh, dammit, you're on Emi's side, that's right! Crap!"

"Devil King! Prepare to die!"

Who could have predicted that an off-color comment about a budget-priced sports bra would cause such an abrupt end to his dreams of world domination?

That pointless pang of regret was all that passed through Maou's mind. None of this "life passing before his eyes" stuff. That was for humans.

He had nowhere to run, no way to dodge Emi's lightning-fast strike. His only recourse, though he knew it was useless, was to heft the apple in his hands upward, blocking the holy sword as Emi swung it from heaven above.

"Huh?"

But the air-rending, earth-shattering blade of her sword never quite got around to neatly halving Maou vertically.

Fearing the worst, Maou slowly turned his face upward.

"......"

He saw Emi, eyes like small dots as she looked at the apple between her sword and her nemesis.

"...?"

Maou was at a loss, but still unable to move.

"Y-your Demonic Highness...rrngh..."

Ashiya spoke up for him, only now recovering from his tumble downstairs.

It was an odd sight he was met with. The Devil King, guarding his head with a giant apple. Crestia Bell, hands to her cheeks in surprise. Emilia, her holy sword still aimed downward. And:

"Is that...?"

But what particularly grabbed his attention was the human hand that just grew out of the apple.

Or hands, to be exact. Two of them, infant-sized, popped out of the large, round apple, arms following behind them.

"Uh."

"Wha..."

"What the hell is *that*?!"

Ashiya and Suzuno grunted inscrutably. It was Emi, in the end, who shouted loud and clear.

Seeing hands grow out from an apple was nothing short of astonishing. Maybe this really *was* a fruit-shaped demon after all. It was entirely possible.

The biggest problem, however, was that these hands, unmistakably those of a human baby, had stopped the full brunt of Emi's holy sword in its tracks.

This was not a matter of Emi hesitating or letting up at the last moment.

She was in a state of white-hot fury, so not even she had considered whether she could really slice through both the apple and Maou in one swipe. That should have been more than enough to at least cleave the fruit in two, though.

Emi reared back in a panic, just as Suzuno removed the hairpin from behind her head.

"Light of Iron!"

As she spoke, the cross-shaped hairpin in Suzuno's hand instantly transformed into a gigantic, holy, power-driven war hammer.

Just like Emi a moment ago, Suzuno was on high alert, tense and wary against this unknown foe.

Staggering to his feet, Ashiya took a moment to figure out what to do.

But even with his experience as chief commander of the Eastern Island invasion force and his reputation as the demonic horde's most brilliant strategist, he had never prepared for the situation of the Devil King pinned beneath an enormous apple with arms as it confronted the holy sword–wielding Hero.

Suzuno, for her part, appeared similarly hesitant, not moving an inch, hammer readied in her hands.

"...Uh, so, like, what just happened?"

Only Maou, unable to see the other side of his apple, lacked a full grasp of the scene. He warily looked around him, fruit still held high.

"M-Maou?"

It was Urushihara who finally responded, on his feet and looking on from the corridor guardrail.

"I think you, uh, maybe wanna put the apple down for now."

"The apple...? Aghh! What're *those*?!"

Maou gradually lowered the apple, only to be greeted with the sight of two infant arms groping around in the air. That earned the fruit an unceremonious toss to the ground.

"Ahh!"

The group around the mystery object gasped in unison, instinctively afraid of what kind of damage a jolt like that could do. Then they watched as the giant apple plaintively rolled across the ground.

"Ah, ahhhh...!"

Emi, caught right in the apple's sights, sprinted off without skipping a beat.

But the apple pressed on. Worryingly so. Maou hadn't thrown it with *that* much momentum. And he didn't curve it like a baseball so it'd follow Emi's path, either.

"Yeaaggghhhh! What, what, *stop* it!!"

The apple merrily chased Emi around the apartment building's front yard, flailing its arms like propellers.

Maou and Suzuno, no new ideas coming to mind in response to this, simply watched.

Finally, the apple settled down in the middle of the yard—finally out of juice, perhaps. Emi gasped for breath, cornered like a rat against the concrete fence.

But the fruit refused to give. Pudgy little hands continued to grope toward Emi's direction, even with the apple now firmly in stasis.

"Hey, uh, Emi, you gotta admit, it's got its eyes on you, or hands or whatever, man."

"*Huff...huff...* Wh-who does? Get it away from me!"

Emi's rage toward Maou was now dissipated, replaced with frantic confusion over this shocking turn of affairs. Her eyes darted pointlessly between the sword in her right hand and the arms extended her way.

Those arms were strong enough to withstand the full brunt of a holy sword.

Or, to be more exact, it felt like some kind of cushioning force stopped the blow, like when you slap your palm against the surface of water.

Emi was beginning to get the impression that she had a lot more enemies impervious to the Better Half than expected. If this apple was one of them, that implied it was related to the heavens, or Sariel, both intent upon seizing her sword.

It made sense in her mind, enough so that she opted to dispel the sword into her body for safety's sake.

That happened just in time for the next cataclysm.

The moment Emi's sword was gone, the groping hands instantly slumped to the side, as if exhausted of power.

Watching them drop like a stringless puppet summoned another scream from Emi's throat as she backed away.

"Yaghh! *Now* what?!"

The apple unpeeled itself, was what, the yellow skin unraveling like a tightly wrapped bandage.

Underneath this shell, built like a reinforced shelter to protect its contents, the apple was hollow. And there, in front of everyone except Chiho, the giant arm-toting apple said:

"...*Bipf!*"

It was now a small girl, its stifled sneeze ringing across the dumbfounded Villa Rosa Sasazuka front yard.

"......"
"......"
"......"
"......"
"......"

Everyone was stunned at this latest metamorphosis.

Not even able to gauge each other's reaction, the group's eyes fixated upon the baby that appeared from the apple.

"...*Bipf!*"

As if responding to her second sneeze, the yellow skin discarded around the girl once again floated in the air around her, leisurely changing shape until it transformed into a yellow dress that fit snugly over her, like she was wearing it the whole time.

"Mm?"

Maou was the only one to notice the emblem that appeared on the girl's forehead the moment the dress took form. It was purple in color, shaped like a crescent moon. "Ooo!"

And then it disappeared in another instant.

The girl scratched her forehead a moment, right where the emblem had been. Then she looked around her surroundings, making the pudgy little hands that stopped Emi's holy sword cold into fists, with which she lazily rubbed her eyebrows.

After a moment of staring into space, she laid down on the ground...

"...*snif...*"

Then fell asleep.

The Lord of All Demons, the half-angel Hero, the Great Demon General, the Reconciliation Panel cleric, and the fallen denizen of heaven looked on.

All of them, each born from similarly outrageously unlikely circumstances, found it equally impossible to comprehend what they had just seen.

"All right... *Hold up.*"

Maou, much to his credit, was the first to snap out of it.

"Wha, what, what on, what kind of, who..."

His speech, however, had yet to crest the waves of confusion ravaging his mind.

"How, how, I don't know, how would I...?"

Emi was no different.

"Ma-Maou!"

Urushihara managed to squeak out a shout from his vantage point upstairs. Suzuno and Ashiya shuddered at the sudden thunderbolt of speech as they looked upward.

But Urushihara's eyes were turned far away, toward the Sasazuka rail station.

"Dude, someone's coming!"

The words were enough to propel everyone back into an ad hoc silence.

Regardless of what this apple girl was all about, there was no way to tell how many people witnessed that huge flash of light. No matter what, they had to avoid the neighbors' prying eyes.

"H-hey, Emi!"

"Wh-what?!"

"Get this...this kid? She's a child, right? Get her upstairs!"

"Wh-why *me*?!"

"She's a girl! So're you! Pick her up! I've never carried a human baby before!"

"What, you think *I* have? I mean, I hugged one once, okay, but she hadn't been lying in the dirt when I did!"

"Hero! Devil King! How foolish the both of you are!"

Suzuno sprang into action.

Gently, taking care not to wake her, Suzuno used her well-practiced hands to pick up the apparently supernatural girl, now fast asleep after giving the neighborhood the shock of their lives.

"Ooh, good one."

"Clerics such as myself must learn how to handle the young for their baptismal ceremony! You! Alciel! I wish to bring her up to Devil's Castle! Bring some bedding out!"

"D-don't you order *me* around, Crestia! Ow ow ow ow…"

Ashiya grumbled to himself as he painfully lurched up the stairs.

Following behind, Suzuno deftly removed her zori sandals at the base of the stairway, climbing up each dust-ridden step in her white *tabi* socks.

"Hey, you go up there, too, Emi! Why'd Suzuno take her sandals off? Bring them up to her!"

"Probably to keep from slipping, I'd guess! …Whoa! Bell! The bag!"

Grabbing the things she and Suzuno dropped when the Gate opened, Emi awkwardly climbed the stairs.

"That, and… Hey, Chi! Chi, what's up? I haven't seen… Huh?"

Maou, at this point, finally realized that neither Chiho nor her trademark panicky voice had played any role in this affair.

Looking around, he spotted her right where he had shaded her from the Gate's light, staring into space in front of the tree.

"Uh…hello? Chi?"

Wild supernatural events like these shouldn't have been enough to put Chiho in a stupor by this point.

Did the torrent of light from the Gate have some damaging effect on Chiho, totally unprotected against demonic or holy energy? The dreadful thought crossed Maou's mind.

But, looking more closely, a twinge of red crossed her cheeks as a content smile spread across her lips. She was lost in reverie.

"Hey, Chi? Chi?"

"…We did it."

"Huh?"

He brought his ear closer to pick up her whispering.

"Maou…*held* me. He went up and held me tight. Hee-hee! So tight…"

A hand went to her relieved, joyful lips as she whispered.

"Ahhhhhhh…" Maou groaned plaintively to himself. "Hey!"

"Agh!"

He had clapped his hands in front of her face, eliciting a shout.

"Please, Chi, back to reality!"

"Ahh! M-Maou! I, uh, I, that—!"

"Yeah, yeah. I'm sorry, but we don't have time to chat about it over coffee, okay? Let's go back to Devil's Castle!"

"Um? Ah, ah, ah! M-Maou! Hand, hand!"

Unwilling to wait out Chiho as she navigated the road back to reality within her brain, Maou grabbed her hand and ran up the stairs.

Everyone, including the apple girl, was now ensconced inside the Castle, each exhausted to the hilt for their own individual reasons.

＊

With the apple girl to one side—sleeping peacefully on her back atop a limp blanket—the demons, non-Earth humans, and high school teen silently consumed their ice cream.

To be exact, Chiho more picked at her ice cream, her mind on other affairs. The other five were wolfing theirs down in a futile attempt to flee reality.

Emi was the first to finish her cup.

"Okay, well, I need to go, so—"

"*Wait* a sec!"

Maou grabbed her leg before she made it any closer to the door.

"Hey! Let go of me!"

She tried to shake him off. Suzuno pointed a finger in the air.

"Sshhh! You're going to wake her, Emilia!"

Emi meekly sat back down, her face resigned.

"...Bell and I don't have anything to do with this! You guys figure something out yourselves!"

"...Like hell it doesn't! That baby girl made a total beeline for you!"

They kept their argument to a well-advised whisper.

The apple, back in pre-infant mode, had indeed all but called for Emi by name. Whether it was attracted by her holy energy or just happened to be rolling in her direction was unclear, but considering she was drawn to Emi almost from the moment she drew her holy sword, the former reason was more likely.

"You have to take her with you! Or at least, like, stay here until we figure out what's going on!"

"Forget it! You know what happens whenever you try to ensnare me in your crap? Nothing *good*, that's what! I want out of here, as soon as I possibly can!"

"His hands... So *tight*..."

Chiho continued staring into space next to the raging feud.

"You think *I* like this, either? You, constantly butting into my daily life and making me solve all of your problems? I'm *sick* of it!"

"Well, you're sure gonna have to do it now, aren't you?"

"Like hell I am! You made that mess yourself, lady! And now I'm gonna make you *sleep* in it!"

"Stop being gross! I always live up to my promises! It's not *my* fault if you keep pretending I promised you the world and a half!"

"Will you quit acting like—"

"Both of you, be quiet! You're going to wake her up!"

Ashiya softly took them both to task. Their voices had gradually ratcheted up in volume as they quarreled.

"So tight... Maou's hands... So big..."

"...What happened to Chiho, exactly?"

"She's been that way ever since we all came in here."

"Silence, Lucifer. Nobody asked you."

Suzuno groaned as she placed a hand upon her temple. Outside of Ashiya and his attempts at defusing the situation, there was nobody she could rely on.

"This is all *your* fault for lighting that freaky fire anyway! You called her over here like all those customers when you put that dumb tree out at MgRonald!"

"How is *that* my fault?! And what's the tree got to do with it?! You didn't even know what a *mukaebi* was! What right do *you* have to whine at me? That stuff's common knowledge in Japan! It's got nothing to do with me!"

"Hah! I knew it! You really *did* summon her! Whatever fumes of demonic power you've got left must've reacted to another traditional Japanese ceremony! *You* brought her here; *you* take responsibility!"

"What the hell d'you mean by 'fumes'?! I've got a *strategic reserve*, dammit! You could at least *try* to help out a little whenever trouble shows up!"

"Help out? As if I've never done *anything* for you before now?!"

"Well? *Have* you? 'Cause lately, it's mostly been you stickin' your neck in my business and gettin' nailed to crosses and stuff!"

"*What?!*"

"You wanna go, or?!"

"Will the two of you shut *up* already?!"

Suzuno, no longer able to bear the vitriolic (if still markedly hushed) war of words between the Hero and Devil King, mercilessly aimed a Light of Iron attack upon both of their heads.

Ashiya and Urushihara had no way of stopping her.

"Agh! Wait! Sorry!"

"Hey, if you're trying to be funny, then *rngh!!*"

The hammer hit more squarely upon the taller Maou's forehead.

There wasn't much strength behind it, but even a regular, nonmystic hammer could be a murder weapon in the right circumstances. Maou grimly stared at Suzuno, eyes welling up with tears.

"Nnnh... Aphh!"

Time stopped at the quiet yawn and the rustling of movement.

The apple girl sat up, yawning as she rubbed her eyes for a few moments. She looked around the room before her eyes settled upon Maou's.

"Uh... Hey."

Maou dared a greeting as his bleary eyes took in the scene.

"Oooo?"

It was hard to tell if his message came across, but she should have understood the nuance of it, at least.

"...Hell-oooo."

He shouldn't have worried. The girl's voice was halting, but it was clearly the simple Japanese of a child—not the Japanese that Maou and Emi relied upon their idea-link skills to cultivate when they first arrived here.

Maou, unable to understand how this girl from the Gate became so erudite in minutes, approached slowly, to keep from scaring her.

"Y-you can speak Japanese?"

"Mm, a li'l."

"A little, huh? Hmm. I see."

Maou nodded distractedly, then turned around, looking for someone, anyone, to step in. He was greeted with silent eyes from Emi, Suzuno, Ashiya, and Urushihara, all urging him to continue.

A bit frustrated by this, Maou drummed up some more courage and turned back toward the apple girl.

"So, uh, what are you?"

"Ooo?"

The apple girl looked back at Maou, bewildered, perhaps not understanding the question. Maou winced internally.

"No, uh…I mean, your name. What is, uh, your name?"

Maou recalled his work training, pretending the girl was just another precocious child at the counter next to Mom.

Now the girl's eyes flickered thoughtfully. She yawned another little yawn before answering.

"Alas Ramus."

"Alas Ramus?"

"Mm, Alas Ramus… *Bipf!*"

Another slight sneeze. Perhaps it served to wake her up; her half-opened eyes were now wide and clear as her head swiveled this way and that.

"Ah!"

Urushihara and the gang reared back at this sudden burst of activity, but Maou, a bit more used to unexpected behavior from customers' children, successfully retained his composure.

It gave him his first chance to take a closer look at this girl calling herself Alas Ramus.

In human terms, she was no more than a year or two old. Her hair was silver, the rare sort that was light enough to reflect the sun's rays, but a single tuft of it was purple at the end, as if dyed. Her eyes shone violet as well.

Maou's eyes turned toward the girl's forehead for a moment, but nothing was on it any longer. Saving that concern for later, he tested out another question.

"So, Alas Ramus, where did you come from?"

"Mm, h...home?"

After a moment, she had responded with a question of her own, one patched together with a couple of indistinct words.

"Um... Oh, home? Well, yeah, I guess you did come from home... but... Like, where is your house?"

"Hou... House? Don't know 'house.'"

Maou scrutinized the questions in his head carefully.

"...Do you have a mother or father?"

"Mo...fa?"

Alas Ramus shook her head, confused. Either she didn't know, or the words were too long for her.

"Well, I mean...uh, can you tell me about your mommy and daddy, Alas Ramus?"

This was a lost child, one who at least seemed human enough. It wasn't much of a leap to ask about her parents.

"Daddy is...Satan."

Assuming the answer was anything but *that*.

Maou immediately felt the eyes of everyone in the room fixed upon his back.

"I see, your daddy is Satan. ...Wait."

"Did she..."

"She just said..."

"'Daddy is Satan'..."

"...Right?"

"M-Maou?!"

Chiho, lost in her own little world up to this point, quickly snapped back to reality, all but lunging toward Maou.

"You, you, you had a *child*, Maou?!"

"Whoa, whoa, whoa, hang on a sec, Chi!"

"Is…is it one of those things?! Did you have a wife and kids back when you were Devil King?!"

"No! Nothing! So just calm down for a bit! I've never had anything like that!"

"Is…is that true, Your Demonic Highness?!"

"Oh, come on, Ashiya! Don't start on me, too!"

"My liege fathering a child out of wedlock would be earth-shattering news across the demon realms! She must be provided with the most gifted of tutors at once in order to prepare her for the throne! And yet you've kept this child from my knowledge for… well, obviously *months*, at least! What is the meaning of this?!"

"Wait! Why is everyone so freakin' convinced that this is *my* girl?!"

"But, oh, what sort of devilish strumpet did you have liaisons with, Your Demonic Highness?! Our forces were mostly comprised of men, but did this saucy encounter occur before we invaded Ente Isla?!"

"No! I'm telling you, it's not like that!! …Hang on."

Near Maou's hand, as he was interrogated in stereo by Chiho and Ashiya, the girl who called herself Alas Ramus climbed out from under her blanket.

"…Nff!"

Both hands clinging to the tatami mat floor, she scrunched her doe-eyed face courageously as she slowly, tentatively tottered up to her feet.

It became clear, if not particularly useful to know, that she was old enough to stand up by herself.

Swinging her arms and legs back and forth with all her might, Alas Ramus made an unbalanced dash across the several feet between her and Maou.

Everyone's countenances softened a bit at her fervent efforts, but as their eyes followed her, Alas Ramus proceeded to grab Maou's hand and bring it to her nose, as if smelling it.

"…Daddy."

Then she beamed widely and hugged him.

It is difficult to portray in words the tension in the room at that moment.

Chiho's and Ashiya's faces clenched, mouths agape like a goldfish plucked out of its bowl. Urushihara fled to a corner of the room, hoping to avoid getting dragged into the mess any further. Emi and Suzuno stood blankly, unable to even process the event.

And it went without saying that Maou, the officially certified father of the child, was plunged into the deepest depths of internal chaos.

"W-wait! How come you're so sure I'm your dad?!"

"Daddyyyy."

"*Please*, man, stop throwing any more dynamite into the volcano for me!!"

Maou's mind ran like a well-oiled machine, searching for some way, any way, to mollify the aghast Chiho and Ashiya. After a moment, he came up with the perfect question to break through this morass.

He had no idea that it was merely the prelude to an even deeper, darker abyss.

"W-wait, wait! Who's your mom, then? Your mom!"

Alas Ramus's wide eyes squinted a little as she returned Maou's gaze.

It was the last straw for Maou within grasping distance. The identity of whoever this mystery mother was could give him ample breathing room to prove his innocence.

The girl was no older than two, judging by her appearance. That was right around the time Emilia and the Devil King waged their final battle in Ente Isla. Ashiya and Emi knew that Maou was cornered, on the retreat, and in no way free to enjoy torrid affairs with sly devil temptresses.

"Mommy."

This time, Alas Ramus responded without repeating the question.

As she spoke, a pudgy arm raised itself into the air, finger confidently pointed ahead of her.

The rest of the group followed her arm. She apparently had full control of her hands and fingers, not that that mattered, either.

"…Eh?"

Emi was standing right where she pointed.

"Uh… M-m-me?"

In a single instant, Emi's face was whiter and more drained of blood than any other.

It was the dead of summer, but the air in Devil's Castle had completely frozen over.

"Daddy. Mommy."

Then, as if striking the final blow, Alas Ramus clearly pointed to Maou and Emi in order.

The pair stood dumbfounded, unable to parse her behavior.

"…………ooh."

Ashiya fainted on the spot. Urushihara rose to help him.

"Aghh! Ashiya! Ashiya, don't conk out on me! You okay?!"

"Yu… Yu, yu, yu, Yusa?"

The cup of ice cream in Chiho's hand, still largely full, was crushed in her iron grip.

"The Devil King is the father, and the Hero is the mother? This is nothing short of a cataclysm…"

Suzuno's observation perfectly summarized the mad fury that commenced soon after.

And on the ground, oblivious to the chaos, Alas Ramus stood between "Mommy" and "Daddy," waving her arms back and forth gleefully.

# THE DEVIL KING EXPERIENCES A LIFESTYLE CHANGE

It was the next afternoon, the day after the incident that turned Devil's Castle upside down.

Chiho checked out the scene around the Villa Rosa Sasazuka apartments for just a moment before modestly tapping on the door to Room 201.

She heard someone fumbling around inside as he slowly approached the door.

"Ashiya?"

As she spoke up, the door unlocked and opened to reveal Ashiya's gaunt face, crow's-feet cascading below his eyes.

"...Hello, Ms. Sasaki..."

The fatigue was written all over his voice, now completely bereft of his usual haughty resolve.

"Is she okay right now?"

"...She finally fell asleep a moment ago. Come on inside."

"All right. Thanks."

They took care to keep their voices hushed as Ashiya closed the door behind them.

Removing her shoes, Chiho stepped inside, then crouched down to gently place the plastic bag she was carrying on the floor.

The rustling of the plastic seemed like an air horn in the silence.

Ashiya leaned down on the other side, just as a motorcycle roared down the street outside.

Ashiya and Chiho held their breath for a moment as they turned toward Alas Ramus, napping beneath the shade provided by the bamboo blinds. She remained motionless, in a deep sleep.

The pair breathed a sigh of relief before their faces turned serious once more.

"Here… I bought pretty much whatever I could think of."

Chiho fished her purchases out of the bag, again taking extreme care not to make any noise.

"Powdered milk… Sugar-free yogurt… And a few different brands of microwaveable baby formula to test out. What did you do for dinner last night?"

"…Crestia gave us some udon noodles yesterday. We minced them up and boiled them with an egg and some ground-up fish. That was soft enough for her to eat. She didn't have any trouble chewing it, and she can drink water all right, so I think we are safe feeding her human food."

Chiho nodded slightly as she continued emptying the bag.

"Here are some sterilized wet tissues for cleaning up any accidents. And here's a children's toothbrush. Don't use any toothpaste, though; not until she's able to spit it out by herself. I got a bottle of mineral water, too."

"Toothbrush… Ah, yes, we didn't brush her teeth last night. Why such a small bottle of water, though? How is it different from regular mineral water?"

"It's a special oral rehydration formula for infants."

Ashiya's heavy eyelids blinked at the unfamiliar term.

"It's hot out right now, right? If she gets dehydrated, you can have her drink this to maintain her salt and blood sugar levels. It's kind of like a sports drink for little kids."

"How is it different from the adult version?"

"It's made so that children can easily digest it. You can make it from tap water, too, but you don't have a water filter installed, do you?"

Chiho's eyes turned toward the lone sink in the Devil's Castle, its barren metal faucet wholly unadorned of any filtering device.

"Tokyo's tap water is supposed to be a lot better than it was way back when, but that's not much help if the pipes in your home are old and rusting. She started out as, like, an apple and stuff... I figured she'll need to have the cleanest water we can give her, so. This is meant for emergencies, though, so we can't just have her drink this."

"...I see."

Ashiya nodded in admiration.

"When you *do* give her something to drink, put it in this."

The next item out of the bag was a plastic cup, a large plastic sipper straw sticking out the center of its lid.

"There's a valve inside the straw that keeps the drink from spilling if you drop it. If she can talk that much, she probably won't have any problem with this. ...Though, do they even *have* straws in Ente Isla?"

"There were... I believe. It was a human thing; I paid it little attention. Emilia and Crestia would know..."

"Well, if Alas Ramus doesn't know how to use a straw, try this instead."

Moving on, Chiho took out a drink box labeled CHILDREN'S BARLEY TEA.

"Does it make any difference whether it is for children or adults?"

"Oh, a big difference. Whether it's brewed hot or cold, the barley tea sold in stores can be too bitter for children a lot of the time if it isn't made right. That, and more important, this drink box comes with a straw, so she can use it for practice if need be."

"Practice?"

"Right. So what you want to do is squeeze the box in the middle so that just a little bit is pushed out the top. That way, the baby will realize that sucking at the straw will make the drink come out. Then she'll get curious and figure it out for herself."

"......"

By now, the look on Ashiya's face was one of awe as he watched Chiho.

"And all the rest of this is diapers!"

Chiho pointed toward a pile of diapers of assorted shapes and sizes.

There was a pull-up type for older children, the traditional kind fastened together with tape, and then a dizzying array of other brands, each apparently boasting its own style and list of materials.

"So you can try these out, one after the other, and use whatever works the best for her."

Ashiya, accepting the pile of diapers, turned his face away, emotionally overwhelmed.

"I... You... You have been such a tremendous help to us, Ms. Sasaki. I, Ashiya, have no way to express the gratitude I feel for your selfless support..."

"Oh, don't be so melodramatic!"

"No, I...I mean it. In fact, if you will it, I would gladly recommend you for the position of Chief General of my liege's regrouped demon forces once he regains his powers within Japan!"

"I'll...pass on that, thanks."

Chiho internally questioned what kind of recruitment standards Ashiya had if he was willing to appoint her to the top command in exchange for taking a walk down the baby aisle in the supermarket. It unsettled her slightly.

"Besides, all I did was use some of the money Maou gave me to shop for a few of the things you need. Oh, lemme give you the change and receipt. Could you give this to Maou for me?"

"...Yes. Yes, I most certainly shall. I, Ashiya, stake my very life upon it...!"

Chiho smiled a bit as Ashiya fulfilled his blood promise and accepted the change.

"It was kind of fun, too, so..."

She looked toward Alas Ramus, still sound asleep.

"My cousin on my dad's side got married, and he's already had a kid. Whenever I come to visit, I like helping out with him while we're playing around together. His wife taught me a lot about this kind of thing while we chatted."

"I...see! Is that how you learned...?"

"Yeah. That, and...um..."

Just as she concluded her trip down memory lane, Chiho suddenly grabbed her left hand, her cheeks glowing red as she hesitated to continue.

"And I... I thought...someday, with......Maou.........I wouldn't mind that..."

"Um, Ms. Sasaki?"

"Huh? Oh, uh, um, um, never mind never mind never...!"

She flailed her hands and shook her head, her face bright red. Luckily, she noticed something that gave her an opportunity to rapidly change the subject.

"Oh, but did Urushihara go somewhere?"

Urushihara, the consummate listless lout, the resident money drain in Devil's Castle, the angel who fell both from the heavens and commonly accepted standards of cleanliness, was nowhere to be seen.

That, and the desk he was always found crouched over was gone, along with the laptop computer that rested on top of it.

"He didn't...escape from you, did he?"

Anyone who knew Urushihara would never imagine the man finding a job, or going out shopping, or making any other positive move with his life. Besides, his criminal past meant he was still in no position to walk around his surroundings in broad daylight.

"Pfft... If he had the guts to attempt something like that, do you think I would be as exhausted as I am?"

Ashiya's temple twitched in time with the edge of his lips. He let out a deep, pensive sigh.

"...As I am sure you could imagine, Ms. Sasaki, the volume and frequency of Alas Ramus's crying overnight was beyond anything we could have imagined."

With a newborn infant, being up and wailing half of the night was just part of the package. But for a child who could speak and understand her surroundings to some extent, outbursts like that represented a demand for some particular need.

Family needs forced Chiho to return home that evening. She had no idea what transpired after that.

Judging by the extent of Ashiya's fatigue, it was hard for her to remain optimistic.

It gave Chiho a chance to recall everything she did witness before she had to leave.

✳

For her (apparent) age, Alas Ramus was picking up on language remarkably rapidly.

That much was clear between "Daddy is Satan" and her fingering Emi as the other side of the couple.

But Emi, after regaining control of her rational thoughts, fervently attempted to prove her innocence, just as Maou had denied everything.

Despite the initial chaos, the other four people in the room never truly thought there was something going on between Maou and Emi. The Hero and the Devil King were like oil and water. Two identical poles on a pair of magnets. They couldn't...interact, not in the least bit. Alas Ramus's age level made that particularly and abundantly clear, and more to the point, neither party had any recollection of the events that would've been required. It would have led to utter chagrin if they did.

Still, it was only natural that after having been turned away by both of her certified parents, Alas Ramus plunged into a fiery, cacophonous crying fit.

Maou, still bewildered to the core, tried his best to keep the girl serene.

"Hey... Hey, calm down, Alas Ramus. Your mommy and daddy are right here, all right? Me, and that girl over there."

"Erraaggghhhhh! Satan, Daddyyyyaaahhhh!!"

She was crying and screaming simultaneously out of her tiny mouth, creating a noise akin to the shrieking of hell.

"Oh, man... Hey, what're we gonna do about this?"

"......"

"Hey, Emi..."

"......"

"...Hey!"

"Agh!!"

Maou clapped her hands in front of Emi's confused, downtrodden face.

Surprised, she fell to the floor, almost into Suzuno's hands.

"Mwaaaammmmiiiiieeeee!!"

Alas Ramus, face covered in tears and snot, chose this moment to fly into her arms, shouting.

It sounded like the guttural groan of some enraged beast, but she appeared to be saying "Mommy" as she clung to her.

With no escape in sight, Emi pulled the child upward.

"Weeaaaaannnnnggggghhhh!!"

"Whoa, hey, uh..."

With a thunk, she thudded into Emi's arms. She was heavier than she anticipated.

To a Hero, a crying child seeking companionship was someone who required protection at once.

But *this* girl? A girl saying Emi was her mother? Emi, elbows bent oddly as she attempted to wrangle the ball of forlorn rage in her arms, had no way to deal with this unimaginable situation.

"What am *I* supposed to do about this?! ...Ah!"

Emi, at her wit's end, turned her eyes upward.

"...Don't just *stare* at me like that!"

There she found the rest of the group watching her with every fiber of their bodies, on the edge of their figurative seats, waiting to see what happened next.

"Uggghh... You people haven't forgotten already, have you? This child stopped my holy sword without a scratch. She can't be any *regular* kind of baby, all right?"

"Yes, Emilia, but stating the obvious will do nothing to improve our lot. Think of this child, this mere babe, seeking out the only mother she knows in life."

"Bell! Quit lecturing me like an advice columnist! This is *your* problem, too!"

"Weeeaaaannnnhhh!!"

"You should be happy for this, Yusa! I almost wish I could take your place, even!"

"Yeah, I'm sure, Chiho! Probably for different reasons, too, am I right?!"

"Mrraaaammmmiiieeee!!"

"I *told* you, I'm not your mommy or anything... Please..."

Signs of resignation began to flash across Emi's face as she slowly, gingerly, put her hands on Alas Ramus's shoulders.

For now at least, just to calm her down, she tried lifting her into her arms...and found her much lighter than she imagined, this time.

"......"

It was honestly a shock, how heavy she felt when she jumped on her. And now this.

Her skin and body frame were soft, so soft that the slightest application of force seemed enough to snap her apart. The memory of Emi's sword meeting its match flew away from her mind as she timidly lifted Alas Ramus. The child latched on to Emi's chest and turned her face upward.

"......"

Emi looked downward, now fully defeated. A silvery bridge of snot arched between Alas Ramus's nose and Emi's shirt, glistening in the light.

"Ngh...*snif*... Mommeee!"

Even as she quivered and cried, her large eyes sought out Emi's face, pleading in their young, immature, begging way for protection.

"O-okay, okay... Ugh, what am I gonna do with you...?"

Emi, thoroughly beaten down, gave Alas Ramus her first true full-body hug.

The girl placed her chin on Emi's shoulder as she clung tightly to her neck and shoulders, the baby fat on her arms soft against her body.

"Ennghh... Mommy...uwahhh..."

The sobs wrung themselves out into Emi's ear as serenity returned to her face.

It was cute. Less than welcome, but cute. But unwelcome. That was Emi's honest take.

She rubbed Alas Ramus's yellow dress calmingly as her eyes turned to Maou.

"So...what're we gonna do now?"

"What? I dunno, what *are* we gonna do?"

"I asked first!"

"Not that it matters, but you sure give a mean hug, you know that?"

"...You realize that's just tightening the noose around my neck, right?"

"Hey, uh, if I could ask a question, how come that girl knew Maou was Satan?"

Urushihara gauged Maou and Alas Ramus.

"I mean, *I'm* one thing, but Maou as a human looks pretty different from his demon days."

"Don't ask me. She smelled my hand just now, but maybe there's something about that only she could tell, or something."

"Dude, the only thing she could've smelled from *your* hand was MgRonald fry oil."

"So what? That smells *great!*"

It was not exactly the retort Urushihara expected.

"...But, man, I guess we're stuck with this, huh?"

As he spoke, looking at Alas Ramus, Maou's face suddenly grew glum.

She was almost out of Emi's arms before wriggling back into position, grabbing on to her neck. Emi offered Alas support from the bottom in response.

"I know!"

Chiho raised her hand.

"This must be like imprinting, right? She must think Maou and Yusa are her parents because those are the first people she saw."

Maou shook his head in response.

"It looked kinda that way, yeah, but she wouldn't have instinctively known my name, too. She said 'Satan,' and I *know* that apple wasn't around to hear that. Or did she?"

"Oh…guess not."

"I mean, Satan is a pretty common name to give a demon where I come from, but she just plopped right down here and called me Satan. I kinda doubt she's referring to anyone else."

"So…so do you have any recollection of Alas Ramus at all, then, Maou?!"

"Chi, Chi—this isn't a custody battle."

Chiho's sudden obstinacy wore on Maou. Suzuno prompted him to continue.

"It strikes my curiosity to hear that Satan is a common name in the demon realms…but what are you trying to say?"

He nodded in response.

"Well, here's the simplest theory. Somebody did up Alas Ramus into that protective apple thing and sent her over to me. And…"

"…And whether that somebody's friend or foe, we should probably expect a visit soon. Right?"

Emi, still holding the toddler, gave Maou a suitably stern look.

"Yep. Pretty much. And I hate to say it, but you're probably involved in this as much as I am, too. Yet again. No way that girl's got any demon in her."

"…Thanks for reminding me. I feel bad for Chiho alone, though… getting her involved in all of this."

"Don't say 'alone.' How 'bout expanding that to us, huh?"

"W-wait, what do you mean? I don't get what you mean by 'Yusa's probably involved.'"

Emi, in response to the worried Chiho, looked at her right hand, which was currently embracing their tiny, otherworldly visitor.

"This kid stopped my sword. She reacted to me when I had my holy sword out. That much is all I need to know. You remember how Sariel wanted his hands on my sword, Chiho."

It seemed hard to believe, but the archangel Sariel kidnapped both Chiho and Emi as part of his attack just a few days previous. He attempted to use his Evil Eye of the Fallen to all but rip the sword out of her body.

"Sariel never said why he wanted the holy sword so badly. And no way am I gonna let him have it—not as long as this penniless Devil King lives and breathes. And now, with all those questions still unanswered, we have this kid who could stop a holy sword. It'd be crazy to think that *wasn't* related somehow."

"Hey, stop weaving little slams against me into your long-winded diatribes, all right?"

Emi, ignoring Maou's observation, turned to Chiho.

"Oh, speaking of which, how's Sariel been the past few days?"

"He's gaining a lot of weight."

Her reply was to the point, certainly.

"Huh?"

"Well, I mean, he's going to MgRonald multiple times a day so he can see Ms. Kisaki. And he orders a supersize combo every time! I can totally tell Ms. Kisaki's just acting nice 'cause he's helping her reach our sales targets. But anyway, you'd be amazed how much of a gut's starting to show up after just a week."

Sariel, his mission thwarted by the rebirth of the Devil King, had decided to take his cover story on Earth—as Mitsuki Sarue, head manager at the Sentucky Fried Chicken in front of the Hatagaya rail station—and make it his permanent gig.

Smitten at first sight with Mayumi Kisaki, manager at the nearby MgRonald and Maou's direct boss, he had now completely forgotten about his mission, and the world of heaven itself. His new goal was to travel to MgRonald daily and make Kisaki his own.

Kisaki wasn't there all the time, though, leading to some awkward encounters whenever Maou was supervising a shift. But Sariel was resolute. He was willing to take the fall from heaven, as he put it, to make his love for Kisaki a reality.

What was more, despite the rampage of just a week or so ago,

Sariel was now almost eerily congenial toward Chiho and Maou. He must have surmised, and oh so correctly, too, that the entire crew was reporting every move to Kisaki.

"...Well. I don't know if that slopeheaded angel is involved with this or not, but if we get any more trouble, the farther away *he* is from it, the better. That guy routinely gets in my way, after all."

"I...I doubt that Sariel is directly related to Alas Ramus, regardless of his past behavior."

It was Suzuno who interjected.

"He most certainly did not use up his holy magic powers in our previous battle. He remains here by his own free will. If he and Alas Ramus were aware of each other, he would have come to us at once."

The observation struck a nerve. Unprompted, Urushihara turned on his surveillance webcam, Chiho peeked out the kitchen window to the outside hallway, and Ashiya shot a quick look out the front door.

"Besides, 'Alas Ramus' means nothing in the heavenly tongues. It is human—the very language spoken in Ente Isla."

"Oh?"

"*Alas* means 'wing.' *Ramus* means 'branch.' Both are terms from Centurient, a language used only in Isla Centurum."

Centurient, literally the "central trade" language, was an international auxiliary tongue created to encourage common standards and trade in Isla Centurum, the central city that linked trade routes from every direction of Ente Isla.

The language was spoken chiefly by politicians, high-level Church clerics, and merchants involved with international trade, but—in theory, at least—it was a common language that would make one understood across the entirety of the world.

"This tells me that there is a set of parents somewhere in Ente Isla, a mother and father who loved their child enough to give her such a deeply meaningful name. Whether they are human or angel, I cannot say. I sincerely doubt she is demonic in origin, but..."

But who named her that, and for what purpose? There was no way to tell. Maou looked on sternly.

"So how 'bout I summarize everything we know? We've got this kid, Alas Ramus, whom we know nothing about. And we've got no way to respond. We just have to wait for this friend, or foe, or whomever to show up."

Emi and Suzuno listened on, a rarity when Maou was speaking. Urushihara picked up where he left off.

"Yeah, so basically, that brings us back to the first problem. Who's gonna take care of the girl?"

For a moment, the thudding truth made all sound, even the whine of the cicadas outside, disappear from Devil's Castle.

"Did she fall asleep? She's been pretty quiet."

Maou noticed Alas Ramus's head, still resting on Emi's shoulder.

"...I just hope this little girl isn't wrapped up in some kind of weird conspiracy."

With a sigh, Emi patted her back as she rested.

"Kinda too bad, though, huh? If it weren't for that weird apple shell, she'd just be a normal baby. Wouldn't you, huh?" Leaning down, Maou lightly pinched one of her cheeks.

Emi winced in dread.

"Don't do that! We just got her asleep."

He pulled his arm back as Chiho watched on. It dawned on her that this was looking awfully like the birth of a fully fledged family unit.

"Aww, you really got it good, Yusa..."

It was a pleasant image to behold, but the jealousy bubbling within her refused to stay bottled up. Her cheeks puffed up in possessive rage.

"Chiho, Chiho, your feelings are painted on your face!"

Suzuno managed to pull her from the brink just in time.

Emi, keeping her distance from Maou (who seemed to enjoy playing the weird uncle in this family all of a sudden), sighed again.

"Well, I can't take her in. I'm a single woman with a job. I can't watch over her all day."

"Perhaps, but having another mouth to feed within Devil's Castle will stretch our finances to bursting. Plus, as three men under one roof, I feel we are ill-suited for the business of child rearing."

Ashiya fired back briskly. They were three men in a tiny AC-less room, one of whom did little besides eat them out of house and home. It couldn't have been a less suitable place for an infant to live.

Chiho looked as apologetic as Emi.

"I'm sorry… I really want to help you out, but I don't know how I could get my mom and dad on my side."

"There is no need to feel tormented, Chiho. This, after all, is an Ente Isla matter."

Suzuno placed a reassuring hand on her shoulder.

"Seeing a young, abandoned child go from home to home through no fault of her own would be difficult indeed to stomach. I would certainly not mind taking her in. I am not particularly employed at the moment…and I have experience with great numbers of children from the past."

Suzuno may have looked about as old as Chiho—younger, even— but considering her career and high post in the Church, she was likely the oldest of all the women.

The rest of the gang never pursued the question, out of an instinctual sense that doing so might threaten their very lives. But given Suzuno's maturity and Church cleric position, she was clearly the best qualified for the job.

Besides, something clicked with the mental image of Suzuno beavering away at her housework, the trademark headcloth and the apron covering her kimono, Alas Ramus snug in a carrier slung over her back.

It brought expressions of relief to the faces of Emi, Ashiya, Chiho, even Urushihara, despite his total lack of interest in even pretending to care about the kid.

"……"

Only Maou's face remained clouded.

Things seemed to be settled—a baby somehow linked to the Better Half holy sword, now in the able care of a top Church official—but Maou furtively shifted his gaze among Emi, Alas Ramus, and his own hand several times.

"…Um, Maou?"

Chiho, as could have been guessed, noticed first.

"Is there…something wrong?"

"Yeah, there's one thing I'm not quite comfy with… Two, actually."

He turned to Emi, not even giving Chiho a glance.

"Maybe I'm just overthinking things, but…"

Then he brought his hand to his own forehead. Chiho's eyebrows arched down in confusion over what his aim was. He continued on, whispering as he collected his thoughts.

"…Why didn't she say 'Mommy is Emilia,' too…?"

"Huh?"

Chiho's eyes opened wide. This was rolling the conversation back quite a long distance. But more than that, it sent an indescribable pang of pain shooting across her heart.

She tried her best to send it packing. She knew "Emilia" was Emi's real name. She also knew that, to Maou, Emi and Suzuno were enemies.

But a new doubt loomed large in her mind.

"I wonder if the day will come when I'm no longer 'Chi' to him…"

She was just a normal teenage girl. No special powers to speak of. The only thing that made her stand out was her knowledge of him and his little clique's secret.

Ignoring the fact that he had yet to give a straight answer to her confessions of love, when Sariel kidnapped her, Maou referred to Chiho as a "valuable member of my staff."

That was all it really was, at this point. Whether at work or in his private life, she was just this girl that Maou kept finding himself in the position of protecting.

Her logical self, telling her that she had to be more aware of her place, collided with her emotional self, yearning to be called by name. The two sides squeezed against her chest.

"Hm? What was that, Chi?"

"…Sorry. Nothing."

Embarrassed at letting her own desires take priority, Chiho edged a step away from the ring surrounding Alas Ramus.

Maou never noticed a thing, of course, as he ruminated for a moment. Then, he unleashed another bombshell.

"Right. So it's settled. We'll keep Alas Ramus in Devil's Castle."

✳

"...So where's Urushihara, then?"

Chiho asked a second time as she pondered over yesterday's events. The reply came from an unexpected angle.

"Ugh, dude, it's so hot. You got that food ready yet, Ashiya?"

The closet door clattered open, revealing a sweat-soaked Urushihara.

"Oh, hey, *you're* here, Chiho Sasaki?"

Chiho was rendered speechless at the suddenness of the scene.

Urushihara had brought his computer, a flashlight, and a small electric fan into the closet. Hopping off the middle tier, he trudged over to the fridge, took out a plastic bottle of barley tea, and returned to the closet.

"Well, uh, make yourself at home, I guess?"

With that, Urushihara—more useless than a Roomba on an ice rink—shut the door.

"...Ashiya..."

"I saw nothing."

The response was instant, if nearly comatose.

"As long as he remains out of sight, everything is fine. My liege and I took turns attempting to assuage Alas Ramus last night, but her wailing never stopped. Hour after hour, it was 'where's Mommy, where's Mommy'.... Ever since last night, Lucifer has spent most of his time in the closet."

"Well, we can only hope Urushihara dries up and turns into a prune, I suppose."

Chiho sympathized with Ashiya from the bottom of her heart.

Suzuno was dead set against Maou taking on Alas Ramus at first. But the girl herself, upon awakening, said she wanted to be with Daddy—and with that, Suzuno stepped aside with surprising grace.

She didn't forget to make one point clear to Maou, however:

"We must respect the desires of the child herself. However! If you do anything that has an ill effect on this infant's education, I will seize her immediately."

Suzuno had the strength to back up her threats, given that her holy power was stronger than all three of the demons combined at the moment. That, and she lived next door.

But the real problem here was the "Mommy" factor. Emi, unlike Suzuno, didn't live within earshot.

Once Emi saw Alas Ramus's contentment at staying with Maou, she proceeded on with her original plan of going out to shop with Suzuno, reasoning that the most pressing issue had been solved. Alas Ramus, however, quickly showed signs of unrest.

"Mommy, don't go again!"

Emi was at a lost to respond to the tearful request.

"...?"

It threw Maou a bit as well, but he quickly took an admonishing tone.

"Hey, listen, Alas Ramus... Mommy's just going out for a while, all right?"

"Going out?"

"Right. Yeah. She'll be coming back, okay?"

"...Really?"

The child's pleading gaze made Emi hesitate. Maou, watching from behind, attempted to telepathically communicate *Lying or not, just SAY it!* to her.

"R-really. I'll be back soon, all right?"

"Okee. I'll wait."

Apart from Urushihara, the sight of Alas Ramus meekly nodding at Emi's words was like a stake through the hearts of everyone in the room.

After all the hectic events of the day, it was almost evening by the time Emi and Suzuno finally left. Chiho had to leave soon after. That was the last she knew of the situation.

"So Yusa never came back?"

"No, she did, along with Crestia…but that only made things worse."

"The child's intention was to sleep together with Emilia."

The Devil's Castle door opened to reveal Suzuno, carrying yet another shopping bag.

"Oh, Suzuno!"

"I've brought the bento boxes and nutritional drinks you requested, Alciel."

She curtly offered the bag to Ashiya, who sluggishly leaned over to take it.

"…Do not expect any thanks. How much was it?"

"One gingerspice pork bento from Orion. Five hundred yen. You can have the nutritional drinks. Those were part of my stockpile."

"……"

Ashiya silently plucked a five-hundred-yen coin out of his pocket, handed it over, then stood up and removed the lid to his bento lunch.

"…I hope you don't mind if I have some lunch, Ms. Sasaki."

"Huh? Oh! No, not at all! Go ahead."

"Hmm? Food?"

Urushihara, smelling out the ginger, opened the closet door just wide enough to stick his face out.

"Silence, wastrel."

The look on Ashiya's face, and the tone of his voice, truly befit the terrifying name of Alciel, the Great Demon General who had conquered all of Ente Isla's Eastern Island in the space of a year. It was enough to strike Urushihara uncharacteristically dumb as he retreated behind the closet door.

"I have to admit, Ashiya, I'm surprised to see you actually shell out the money to get something from Orion Bento delivered."

Chiho wiped away a tear. The thought of what kind of hell he must've gone through if he was too fatigued to even care about keeping frugal with his food budget made her shudder.

"The child's crying fits last night were grueling to endure. Even with a wall between us, I was woken up multiple times."

Taking a closer look, Chiho noticed that Suzuno had applied an atypically full array of makeup today.

That was rare. Extremely rare, in fact, given that she usually walked around in public with no makeup whatsoever; last night must have had a serious impact on her. The corners of her eyes sagged low with exhaustion.

"And her fury was even more unrestrained this morning. She made every effort to keep the Devil King from reporting to work. Emilia had left and never came back, so she must have assumed the Devil King would pull a similar escape."

"Oh, no... But it's not like Yusa can just stay over all the time either, huh?"

It was easy for Chiho to surmise that Emi would never stoop as low as sleeping on the floor of Devil's Castle. That'd likely apply even if she wasn't the Hero and everything.

Emi actually *did* stay over once, long ago, but what Chiho didn't know wouldn't hurt her.

There was always the option of sleeping in Suzuno's room, but that presented its own difficulties.

Suzuno had no shower or anything, of course, and she retained only the barest minimum of toiletries in her room. Given the midsummer weather, a bath and a change of clothing would be a must.

But with Emi still making regular stops at her condo in the Eifukucho neighborhood of Tokyo, the public bath in Sasazuka would have been long closed by the time she returned. And there was no way Emi would report to work the next day without bathing.

"Emilia is not without concern for our plight, of course, but it seems that not even she can fend off the vagaries of reality."

Suzuno produced a mobile phone from beneath her sleeve and showed the screen to Chiho.

It showed a text message from "Emilia" reading:

"I'm sorry, can you take care of her? I'll show up tomorrow."

Chiho was less interested in the message than the presence of the phone itself. She gave Suzuno a glance.

"You bought a cell phone, Suzuno?"

"Mm? Ah, yes, yesterday. Emilia taught me a great many things."

"Oh, wow! Hey, let's trade numbers while we're thinking about it! You went with DokoDemo for your carrier, huh?"

Suzuno's phone was the once-ubiquitous flip-open type, a fair bit behind the times by now.

"N-numbers? Hmm. How does one do that? I think there is some kind of infrared light-gun function that can transmit the number over..."

She tapped away intently at the phone for a few moments, as if controlling a giant robot by remote as it faced off against a city-destroying monster. Eventually, though, she resignedly handed it to Chiho.

"...I apologize, Chiho. I am all too unfamiliar with this. Please perform the required deed for me."

"Okay, but are you sure you don't mind me using it?"

"It is quite fine. I have only just made the purchase, and Emilia's is the only name we added to the directory."

Chiho, while no gadget genius, figured she had enough phone experience to figure out the basic functions with a little experimentation.

But, as she opened up Suzuno's phone, she was greeted with a somewhat unfamiliar scene.

Emi used one of DokoDemo's flip phone models herself, but compared to her model, the text printed on the phone buttons was quite a bit larger.

That, and there were three large, conspicuous buttons, labeled "1," "2" and "3," on the very top of the keypad, something Chiho had never seen on her phone, her family's phones, or any of her friends' phones.

The clincher, though, was the button on the lower-left labeled "Help."

"Suzuno, is this...DokoDemo's 'Jitterphone 5'?"

Suzuno nodded, her face betraying her surprise. "Good heavens, Chiho! You could tell what model it was with a single glance?!"

"Well...*this* one, yeah."

"I had no particular interest in this or that model. As long as I could make calls, I would be content with anything. That, and I have little confidence in my ability to operate machinery, s  I requested a type as easy to use as possible. That is what they pro  ied me."

There was a misguided twinge of pride in Suzu   s explanation. Chiho decided to put the whole thing behind I

The TV ads mostly depicted elderly retiree   ing vacantly as they gushed about how easy it was now to nag their grandkids in the big city, yes. But it wasn't like Japanese law defined a minimum age for Jitterphone owners.

Discovering the IR transmitter on Suzuno's phone, Chiho lined it up with her own phone's sensor. In half a second, they had traded contact information.

"And there we go! I sent my phone number to you, too, Suzuno."

"My thanks to you. My knowledge of telephony before I came here was limited to large, black, rotary-dial models. The instruction manual was so full of unfamiliar terms, I simply wanted to throw my hands in the air!"

Suzuno sheepishly accepted the phone as she spoke.

"…Daddy!"

Everyone in Devil's Castle shuddered and turned to the source of the interjection.

Alas Ramus, put to sleep just a moment ago, was now stirring, her sleepy eyes gauging her surroundings.

"Grkkk…"

Ashiya, caught off guard, let out a muffled groan as a piece of ginger-spice pork lodged itself in his throat.

"Where's Daddy?"

Failing to find Maou or Emi among the grown-ups surrounding her, Alas Ramus's face grew visibly redder as the group watched her erupt into large, globular tears.

"Daaaaaaaaddyyyyyyyy!!!"

The explosion followed soon after. Forcing the pork down with a swig of barley tea, Ashiya hurriedly tried to assuage the girl's fears, but was left to pat her head awkwardly as the firestorm of tears raged on.

"Here, let me look."

Chiho, the only coolheaded person in the room, brushed the limp Ashiya away.

"Ashiya, this diaper…"

The diaper Alas Ramus sported was starting to look distressingly swollen.

"Ah, yes, I purchased that yesterday."

Suzuno spoke up.

"After Emilia left, Alas Ramus had quite the little accident. I failed to consider hand-washing her clothing, and the pharmacy was closed by then, so I had to visit the convenience store by the rail station…"

Next to the Devil's Castle john, a small pile of diapers was strewn around a hastily-torn plastic bag.

"…Ashiya, you should really know better."

"What…what about?"

"I mean, of *course* she's crying. You didn't change her diaper once since last night, did you?"

Chiho's voice was harsh and chiding as she took out a clean diaper and spread it on the floor. In a moment, Alas Ramus was lying on top of it.

"There should be a bottle in my bag that looks like a big medicine dropper. Could you fill it up for me? Tap water's fine."

"Y-yes, but, um, the pipes are hot right now, so it's going to be a shade lukewarm…"

"That's even better. Hurry!"

As Chiho nimbly gave orders, Ashiya and Suzuno watched as she grabbed both of Alas Ramus's legs with one hand, lifted them up, and undid the tape on the diaper with her free hand.

"All right, how about we get you nice and clean?"

Accepting Ashiya's bottle, Chiho pointed it downward and slowly squeezed. Ashiya and Suzuno was thrown off guard for a moment, but the diaper absorbed all of the excess flow.

Putting the bottle down, Chiho used a wet tissue to wipe away the remaining waste, tossed it alongside the old diaper, and lifted Alas Ramus's legs just a little higher to bring her into position.

Showing the one-handed dexterity none of her onlookers knew she had, Chiho gently placed Alas Ramus's rear end upon the new diaper, then briskly taped it shut.

Before they knew it, Alas Ramus—crying with the strength of a mile-wide tornado just a moment ago—had stopped.

Ashiya stared at the girl and her caretaker, eyes like saucers.

"...She was crying out for Emilia, so I reasoned she was just feeling lonely..."

"Well, I'm sure she *is* lonely, but babies don't really have a lot of different ways to express their concerns, you know? If something bad happens to them, all they can do is cry out, the only way they know how."

Chiho balled up the old diaper with the rest of the trash and threw it into the burnable-refuse bag. Using another wet tissue to wipe her own hands, she picked up Alas Ramus and brushed cheeks with the red-faced child.

"There, see? Feels a lot better being clean, right?"

"Oooo."

It was hard to tell if Alas Ramus was agreeing or simply growling to herself, but she responded to the question nonetheless.

Now it seemed clear. The cause of Alas Ramus's endless carrying-on last night wasn't emotional, but physical. Around her rear end, to be physically specific.

"It'll be all right, okay? Daddy will be home soon, and...um, Mommy...too, okay? So be a good girl until they do!"

Chiho felt an odd sort of psychological barrier keeping her from calling Emi "Mommy." But there was no point brooding over it. Keeping Alas Ramus warm and supported took priority.

"Okee!"

Her eyes were still tearful, but Alas Ramus flashed a meek smile as she looked straight up at Chiho and nodded.

"Awww... There's a cute little girl."

Chiho couldn't help but grin as the child fervently brushed away her tears with her little hands.

"Hmm...?"

Just then, Chiho noticed a purple, crescent moon–shaped mark appear on the placid Alas Ramus's forehead. Her entire body emitted an ever-so-faint glow, the same color as her yellow dress.

It was barely noticeable, and it disappeared in the blink of an eye.

Chiho sighed. The event didn't seem to bring about any major changes, but it was a timely reminder that this infant was a being from another world.

Still, all she could do was approach Alas Ramus with the kind of love she thought she needed. She hugged her tightly.

"Ahp!"

Alas Ramus blurted out in surprise.

Watching on, Ashiya put his hands on the floor, all but defeated in spirit.

"Truly, I am no match whatsoever for you, Ms. Sasaki... How embarrassing it is! Yes, embarrassing to let my previous name as the demon forces' master strategist go to my head...! And such deft maneuvering you demonstrated to me in the way of diaper application... Truly, the scales have fallen from my eyes..."

The universe may be a vast, inscrutable place, but it still seemed fair to say Ashiya was the first and last demon to ever be asked to change a baby's diaper during his quest to conquer the world. Even so, he deeply regretted the dishonor he showed at failing the task.

Chiho, unable to find the words to console him, turned to the wall clock in an attempt to distract him instead.

"When do you think Yusa will come back?"

"Once her work is complete, I would imagine. No sooner than six in the evening."

"You know Emi's work shifts, Suzuno?"

"No, but I did lie in ambush for her once."

Chiho had no context to rely on for this sudden confession, but a glance at the bag she brought in reminded her of something.

"I'm sorry, Suzuno, but there's a notebook with a pink cover in my bag. I stuck a piece of paper right under the cover, but could you get that out for me?"

"Certainly. One moment... Is this it?"

Suzuno unfolded the paper for Chiho, her hands occupied with holding Alas Ramus still at the moment, and presented it to her.

"Lemme see... Today Maou's shift supervisor from morning until past the lunch rush. Kisaki's scheduled to show up after that, and... Oh, he's getting off early today. Four PM, it says."

It was a handwritten shift schedule, drawn up by Kisaki for her staff as a portable version of the on-site attendance spreadsheet. It was currently two thirty in the afternoon, according to Chiho's phone.

"...Oh, I know! Say, would you mind if I took Alas Ramus to MgRonald?"

"Pardon?"

"What?"

Neither Ashiya nor Suzuno were capable of a yes-or-no answer.

"Well, I think she's gonna be pretty bored, cooped up in here all day. Maybe if we took her on a walk, she'd get in a better mood and remember something about her past for us. That, and she can get to see 'Daddy' quicker, too."

"Daddy!"

Alas Ramus, in Chiho's arms, quickly brightened at the word, raising her arms in delight. She truly loved Daddy like no other.

But Ashiya raised his head up from his depressed stupor to object.

"I do not understand why my liege decided to take Alas Ramus in, but as long as we do not know the origin of this child, I feel it dangerous to bring her out in public..."

"No. I agree with Chiho. We may have had quite a tumultuous time with her, but if we wish to make any progress, I feel we need to seize the initiative. The societal mores of this country would likely grow unfriendly before long to the idea of you caring for an unknown child. What if Alas Ramus fell ill? Would you take her to the doctor uninsured, without any documentation to prove you are related?"

Ashiya fell silent to this justifiable counterpoint.

Suzuno looked at Alas Ramus, comfortable within Chiho's arms, the bawling from before now a near-forgotten nightmare of the past.

"There is nothing to fear. I am confident enough that I can handle myself against your run-of-the-mill angel or demon. Once things are set into motion, we can decide what to do once circumstances change. That would be good for her, and for you as well, no?"

"…Yes. But…"

"And also note, Alciel, that no matter what our situation is, no matter how we clashed in the past, we are all in agreement right now on one central point—that we need to keep Alas Ramus protected, heart and soul."

"Dude, *I* never said that."

Everyone ignored the voice emanating from the closet.

"*In* which case, I think it a fine idea to take Alas Ramus outside. It is the best thing for her health and happiness."

Suzuno's gaze turned toward the closet.

"I also feel that *his* presence is having a deleterious effect on her upbringing."

"Agreed."

Chiho nodded eagerly.

"Hey, stop ragging on me!"

He was aware of the pejoratives against him, but it still wasn't enough to lure him out—a telltale sign of how unwilling he was to improve his attitude.

"…Very well. But as my liege's faithful servant, I cannot simply pass off the child he agreed to take care of without a second thought! I will come with her. On that condition, she may go outside."

Ashiya wolfed down the remainder of his bento with remarkable speed as he spoke, mumbling the words as he drained one of Suzuno's energy drinks.

It was a difficult sight to believe, considering Ashiya's usual anal-retentiveness about table manners. But, the instant the drink was emptied:

"Nh!"

With a groan, Ashiya collapsed flat on his back.

"Ashiya?!"

Chiho hurried to his side. Ashiya stared into space for a moment, clearly in pain, before gently closing his eyes, as if breathing his last.

"Ooo, Al-cell sleepy!"

The carefree Alas Ramus was in stark contrast to the aghast Chiho. Suzuno couldn't have put something in that drink to strike a final blow against the demons. Could she?

"Grrrnnnkkk..."

But, the next moment, Ashiya let out an enormous snoring sound, mouth wide open.

"...Well, that was the telling blow, I suppose."

Suzuno shook her head in disbelief.

"I woke up several times last night, and I was in another room. Listening to Alas Ramus's wailing from inches away must have pushed Alciel over the brink."

Warily watching the closet door, Suzuno picked up the small bottle Ashiya dropped as he fell.

"Emilia gave this to me yesterday. It was not the gentlest approach, I grant you, but without this, I doubt Alciel would ever allow himself any rest. Illness would come soon after, and I have noticed by now is that whenever Alciel is too ill to go on, the demons around him have a tendency to make things even worse."

Suzuno was pointing to the energy shot in her hand. The bottle read "5-Holy Energy β," a brand wholly unfamiliar to Chiho, and its ingredient list was written in a script she had never seen before.

"...What's that written there?"

"The Ente Islan language. Think of it as a sort of...relaxant, for demons."

Judging by Suzuno's careful eye on the closet door, Chiho surmised this wasn't something she wanted her demonic neighbors knowing about.

"Hey, that reminds me..."

Chiho looked at Alas Ramus, then Ashiya, his snoring reminiscent of a jet engine.

"Alas Ramus... You know Ashiya's name, don't you? You said 'Al-cell.'"

"Ooo?"

Alas Ramus, still in Chiho's arms, held a finger in her mouth as she returned Chiho's gaze. Chiho thought a bit as she looked into those large, expressive eyes.

"Alas Ramus?"

"Yeh?"

She raised a limber arm. Even that was enough to make Chiho smile.

"My name is Chiho."

"Chee-o?"

"Chi-ho. Although Daddy likes to call me 'Chi.'"

"Chi-cha!"

Alas Ramus's face brightened, as if she was reminded of something.

"Daddy's friend!"

"Now, now, Alas Ramus..."

Suzuno interjected from the side.

"Chiho is more of an elder sister to you. 'Chi' would be far too informal."

"Oooo? Oo?"

"Try it. Call her 'Chiho, my sister.'"

Alas Ramus, apparently taking the criticism to heart, tensed up her body and looked straight at Chiho's face.

"Chio...mmm..."

She tried to ruminate over Suzuno's command.

"Chi-Sis!"

That was her final interpretation.

"Oh, that is *so cuuuuute*!!"

Deeply moved by this show of affection, Chiho rubbed cheeks with Alas Ramus once more.

"Chi-Sis, Chi-Sis..."

The child repeated it over and over, pointing a finger at Chiho to make sure she had it right. Then her eyes turned to Suzuno, adjacent to her...and she stared. And stared. And stared.

"...Oo."

"Wh-what...?"

Suzuno swallowed nervously, bowled over by this odd confrontation.

"And you know who this lady is? This is Suzuno. She's kind of a big sister, too."

Chiho, picking up on what Alas Ramus was thinking, came to the rescue. Running this data through her internal computation engine, the child quickly came up with her reply.

"Suzu-Sis!"

She defiantly pointed at her, daring her to claim otherwise. Waves of crimson flooded toward Suzuno's face.

"Suzu-Sis... Mm. Oh. Hmm. No. That is fine, but... Mm."

"Chi-Sis, Suzu-Sis!"

Alas Ramus shouted the names, one after the other, as if attempting to fuse them into her brain. The last time she did that, it was with Maou and Emi.

"Awwwww, I can't get *enough* of you!!"

"There...there is no need to parrot it endlessly like that...! And stop looking at me with those eyes! This is unfair! She is just too darling to bear!"

The women blushed with glee as they cackled to each other.

"...You girls are acting *so* stupid."

They were crudely interrupted by a sudden voice from the closet. The two of them glared back grimly.

Straddling Ashiya's unresponsive body, Suzuno stood in front of the closet door and gave it several loud smacks with her palm.

"Agh!!"

She could hear the surprised Urushihara flail about inside.

"I presume you heard us. Chiho and I are going to take Alas Ramus outside. Tell that to Alciel once he wakens. We will return by the time Emilia or the Devil King are finished with work."

"All right. Fine. Dude, you really scared me. If anything goes wrong, I'm not here, okay?"

"That is the fervent wish of all of us, but surely you could serve as our walking, talking memo pad, at least."

"...Since when are you all in the same clique now? It's like, there's me, and then there's everyone else. You girls are human!"

"I invite you to ask the question to yourself. Even the bitterest of foes may unite for a common cause at times. But there is *no* common cause to be found in defending you!"

"Luciffar, useless?"

Alas Ramus quizzically watched the closet-door conversation, referring to Urushihara by his real name.

She made herself heard through the door, apparently. Suzuno could feel the agitation from the other side. Then she left one final parting shot.

"Children do pick up on things quickly, do they not? And they are so *honest*, too."

✳

Three PM.

A shout rang out, echoing across the MgRonald eatery near Hatagaya station.

"Daddy!!"

The shout, clearly pointed in a carefully aimed direction, coursed its way directly toward a single individual.

Everyone inside looked at the source of the sound, then where it was directed. Then time stopped.

One crewmember forgot all customer service duties. Another lost his grip on the tray he was carrying. A third forgot to remove her finger from the drink dispenser button, sending orange juice overflowing into the drain below.

The beepy little jingle that indicated a batch of fries was done cooking played over the farcical scene from the kitchen.

The target, stabbed by a heartrending bolt of lightning, stood there in confusion for a moment, looking like he neither believed his eyes, nor his ears, nor in the inherent fairness of the world itself. The color returned to his range of view the moment every crewmember in the restaurant turned their eyes toward him.

"!!!!!!"

It was the very definition of a silent scream.

From the other side of the counter, Sadao Maou was instantly shot forward by an invisible catapult, flinging him at light speed toward the source of the thunderbolt.

"Daddyyy!"

Chiho and Suzuno stood there by the doorway, frozen by this instantaneous change in atmosphere. In Chiho's arms, there was Alas Ramus, the tiny little apple girl, who must have thought her beloved daddy was rushing toward her for a warm embrace.

"Hooowwww *coooooouuuuld* yooooooouuuuuu?!"

Maou confronted the pair of women, his face so white that he was liable to pass out, foaming at the mouth, at any moment.

"Why did you bring *her* in here?! This... I mean, this isn't even funny!"

"Um... I'm sorry. I just thought it'd make Alas Ramus happy..."

"She was crying out to see you. And we thought a chance of scenery would help stimulate her past memories. So we brought her here."

Chiho, sensitive to the gestalt around the dining area, began to consider whether this visit would have dire consequences for her. Suzuno couldn't have cared less.

Alas Ramus, clearly in Suzuno's camp, started squirming in Chiho's grasp, hands reaching out for Maou.

"Daddy, Daaaddy!"

"Agh! Hey, stop moving around..."

"*Please*, stop repeating that!"

Maou found himself providing support for Alas Ramus, who had almost managed to wriggle herself free of Chiho's embrace.

"Daddyyyyy!"

The expression on the girl's face as Maou approached exploded into a broad, guileless smile as she coiled her arms around his neck.

"Daddy! I'm here!"

"You, you, you sure are, ah-ha-ha-ha-ha-ha-ha!"

Behind Maou and his dry, crackly laugh, the crewmembers didn't even bother to speak in whispers.

"That's Maou and Sasaki's kid?"

"Dude, no *way*. If Maou actually did that, I'd take him out on the street and strangle him."

"Where's Kisaki? 'Cause, man, if she hears about this, it's gonna be a horror show."

"Ah, crap crap crap, the fries are burning!!"

Curiosity, panic, and speculation were legion.

"Ha-ha-ha-ha-ha... Maou, I'm, I'm sorry if this is bad or something..."

Alas Ramus's smile was a poor match for Maou's twitching death mask. Chiho, noticing the enormous shadow sidling toward the man and the child, looked even more frozen than Maou.

"What is it, Chiho? You look ill. Has the heat affected you?" Not even Suzuno's misguided concern reached her ears. It was understandable, given what she saw behind Maou.

"Helloooooooooooooo, Marrrrrkkooooooo!"

Mayumi Kisaki, MgRonald manager, was standing there, her face resembling a Noh actor's terrifying mask.

"Eep!!"

"Oo?"

Maou arched his back, going bolt upright so quickly that his spine almost burst through his chest.

"If my eyes aren't deceiving me, that little girl Chi just brought in called you 'Daddy,' didn't she? *Hmmmmm?*"

Maou, realizing that Kisaki's near bestial tone of voice immediately precluded any attempt at objecting, lying, or any other defense, gave the only answer he could.

"...She did."

Chiho stood alongside him, both pale as a sheet of paper, as they waited for the next thunderbolt to rain down.

But, even after several seconds, Kisaki showed no signs of movement. Slowly, Maou turned around, expecting the blow to come at any moment.

There, he saw Kisaki, neither angry nor smiling, sigh as her eyebrows furrowed in distress. Then, her face surprisingly somber, she turned toward not Maou, not Chiho, but Suzuno.

"You're Maou and Sasaki's friend, aren't you? …Kamazuki, right?"

Suzuno meekly nodded.

"Would you mind if I spoke with Sasaki for a few moments?"

"I… You may… I mean, sure. Anytime."

Suzuno struggled to adopt her speech to Kisaki's more modern ears. It proved just as difficult as the last awkward time they met.

"Thank you. Hey, Marko, show Ms. Kamazuki a seat for me. I'll take the baby."

"Uh? Um, okay, but…"

Without asking further permission, Kisaki lifted Alas Ramus from Maou's hesitant arms. For a moment, he was relieved to find the child smiling and comfortable in her hands, not at all the ball of fury he expected.

"Could you go to the staff break room for me, Chi? You, too, Marko, once you're done seating her."

That made the blood drain from his face yet again.

Chiho was no different, apparently, pensively following behind Kisaki as she strode behind the counter.

Maou was left to watch with Suzuno.

"…My apologies. This was, perhaps, too shallow-minded of me."

Even she was a little thrown by the chaos they had unwittingly seeded.

"Nothing 'perhaps' about it, man…but I guess I got nothing to whine about. You were just trying to help her, so. Feel free to sit down over there wherever. You won't have the AC blowing on your face that way."

Maou pointed out one corner of the dining area. Suzuno remained fixated on Maou.

"I assumed you would be angrier."

"Oh? What do I have to be angry for? I mean, like, it kinda blew up in your face, but if anything, I gotta thank you for lending a hand. Sorry 'bout this."

Maou looked Suzuno in the eye, trying to sound as sincere as possible.

"…I do not need a Devil King patronizing me." Unable to accept his honest feelings, Suzuno turned her back to Maou as she launched the barb.

Where did the Lord of All Demons get off, looking her in the eye every single time he dared to express appreciation to her?

"Hey, what kind of Devil King would I be otherwise? Just wait there in one of those seats for me…"

Just as Maou's eyebrows furrowed at Suzuno's response, a customer stepped through the door.

"Whew… Three in the afternoon, under the blazing sun! The moment when my goddess of beauty will provide me with the sweet, sweet ice cream that so deftly, so immaculately cools and quenches my heart!! Oh, my beloved goddess! I have come to you today, at this moment, to bring my love to your soul!"

The loudmouthed pervert loudly, pervertedly, strode in, spewing his loud, perverted oratory the entire way.

It was Mitsuki Sarue, manager of the Sentucky near Hatagaya station—formerly Sariel, the angel who fell from heaven at the sight of Kisaki's beauty. By now, he was a notorious fixture around this MgRonald location.

Chiho mentioned that he showed up for nearly every meal. This apparently included snacktime.

Sariel, blessed with handsome features but little else, ran his large, purple eyes across the dining area before noticing the goddess he swore eternal loyalty to in front of the door that led to the break room.

That, and what she had in her hands.

"Gnrahh!"

With an odd, guttural groan, Sariel froze solid, no longer in need of soft serve to cool him down.

"My. He *has* gained weight."

It had been several days since Suzuno last met Sariel, but already there was an obvious, unnatural puffiness around the diminutive angel's cheeks and neck.

Suzuno's observation gave Sariel notice that she and Maou were right next to him. He brought his head up like a half-broken puppet to face them.

"Have...the heavens forsaken me?"

He was asking the wrong couple. It didn't stop him.

"Is this the punishment of the gods, exacted upon me for abandoning my post? Has the heart of my eternal goddess already been...*struck*, by the arrow of another man? Has she returned this man's advances? And, by all that lives in heaven, is that the blessed, crystalline symbol of their love that she bears?!"

Maou was unsure how to explain his way out of the obvious conclusion Sariel jumped to. So he tossed the job over instead.

"Uh, you handle this, Suzuno."

"Huh? Ah... W-wait!"

Before Suzuno could lodge a protest, Maou made good his escape into the break room.

"Crestia Bell! Am I dreaming?! Tell me this is a dream! If I have lived in sin up to this point, then I swear I will repent! I know I have been something of a womanizer in the past, but this time, I promise you, I am serious! Please, allow me to confess my sins! Allow me to beg for the forgiveness of the gods!"

"Why is an archangel begging a...a lowly human cleric for confession?!"

Suzuno tried her hardest to temper her words. They were enemies in the past, but he was still an archangel—one who belonged to the religion she served, and worshiped, within. But this archangel, descended into the world of humans, was...well, to put it bluntly, as low class as the Devil King himself.

"*This* must have been what the morning's horoscope meant when it said 'rocky times for romance lie ahead'! Such a merciless, merciless trial the gods have conceived for me!"

Merely thinking about what kind of confessional a womanizing archangel who took horoscopes seriously would utter caused Suzuno no small measure of distress. As a cleric—and, more presently, as a woman—she was less than interested in hearing it.

"…Lord Sariel, do you know at all where that child came from?"

With Alas Ramus clearly in front of them, Suzuno tried striking while the iron was hot.

"Ahh… Joyful indeed, would I be if it were mine…"

It may have been mere ravings from Sariel's mouth as he collapsed to the ground and wept plaintively, but it told Suzuno all she needed to know. Alas Ramus and Sariel had no connection to each other.

"…Well, so be it. Come to me, my lord, and tell me of your sins."

She decided to go through with it, in hopes she could extract some other crucial snippet of information in the process. But the dread over what would no doubt be ejaculated from his mouth was giving her a migraine already.

"…All right."

The voice made Maou and Chiho twitch a bit as they stood side by side, the dread over the upcoming lecture forming knots in their stomachs.

"How old is she?"

But Kisaki's first question was quite unexpected. Maou's manager was cradling Alas Ramus, her experienced arms gently bouncing her up and down.

Maou and Chiho glanced at each other.

"I'm guessing about three… No, she's smaller than that, actually. A little less than two, maybe. Hmm?"

"Um. Y-yes… I think so."

"You think so? You didn't ask her parents how old she is?"

He would have loved to if he could, but there was no way to ask, since her parents were incommunicado.

"…Well, I guess if you asked me how old my niece was, I wouldn't be too sure about that, either. But it's a lot easier to remember what grade in school they're in for some reason, you know?"

But Kisaki dropped the line of questioning, using her own experiences to reach a conclusion instead.

"But anyway, relax. I'm not gonna yell at you guys or anything. Not in front of this girl."

Anyone able to relax in that situation would be a rare talent indeed.

"Now, just so we're on the same page here, this is definitely not your kid, right?"

"No! Not at all! …It'd be kinda nice if it was, but…"

Kisaki refused to let Chiho's descent into reverie slide.

"You're free to think whatever you want, Chi, but there's a time and a place for everything, okay?"

The force behind her reproach, delivered as it was from a smiling Kisaki as she cradled the girl, was still enough to make even the Devil King whimper.

"So you two… You aren't a romantic couple right now, correct?"

"C-correct."

"I, uh, right."

Chiho dared a peek at Maou, nodding only after he gave his instant agreement.

Kisaki smiled wryly at her young employees' responses.

"Did you think I was going to punish you for bringing romance, or your family or whatever, into the workplace? I mean, really, if you guys *were* a couple, we wouldn't need to have this little talk right now."

"Um?"

Maou gurgled the barest of responses to this unexpected left turn.

"I don't care if you asked Chi for help, Marko, or if Chi asked you first. But lemme ask you this. Have you ever thought about what it looks like to people, a girl who's still in high school regularly visiting a man's house to help care for an infant?"

Neither lecturee could hide their surprise at the way this talk was going.

"But…but Maou doesn't have anyone else he can ask. He didn't even really have any stuff…"

"Maybe you…don't understand quite yet, Chi. People… They can be shallow, you know? They can jump to conclusions, and they can spread all kinds of things before you even know it. And, sadly, you can't fight that. Because there's nothing 'there' to fight."

"……"

"!!"

Chiho was about to say something just as Kisaki's eyes turned to Alas Ramus. Maou stopped her just in time.

Whether she noticed it out of the corner of her eye or not, Kisaki's finger was lightly rubbing against Alas Ramus's cheek. The girl laughed excitedly.

"You smell like Daddy!"

"Oh? I do, huh?"

Both manager and child warmly basked in the experience.

"Young people can be a shallow a lot of the times, too. They hear me talking, and they'd probably say something like 'The world doesn't understand us!' But you guys didn't, and I have to praise you for that."

Placing Alas on one knee, Kisaki placed a bracing hand on her stomach, then gently spun around on her chair. The child gleamed once more.

Looking on, Maou took his hand away from Chiho and spoke solemnly.

"I…I don't think I know enough about the world to be able to say that."

With a squeak, the chair stopped cold. Kisaki lifted the smiling Alas Ramus into the air.

"Wheeee! Yaaaaa! Ha-ha-ha!"

The girl rollicked to and fro, clearly excited.

"Well, if you can say that, you're at least half a grown man."

Kisaki returned the toddler to Maou, looked at the break room clock, and shrugged.

"You can go ahead and take off, Marko. It's still a little early, but if it's gonna stay this empty, we're not gonna miss one crewmember too much."

"But… I really…"

"You're this kid's 'daddy,' aren't you? Then quit worrying about another hour's wages and start worrying about the time you spend with her. I'll see what I can do about your request for more hours, too."

With that, Kisaki readjusted her crew cap and strode out of the break room.

"...More hours, Maou?"

Chiho was in the dark.

"Hey, a man's gotta work. I've got dependents now. If this keeps up, I might have to send her to school sooner or later."

Maou lifted Alas Ramus as he spoke, his tone making it difficult to discern how serious he was being.

"So...you're really going to take her in?"

"Well, not take her in, exactly."

Maou gave Alas Ramus a poke or two on her forehead.

"I just figure I'll watch her until I get some answers to my questions. If her parents ever show up, I'll be first in line to hand her over."

Come to think of it, Maou had seemed oddly fixated on the girl's forehead while the gang was arguing over what to do with her.

"You know, Chi... You told me your mom and dad were cool with you coming over to my place, right?"

"...Yes."

Chiho's body tensed up.

She knew that Maou gave Kisaki a great deal of respect—as a manager, and as a full-fledged member of society. Ignoring the question of whether this was a sound decision for a Devil King to make, there was every chance that their boss's advice could change the way he felt about Chiho.

"I want to keep what Ms. Kisaki said in mind from now on...and that's why I need to ask. Would you mind if I...took advantage of that trust in me for a while longer?"

"N... What?"

Chiho, fully prepared to have Maou tell her to stop playing baby-sitter, stared upward, eyes agleam.

"Things are still relatively peaceful right now, but...you know, Emi and Suzuno are still technically against me, so... Right now, here in Japan, if you asked me who's the guy I feel safest in fully relying upon for something... Well, you're about it, Chi."

"......"

"And I know it's kinda unfair to say this without ever giving you an answer to that question, Chi, but...and I know it's gonna be a pain in the ass sometimes...but if you can help me out, I'd really appreciate it."

"......"

"...Chi?"

Chiho stood agape for several moments. Long moments.

"...Hey! Hey, why're you crying?! Chi, I... Hey! Did I offend you or something?!"

A single tear streamed down her face.

Maou flailed in panic over how to respond. Chiho, perhaps only noticing the tear after Maou pointed it out, calmly took out a handkerchief and wiped it away.

"Oh...I'm sorry. I, I just... I'm kind of happy, so..."

"No, *I'm* sorry! My bad, okay? I'm older than you; I mean, I'm the *Devil King*, and I'm still relying on you for everything... Wait, what?"

"I'm happy to hear that. I'm happy to know that you're relying on me, Maou."

"Huh? Ah? Eh? Happy... What? So why're you crying, then?"

The question mark on top of Maou's head ballooned in size as he took in Chiho's smile.

"Hee-hee... I apologize. This is just how human beings behave."

"Well, it makes no sense at all to me. I mean..."

"I know that you can't give me an instant response. I'm prepared to wait as long as you need, and I don't care what you say to me in the end. So..."

Chiho took Alas Ramus's hand, pushing back the tears that threatened to fall once more.

"Chi-Sis?"

"So I'll do whatever I can to help, Maou."

"R-really? Uh... Well, thanks. And sorry."

"You got it!"

Now Chiho was flashing a smile, the best one she could muster. At a loss as to how to respond, Maou turned his crew cap downward to hide his face.

"Hey, Marko, could you open that drawer and get that—"

Kisaki chose that moment to suddenly burst back in the room.

"!!"

Her eyes arched upward as Maou and Chiho instantly froze into statues.

"…Ugh. Guess I better stop hiring women for a while."

There was no way to hide from her. Equal opportunity employment laws did not apply under the Constitution of the United States of Kisaki. She stalked angrily toward the break room desk, removing an envelope from one of its drawers.

"I got these as a newspaper subscription freebie, but I don't have any use for them, so I figured I'd give 'em to you instead."

With a sigh, Kisaki sized up Maou and Chiho.

"You *do* understand what I just told you both, right?"

She perched the envelope on top of Maou's head. Her work done, she left the room.

The pair sighed deeply once the door was closed. Chiho plucked the envelope off Maou's head. The two of them watched intently as she opened it, revealing…

THE DEVIL KING AND THE HERO TAKE A HINT AND HIT THE THEME PARK

"Hey, Emi, somethin' bad happen to you?"

"Huh?"

"I dunno, you've just had this really peeved look on your face all morning."

Emi brought a hand to her forehead as her workmate, Rika Suzuki, made the observation.

"Not some kind of trouble with that Maou guy again, I hope."

Emi flinched back at this, a direct assault upon the very core of her heart.

"Wh-what made you think *that*?!"

"Well, Emi… I mean, whenever you've been troubled about something lately, it's never been about anything *but* him."

"What? No! No, it hasn't!"

"Oh, reeeeeeally? I don't seem to remember you ever acting like this at work *before* I started hearing about Maou."

That was a surprise.

As the Hero, whose ultimate mission would only be complete once the head of the Devil King was on a pike for all to observe, Emi had always tried to maintain a certain sense of urgency within herself, a willingness to fight at all times. In no way was she merrily wasting her time with the trivialities of modern-day human life! Never!

"I mean, like, whenever we went out to eat, you always looked so happy that it made all my own troubles seem like nothing. Whenever we went out together, too. It's really been just a little bit ago that you've been all serious like this."

"Oooooh..."

The false bravado in Emi's heart crumbled instantly.

There was a certain period in Emi's life when everything about Japan, its food and cultural customs, provided a never-ending parade of new and fresh surprises to her. They instilled new values within her on a daily basis. Everything seemed to sparkle in her mind. She felt confident in saying that even with the entirety of Ente Islan cuisine before you, it would still pale in comparison to the variation and quality of food in Japan.

"Oh, wait! I think your AC broke down this time last year, right? I remember you said you had a lot of trouble sleeping in the heat."

"......"

Emi softly placed her head on her desk.

It had been just over a year since she came to Japan. The idea that her concerns had grown so mindlessly trivial almost immediately after her arrival made her descend into self-loathing.

"Oh, and that one time you complained about how DokoDemo was giving you too many hours and you couldn't arrange an appointment with the electric company guy..."

"Rika, you got me, all right? You win. You don't have to keep beating a dead horse."

"Oh? Oh. Oop, I got one."

The call Rika's workstation received covered up Emi's groan, offering her welcome solace for a few minutes.

"So what is it, girl? What're you arguing about this time?!" The moment her call ended, Rika pulled her headset up and leaned over the cube wall to confront Emi again.

"You are *so* enjoying this, aren't you?"

She flashed a resentful look in response. It was nowhere near enough to faze Rika.

"Hey, it keeps the boredom from setting in."

The way Rika never hid her true feelings was both one of her greatest traits and one of her most annoying habits.

"Plus, you know, I hate to leave a friend hanging when she's in need!"

"Something tells me the 'boredom' excuse is a lot closer to the truth."

Emi grinned to herself.

"Things are...well. You know. Kind of a pain. But I can't sever myself from them or anything."

"Ohh?"

"There's a small child involved."

Rika nodded to herself, elbow planted on top of the cube wall.

"Yours and Maou's?"

"Well, that's what *she* says, but... Agh!!"

Emi realized, far too late, that her overly cute attempt to deny all charges only served to dig her own grave.

Even Rika wasn't expecting such a masterful performance. She put her elbow down, eyes open wide as she gauged Emi.

"Wait, what, really?"

"N-no! Not *that* way. I meant... Well, not exactly no, but *no*, okay?!"

"Whoa, whoa, chill! You're not making sense."

Emi attempted to catch her breath as her tormenter attempted to calm her down.

"...Okay, so listen. Seriously this time."

"Oh, I've always been serious!"

She flashed the utterly innocent Rika a look before gathering her thoughts and continuing.

"...So, there's this little kid at Maou's place right now, right? Apparently... Well, he's watching her for someone."

"She related to him?"

"I don't know all the details."

Emi kept her replies deliberately vague. She had to avoid trouble later on, at all costs.

"Do you remember the girl in the kimono you met a little while ago? I saw the child when I came to see her."

"Oh, yeah… She had kind of a rare name, right? Kamazuki or something? Suzuno Kamazuki."

"Yeah, her. She lives right next to Maou, like I told you, so I kind of have to see her, whether I want to or not. So that's how I found out. Anyway…"

Emi placed an elbow on her desk and sighed.

"For whatever reason, this girl thinks I'm her mother."

"Huh?"

Rika craned her head forward. This plot twist was too good to pass up.

"I've never seen her before in my life, and she's all 'Mommy, Mommy'…"

"She's not just, like, really really friendly with you, and that's why she calls you that?"

"No, I… I think she's really gotten it into her mind that I'm her mom, you know?"

Emi shook her head as she looked at Rika, whose previously jovial expression was now one of sincere concern.

"Oof… Yeah, that's a problem. If she was just really clingy, that's one thing, but if she seriously wants to be your daughter…"

Rika crossed her arms, eyebrows cast downward as she leaned back on her office chair, deep in thought.

"Um, I'm sorry if I'm getting morbid or whatever, but this girl… Did her mother die right after she was born or something?"

"Huh?"

The solemn gravity to Rika's voice caught Emi in abject surprise.

"I mean, if she was usually with her mom all the time, she wouldn't start calling other people 'Mommy' after being away just a couple, three days. 'Cause otherwise, either you're, like, her mom's identical twin, or she never had any memories of her mom in the first place."

"That…"

*That's nuts*, Emi thought, but she stopped herself from blurting it out loud.

She hesitated because she herself had zero memory of her mother—and, in fact, didn't know she was alive until just a little while ago.

Now Rika reminded her of some fainter memories, back when she was a child, when she mistook women in her village for her mother multiple times.

Of course, it wasn't even clear yet whether Alas Ramus *had* a family to speak of. But something about her plea "Mommy, don't go again!" struck a chord with Emi. It implied she had been separated from her mother, and for some nontrivial reason as well.

"Was it something like that?"

"Hmm... I dunno. I don't really have the whole story."

"Ah... All right. Well, hell, it's Maou's problem anyway, isn't it? Why do you have to care at all, Emi?"

Now Rika took pains to lighten the mood. Emi was starting to brood too much again.

"I just figure... You know, there's only so much someone like you can do here, and maybe we're both overthinking it, but if you don't have any intention of seeing that stuff through to the end, why get involved at all?"

Rika gave Emi a reassuring pat on the shoulder. As if on cue, the chime signaling the end of the shift rang out, bringing Emi's head to attention.

"Yeah, but I already told him I'd stop by today..."

"Oh, Emi! You're *totally* getting involved, aren't you?"

Rika suddenly grew quite a bit less reassuring.

"Yeaaah... I guess I kinda got caught up in the mood over there, you know?"

"Well, if you're just trying to stick to your guns for no reason around Maou and his buds, that's all the more reason to get out."

Rika always had a knack for striking Emi right where it hurt.

"It, it's not that... Okay, maybe a little...but it's not *just* that."

Even with Suzuno running guard duty next door, the idea of a baby—even one as supernaturally gifted as Alas Ramus—alone inside Devil's Castle filled Emi with concern.

That, and…

"It's not like I'm feeling sorry for the girl or anything but…if it's fun for her to spend time hanging out with me, I don't really see any reason to deny her that…"

Rika, looking down at Emi as she awkwardly tried to explain herself, smiled and shook her head as she removed her headset.

"You always were Ms. Nice Guy like that, huh? For better or for worse."

*Because I'm the Hero*, Emi replied internally.

"Of course, I guess there's really no telling what's good or bad for the kid until she grows up a little more, huh? In which case, why don't you just approach her whatever way you like? Think about what's good for you, not what's good for Maou or whoever."

Suddenly, a murmur of doubt crossed Rika's eyes.

"Say, Emi, you've never pet-sitted for friends or anything, right?"

"…Where'd *that* come from?"

"Well, I mean, you'd be amazed what feeding a dog for a day or two does. A lot of the time, it'll be pure love, you know? So I'm just saying, don't dig in too deep here. Otherwise I bet it's gonna hurt whenever she goes back to her family."

"…Yeah, I'll remember that."

"Well, super! Better get going now, huh? Your beloved bundle of joy awaits!"

"Rika!!"

Emi took the time to remove her own headset before chasing her out of her cube.

"Her family, though, huh…?"

Placing the headset in its place on the desk, Emi stood up.

"Hey, you know, Emi, if you wanna make your time with her special, how 'bout this?"

Already back from the changing room, Rika beckoned to Emi, cosmetics bag in one hand. Walking over, Emi was presented with a handful of paper sheets.

"I didn't know this 'til now, but I guess DokoDemo's sponsoring this joint, so there's a pretty big employee discount."

✳

Six small, rectangular pieces of paper were laid upon the table in the center of Devil's Castle.

"......"

"......"

"Wuzzat? Wuzzat?"

Maou, Alas Ramus, and Emi sat around them in silence.

"Well, coincidence or not, we've got them all together."

Chiho, looking on from the side, seemed to have trouble determining what kind of facial expression to make.

On the table lay six tickets to Tokyo Big-Egg Town, the hybrid amusement park located next to the well-known Tokyo Big-Egg domed stadium in Bunkyo ward.

The envelope Maou received from Kisaki contained a One-Day Passport that unlocked free access to all attractions, alongside two coupons for discount tickets, all provided as part of a newspaper subscription promotion. Meanwhile, the office packet Rika had given Emi contained three coupons for employee-discount one-day passes—even cheaper than Kisaki's cut-rate ones.

Either way, both Kisaki and Rika had provided their own respective methods for a couple and their child to create a few memories.

It was clear to everyone involved that there was no way they could coop up Alas Ramus inside a one-room apartment for the rest of her life. Even if she could deal with it, Ashiya would doubtlessly crumble to pieces sooner or later.

"These will serve us quite well, will they not? An amusement park, after all, is built for the enjoyment of young children, I believe. We could combine these coupons and have quite the ball together."

Suzuno was making perfect sense, but there was a bigger problem at hand.

"Amusement park! With Mommy and Daddy!"

To Alas Ramus, this had all the markings of a family vacation.

*Family*, in this case, referring to Maou and Emi.

Kisaki's act of charity might have been mere coincidence, but Rika had made a concerted effort to put together a set of three coupons. To everyone involved, it seemed like there were ulterior motives afoot.

Maou and Emi, for their parts, remained motionless, their eyes settled upon the tickets.

Both of them wanted to protest against this outing with every ounce of their spirits, but they also knew Alas Ramus, gifted at picking up on their emotions, would immediately start bawling. The paradox had left them unable to take any action whatsoever.

"…Nugh."

Maou's groan of resignation broke the stifling silence. Emi shuddered a bit in agreement.

"Look, if *this* is the kind of thing you're bringing in here, should I take that as you accepting your role in this?"

"I-in what…?"

"Hey, Alas Ramus? I'm thinking about taking you somewhere, but is it okay if Mommy doesn't come along?"

"No! Together!"

Her response came from the soul, strongly enough to rattle both their hearts.

Alas Ramus stood up off Maou's knee to face Emi, almost knocking over a glass of barley tea on the table. Ashiya hurriedly moved it aside.

"Okay, well, how about you go out together with Mommy and I don't come with you?"

"No!!"

Her mouth opened even wider than before.

"…And there you have it. If anyone else has any brilliant ideas, feel free to start convincing Alas Ramus anytime. Me and Emi'll help you out as much as we can."

"Chiho Sasaki, are you willing to see that—*aghh!*"

Urushihara's snark from the inside of the closet was sharply silenced. Suzuno, standing right next to it, had given the door a loud smack.

"But, Your Demonic Highness, if you are together with Emilia and Alas Ramus..."

Chiho stepped up to drive off Ashiya's complaint first.

"...I'm sorry, Yusa, but would you mind going together? For her sake?"

"Uh? Chiho?"

Ashiya, Suzuno, and Emi all looked up in surprise at this unexpected advice.

"I mean, just think of it as watching over Maou to make sure he doesn't do anything weird. That's okay by you, right?"

"......"

"Besides, Maou's never even been to an amusement park before. I mean, he's barely even walked as far as Shinjuku from here in Sasazuka, and that's only two miles or so. Doesn't that make you nervous, someone like that carrying a baby around the city?"

Maou remained silent. He knew Chiho didn't mean to paint him as a poverty-stricken drudge, no matter how successful she had just been at it.

"That, and we still don't even know why Alas Ramus is here in Japan, either. What if there's some other bad guy like Sariel around here and he tries to go after Alas while Maou's wandering around by himself? What if Maou gets killed, even?"

"...You truly would make a fine attorney, Chiho."

Suzuno whispered it softly to herself.

There was no evidence that Alas Ramus's life was in danger, but considering the circumstances that brought her to Devil's Castle, there was no way to claim that Chiho's worst-case scenario was totally implausible.

"But what about you, Chiho...?"

"Oh, I'm fine. You don't have to worry about me. I'm just saying, if we're really worried about Alas Ramus here, we should try to be together with her as long as possible so we don't have anything to regret once it's all over."

Having clearly, curtly, said her fill, Chiho placed her hands on her hips and looked down upon the happy parents. Emi hung her head in resigned disgust.

"Chiho!"

The Sasazuka neighborhood was dark by the time Chiho set off for home, only to have a voice from behind stop her.

"Huh? Oh, Suzuno."

Suzuno was running in from behind, her geta sandals clacking sharply over the murmur of urban life.

"What's up? Did I forget something?"

"No, nothing of that sort..."

Suzuno brushed back the hair stuck to her sweaty brow.

"It may not be my place to say this...but I hope you will not mind."

"What is it?"

"What...? Well, I... I am referring to Emilia and the Devil King, going out together..."

"Ohh... Well, if you're worried about Maou getting slashed into ribbons following some argument with Emi, I guess I can't blame you."

"No, I... There *is* that, yes, but it is not what I mean."

After all the effort spent catching up to her, Suzuno was now annoyingly evasive about her intentions. Chiho, feeling an odd sense of sisterhood with her, smiled.

"I do kinda worry, though. After all, I don't think Yusa hates Maou as much as she says."

The observation would be enough to make Emi faint on the spot if she heard it. But Suzuno chose not to deny it.

"But Maou told me that he's trusting me and all, so..."

"What?"

"...Hee-hee! Oh, nothing."

Chiho put a finger in front of her mouth.

"But if we're going to worry about anybody here, I don't think it's me. Yusa's leaving them alone tonight, too, right?"

"Ah. Yes. She has yet to find the resolve to stay together with them, she said."

"In which case, I bet *he's* gonna pitch a huge fit once Yusa goes home. Ashiya, I mean."

"Alciel?"

Suzuno looked upward in confusion.

"My liege! It is far too dangerous! Please, I beg you to reconsider!"

Chiho's prediction had already come true by the time Suzuno returned to the apartment building.

"Calm down, man. You think that after all this, Emi's gonna choose *now* to murder me in public?"

"Even if Emilia herself poses no threat, think about Ms. Sasaki's hypothesis. What if someone out there should seek to take Alas Ramus's life, in the worst case...?"

"Look, seriously, calm down! If that's true, then it's true whether we go out or not, okay? You think that barricading ourselves in here and locking all the doors and windows is gonna be enough to protect her from some assassin from Ente Isla or the heavens? I mean, eesh, if I'm gonna pee my pants over somebody who I don't even know if he exists or not, I'm gonna die of heat stroke in here *way* before anybody kills me!"

"Your Demonic Highness, the bite of a single termite has the power to make a mighty castle wall crumble!"

"That's not even the right metaphor, man! You're talkin' about trying to block a bullet with a shield made out of cardboard! What're we gonna do if we keep Alas Ramus in here day and night and she winds up like Urushihara, huh?"

"The girl boasts much higher qualities than *that,* my liege! When she finishes her meal, she brings her dish to me for cleaning and thanks me for the food!"

"Oh, so you're saying I'm below Alas Ramus now?!" the shut-in interjected.

"Exactly!"

"Urushihara!!"

"Dude, you guys are being *so* unfair!!"

All the windows were open, allowing Suzuno to hear the entire verbal sparring match. It was enough to bring the headaches back all over again.

"What are you fools squabbling about? I can hear every word!"

"Welcommmmme, Suzu-Sis!"

Alas Ramus raised a chubby arm to greet Suzuno. She was near the door, ripping up some newspaper sheets for fun, totally disinterested in her semilegal guardian's immature whining.

"Oh. Um… Yes. Good to be back."

Suzuno's cheeks reddened once more. The nickname was not one she was used to.

"Suzu-Sis, it's Sepila!"

"Hmm? What is it?"

Alas Ramus pulled at Suzuno's kimono sleeve in order to show her a color page taken from an old newspaper. It was an advertisement for a family minivan.

A photo of the car was printed front and center, cartoony cityscape in the background, as the ad copy touted the massive amount of space inside. The back door was open, with a large flock of helium balloons pouring out the rear.

"Sepila!"

"Hmm…? Oh, um, I see."

Suzuno gave only the most halfhearted of replies, unable to tell what Alas Ramus was trying to say, before turning to Maou.

"Where is Emilia? Has she gone already?"

"Yeah, she left pretty quickly after Chi did. You didn't see her on the way out?"

"No… But it surprises me that her departure has not sent Alas Ramus into a crying jag."

"Well, she promised Emi that she wouldn't act up, so. We're aiming to put the plan into action on Sunday."

"Your Demonic Highness, you must give this more thought…"

"Ketter, Netack, Market, and… no Binah. Daddyyy, no Binah!"

"Uh, what?"

Alas Ramus batted her hand against her beloved car ad as she called for Maou.

Suzuno whispered into Ashiya's ear as she watched from behind. "If you are that concerned about this, Alciel, then let us surveil them in secret."

The suggestion was enough to make Ashiya turn a ghastly shade of white.

"We have more than enough discount coupons. You can, at the least, keep track of their movements."

"B-but…"

Ashiya groaned his disapproval before suddenly taking on a far more brooding countenance.

"Even if my liege took the free pass and Emilia paid her own way, Alas Ramus would receive little in the way of a discount for her child admission. And even at half price, when you factor the train costs into the equation… Depending on timing, they may have to eat at a restaurant as well, and that only makes things worse…"

Suzuno needed no extrasensory psychic powers to guess what troubled Ashiya's mind.

"Look, Alciel."

Suzuno grabbed one of the coupons left on the table, turned it over, and showed it to Ashiya.

"This amusement park charges no admission for entry. Prices are assigned for each of the attractions instead. Even if you did nothing apart from shadow them, the transit costs are all you need to be concerned about."

"Ah… I…I see."

"—So will you all just *go* already? I'll be right here at home, soooo…"

Just as Ashiya was beginning to soften, Urushihara's voice chirped out from the closet. The sound was enough to harden Ashiya's expression once more.

"No! It cannot be allowed! Damn you, Urushihara, you're set to take advantage of my extended absence to purchase more same-day-shipping folderol from that accursed Jungle.com!"

"……"

The extended silence was all the confirmation required.

"If you wish to go, then go. I will gladly stand guard over Lucifer."

"Dude!"

"…What are you scheming here?"

Ashiya glared at Suzuno, face twisted with concern, as Urushi-hara impotently protested behind the door.

Maou, for his part, was silently cleaning up the scraps of newspaper Alas Ramus had strewn around the room.

"I am every bit a resident of this building as you are. If some trouble were to truly befall us, do you think Lucifer would be capable of providing any support by himself?"

"Ngh... You..."

"Whoa, dude, Ashiya, stop acting like you reluctantly agree with her!"

"More to the point, if someone related to Alas Ramus does enter the scene, he or she may not necessarily be the rogue that Chiho suggested. If her true parents were to appear, we must provide an environment for Alas Ramus that will allow us to proceed with things in a smooth, harmonious manner. There is the chance of some ruffian attempting harm upon her, of course...but given the location of the previous Gate that was opened, there is a very good chance of this visitor appearing in Villa Rosa Sasazuka him- or herself. In such a case, do you think Lucifer is capable of handling them on his own initiative?"

"Ngh...nnnnngh."

"Dude, Ashiya, make her take that back! Say *something*, at least!"

"Of course, I suppose we can worry about that once the day arrives."

"Nnnnnnngggggggghhhhhhhhhh."

Leaving Ashiya to redline his brain into oblivion and Urushihara to plead his nonexistent case, Suzuno turned toward Maou.

"And if something should befall you, I suppose there are worse fates than having Emilia come to the rescue."

"Mmm, yeah, I guess so. I might get my demonic power back, too, y'know, if there's a lot of people around."

He had apparently listened in on the conversation as he took care of Alas Ramus.

"Hoad! Tiperay!"

The girl was still flashing the auto advertisement around the room.

"Still, there's not much point worrying about it if we don't know what's even going to happen. I'll just worry about the most likely scenario, which is that absolutely nothing happens and it's just another normal day."

"Hm? How do you mean?"

"What do you *think* I mean?"

Maou gave Alas Ramus a pat on the head. Upon noticing it, she shifted her focus from the advertisement to thrusting her arms upward, trying to grab at the hand.

"I'm gonna keep on working. That's all. If I can't keep this girl fed, then we're screwed, besides."

"Ugh. I can't take this."

Back home, Emi collapsed in the front foyer, not even bothering to remove her shoes.

Alas Ramus *was* a cute, heartwarming child, like any baby her age would be. But, thinking about it, she was still a total stranger, one she had absolutely no personal connection with.

"It's too much for me to deal with..."

She groaned to herself as she fetched the bag she had just flung away, sitting on the edge of the main hallway to remove the fasteners on her sandals.

"...Why am I acting like such a wimp?! I'm just acting as Alas Ramus's stand-in mother. It's not like I'm a c-c-cuh-*couple* with..."

Even talking to herself, the word proved devilishly difficult to blurt out.

"No! No way, no how, not *ever*!"

Putting a final exclamation on her spirited defense to no one in particular, Emi hung her head downward, brushing the hair away from her sweat-covered neck and forehead.

"…I should probably go to the hair salon or something…"

Just as she said it, the cell phone inside her bag began to belt out the *Maniac Shogun* theme song.

Jolting herself to attention, she hurriedly fumbled through her bag and answered the call.

"H-hello?!"

"Oh, hellooooo? This is Emeraaaaalda."

"Huh? Eme?! I-I'm not looking forward to it or anything, all right?!"

"What are you taaaalking about? Oh, did I catch you in the middle of worrrk or somethiiing?"

Emeralda Etuva, Emi's traveling companion on Ente Isla, gave a confused response to Emi's spirited apology.

"Oh, um, no, it's not, not like, it's all right. *Totally* all right."

"Oh? Well, all riiight. You sound pretty agitated, thooough."

Beneath her easygoing manner of speech, Emeralda could be a surprisingly sharp woman. You would need to have at least some shrewdness on hand to retain such a lofty position as hers in the largest nation on Ente Isla's Western Island.

"I just wanted to call you because I'm getting a little worrrried."

"Worried? I-I'm working, all right?! I haven't forgotten about my obligations as the Hero or anything!"

Despite her best intention, everything Emi said now sounded like an excuse.

"…Oh, gooood. *Such* a relief."

"Huh?"

"One of my 'reeds' told me the Church was up to something seeeedy, so I didn't want anything bad to happen to youuuu, Emilia."

"Reeds" was probably the way she referred to her spies. And "something seedy" was probably something related to Suzuno.

"Oh? Well, I wouldn't be worried. There's somebody with the Church here who made contact with me, that much is true. But she's not like Olba. She can listen to reason."

Emi proceeded to give Emeralda a quick summary of her past experiences with Suzuno and Sariel.

Emeralda was leery at the idea of the top Church official making such close contact with Emi at first, but not even she thought everyone at the Church was inherently evil. Emi's summary of how she came on to the scene, and her role in the battle that ensued, seemed to put her friend's mind at ease.

"You made it sound like just another day, Emilia, but that sounded terribly daaangerous, no? That angel is still there with you, yes?"

"Well, yeah, but... We got some strong allies here in Japan, too, let's just say. I don't think we'll need to worry about him too much for now."

She was referring, of course, to the charming, tyrannical despot that managed the MgRonald near Hatagaya station.

"Of course, I still don't really know why they're so intent in getting my holy sword back from me."

"Hmm... And come to thiiiink of it, we've never given much thought to the sword's orrrigins, either. The Churrrch says it was bequeathed to us by the heavens years and years ago, but that's just their storrry, hmm? I had best pursue this question some more on myyy end."

"Thanks. Try not to overdo it, though, okay? I'm sure you have your government work to think about, too. How's the reconstruction effort going?"

"Ooooh, you'd better not aaaask me. I'm likely to whiiine at you for the remainder of the day."

Even before the arrival of the Devil King's forces, the five great islands that formed the land of Ente Isla did not enjoy the most harmonious of relations with each other. Today, with the Central Continent all but ceasing to function as a hub for trade and cultural affairs, one could only imagine all the political infighting taking place among the nations as each struggled to become the next Isla Centurum.

"But it amaaazes me to hear that Crestia Bell, the inquisitor feared as the 'Scythe of Death,' is such a small and demure wooooman! If you think she can be trusted as an ally, well, that is wonnnderful news."

Emeralda's voice turned upward as she aimed to guide the conversation away from darker subjects.

"When it comes to 'small and demure,' I'd say you still take the cake, Emeralda."

"Yesss, well, when I walk around the castle, I am often mistaaaken by the palace guard for a lost chiiild and the like."

Emeralda, just as compact and baby faced as Suzuno, apparently lacked the kind of personal air of dignity that would normally befit her role as court alchemist for the Empire of Saint Aile, which was positioned strategically within the Western Island.

"So was that all you were warning me about?"

"Ah, yes! There was thaaat, yes, but I also had a question for youuu. Has Laila come over there?"

"Huh?"

Emi was caught unprepared for this sudden change of subject.

"She said she was traveling to the marketplace outside of the castle a little while ago, but she's not been heard from siiince. I know she didn't have much freedom to travel arooound much, so I figured if she was going somewhere, it'd be to you, soooo..."

"Well, I mean, even if she did, I don't know what my mother even looks like... But, wait a sec, you were *living* with her?"

"Liiiving, or let's call it... Oooh, I hesitate to use such a term with you, Emilia, but perhaps you would say 'crashing' in my home?"

"Oh... Oh."

Emi failed to come up with any other reaction.

"Well, anyway, there hasn't been anyone else here lately apart from Sariel and that Crestia girl, and... Agh."

Her voice climbed several octaves midsentence at this point.

"Um, listen, um, I don't know if this is related or not, but..."

There was no point hiding it. Emi decided to plow forward, revealing all she knew about Alas Ramus while deliberately skirting around who the girl thought her parents were.

"A small girrrl, done up like an apple? I've never heard of such a person, or devvvil for that matter, and here in the Western Island, we've not detected any large Gaaates opened lately apart from Crestia Bell's."

"You haven't? ...Hmm. I guess not."

Ente Isla was a large place. There were countless alchemists capable of producing a Gate. Emeralda was a top bureaucrat from a powerful country, but she wasn't omniscient.

"Well, sorry, but I don't have any leads here, either. I figure maybe she's related to Laila somehow, but maybe I'm overthinking it. I'll keep my eyes open, though, not that I'm capable of too much at this point."

"Oh, no no no. She was always something of a free spiiiirit, so she may decide to drop by my doorstep todaaay for all I know. I just thought I'd let you knooow. And I'll see what I can dredge up about that child without arousing too much suspiiicion. Bye for nowwww!"

"Oh, wait, Eme…!"

With that, Emeralda ended the call. Alas Ramus was one thing, but Emi had never even laid eyes upon Laila once in her life. Even if she did care, there was almost nothing for her to go on. Excessive worrying about her was pointless.

"…Oh, well, I guess. She couldn't be that dangerous if she's my mother, anyway."

Emi finally removed her sandals and left the front foyer.

Turning on the air conditioner and her TV set simultaneously, she flopped down on a chair.

"…Yeah. I really better hit the hair salon. Don't want to look all sweaty and exhausted in front of him."

She played with her hair with one hand as she muttered to herself.

The TV just happened to be playing an advertisement for some event or another taking place in Tokyo Big-Egg Town.

It was some kind of weird tie-in between one of the Sunday morning action hero shows for boys and a "magical transforming heroine" series for girls.

✳

The next four days passed without incident. Everyone was prepared for something unforeseen to happen with Alas Ramus, but things remained surprisingly routine.

Not even Emi received any further information or contact from the "source" she had leaked her current situation to earlier.

The only very palpable changes were that Urushihara started to proactively bring his dishes to the sink for rinsing—apparently having his hygiene compared unfavorably to a two-year-old's finally got to him—and everyone at Devil's Castle got better at handling the diaper-changing process.

It was irresponsible for the gang to assume that tomorrow would be just as uneventful as today, but the combination of child-rearing and work duties left them with little time to ponder the future.

They had to find a routine they could fall into without too much fuss, or the dual responsibilities were going to suck the life out of them. That didn't apply quite as much to Suzuno next door, but not even she had the time to attend to every little detail.

Either way, however, four days passed without major incident for everyone involved, and Sunday morning quickly descended upon them.

That day, Maou and Ashiya were drummed awake by Alas Ramus at seven in the morning. She remembered that it was the day of their big outing with Mommy, of course.

The demons had reluctantly agreed to meet with Emi at one PM in front of the Tokyo Metro Kourakuen subway station. Emi, try as she did, couldn't get out of her scheduled work shift in the morning.

Maou's work between today and the day they all agreed to visit Tokyo Big-Egg Town was nothing short of punishing.

According to Chiho's testimonial, he was a dervish of activity from start to finish, attending to every MgRonald duty like a man possessed.

He was willing to fight tooth and nail for every yen he could possibly lay his hands upon. The assistant manager hourly wages at MgRonald were nothing to brag about, but it was still *something*.

That meant less time to spend with Alas Ramus, but Ashiya and Suzuno took turns taking her on walks and bringing her to MgRonald, ensuring she remained in a cheerful mood.

Emi, meanwhile, was largely out of the picture. Her sole interaction with the toddler was over the phone, just once, when she gave a call to Suzuno.

It was funny that she could tell it was Emi by voice alone, but in a way, it was funnier how the idea of a telephone didn't seem to faze her at all. She must have been too young for it to bother her.

It was still only nine by the time they were done with breakfast.

"Daddyyyy, can we go yet? Can we go yet?"

Alas Ramus was unable to wait another second, constantly tugging at Maou's arm. Maou lightly brushed her off each time, but suddenly, he slapped his knee in realization.

"Oh, right. Man, I've been working so hard lately, I totally forgot. Hey, Ashiya, I'm going out for a sec."

"Your Demonic Highness, where are you going?"

"Over to Mr. Hirose's. I gotta talk to him about my bike."

Dullahan II was still practically new; it hadn't even been a week since Maou made Suzuno purchase it. What could he have to discuss with its seller?

"About you, that is, little one."

"Oo?"

Alas Ramus tilted her head upward as Maou patted it.

Soon, in no small part so Maou could get Alas Ramus out of the house, the two of them were walking hand in hand, enjoying the Sasazuka morning.

The shutter had just popped open in front of Hirose Cycle Shop at the Bosatsu Street shopping center when they arrived.

"Mr. Hirose!"

"Hmm? Ohh, mornin', Maou! What's...up?"

Hirose was still shaking the cobwebs from his head this early in the morning. The sight of what Maou brought along with his hand was like someone splashing water in his face.

"Hey, uh, you can put luggage racks and stuff on the bike you sold me a bit ago, right?"

"Y-yeah, but...you didn't..."

"Wahbf!"

Maou picked up Alas Ramus, fully enjoying Hirose's quivering response.

"Do you have any seats that would fit a little girl this size?"

They spent the next little while browsing child seats with the dumbstruck Hirose before turning home.

"Man, *that* was refreshing. I couldn't have predicted his response any closer."

In the front yard, still not quite fully lit by the morning sun, Maou then spent the next little while attaching the five-thousand-yen child seat to Dullahan II's front handle.

"That was terribly devious of you, Your Demonic Highness. What if this leads to certain untoward rumors around the neighborhood?"

"Oh, it's fine. I told him I was just watching her for some relatives."

Ashiya still scrunched up his face distastefully. Maou paid it no mind.

"…My liege, may I ask you a question?"

"Yah?"

"There may be little point asking now, but what made you resolve to take in Alas Ramus in the first place?"

"You don't like it?"

"No, not…not as such, Your Demonic Highness, but I merely thought that leaving her in Crestia's care would have presented little in the way of issues to anyone…"

"Yeah, well, I guess it's pretty much you, Suzuno, and Chi taking care of her anyway, huh? Sorry 'bout that."

"No, no, not at all…"

"You know, I just figured that, if something bad *did* happen in the end, I better be the one who steps up and takes responsibility for it. We don't have any proof of anything, and *I* sure don't remember anything about her, but…"

Maou gathered up the remaining plastic alongside the hex wrench included with the chair.

"But, you know, I got a little worried."

He tapped himself on the forehead several times before returning to his room, leaving Ashiya confused behind him.

Ashiya's gaze shifted between the upstairs room and the shiny and new yellow child seat on the bike. He shook his head before following his leader inside.

"Your Demonic Highness, please—*please*—be careful out there! You are dealing with the Hero, and there is no telling when or where she may strike!"

Ashiya made sure to read Maou the riot act before he left. Back in the demon realm, these roles would generally have been reversed.

"Chill out. If things get that bad, I'll just haul ass over to security, okay? Whatever happens to me, I'll make sure Alas Ramus stays safe."

With these words, which did absolutely nothing to help Ashiya "chill out" at all, Maou left the Devil's Castle behind him.

If Maou was the Maou he used to be, he would certainly have walked to Shinjuku, one rail stop away from Sasazuka, in order to save himself 120 yen on the way to JR Suidobashi, the nearest full-on rail station to Tokyo Big-Egg Town. But not with a young child in tow. It'd be far safer to meekly board the Keio New Line from Sasazuka station, pop off to the Toei-Shinjuku Line, switch at Ichigaya to the Namboku Line, then get off at the Tokyo Metro Korakuen station—the nearest subway exit to the park.

He took pains to give himself plenty of time, hoping to avoid getting yelled at for being late, but the sun was already near its highest point in the sky, bouncing its punishing heat against the city pavement.

The shoulder bag Maou normally used for his work commute contained cups, wet tissues, spare diapers, even Chiho's oral rehydration formula. He was prepared for anything, and cheaping out on train fare after all that prep work would have made him look like an utter fool if it resulted in dehydration and other worries.

Alas Ramus was boundlessly excited at the chance to ride her first train, although the roar of the tunnel's echo when they went underground made her betray a little distress.

After accepting all the "so cuuuuute"s the elderly couple at the

Shinjuku platform rained upon Alas Ramus, Maou made the unfamiliar transfer from the Toei-Shinjuku Line to the Namboku Line before getting off at Korakuen and taking the long, long escalator to the surface.

Just as he was about halfway up, a passerby looked up at them from the platform far below, the concern written plainly on his face.

"Nobody threatening nearby... My liege, I swear to you that I, Ashiya, will protect your back from the shadows that lurk among us!"

It was Ashiya. That much was clear from his fumbling, overt stalking. Standing behind a column and peering out from behind it while wearing a pair of cheap sunglasses made him incredibly conspicuous, and the way he paid zero attention to his surroundings apart from his target meant that his mission was doomed from the start.

"You're the most threatening-looking person here, Ashiya."

An exasperated voice erupted from behind his back. Ashiya shuddered.

"You should really get rid of those sunglasses. Did you buy them at the hundred-yen shop? They look terrible on you, and you're sticking out like a sore thumb."

"Ah! Ah, ah, ahhh! Ms. S-Sasaki!"

He leaped backward at the unexpected sight of Chiho, who was sporting an uncharacteristic hat today.

"Wh-wh-wh-when did you come here?!"

The sight of a Great Demon General being so easily discovered by a teenage girl made Chiho wonder what kind of qualifications Maou asked from his demon hordes in the first place.

"I was on the same train as you. Suzuno texted me your plan. ...But, really, if something *does* happen here, aren't *you* more of a problem than Maou is?"

"H-how do you...?"

"You don't have a cell phone, right, Ashiya? How are you supposed to contact anyone?"

"I-I was planning to look for a pay phone, but..."

"...I kinda figured that's what you'd say. If you don't have any way of making contact... Maou doesn't know you're tailing him, right?"

"Um, yes, well, I thought it would be distracting if Emilia found me, so..."

There was no doubting the merits of that suspicion, but it begged the question of why Ashiya hadn't at least tried to prepare a little more for the covert op.

"Well, I can lend you my cell phone if we need it. Let's get going. We're going to lose them!"

Pressed on by Chiho's urgency, Ashiya clambered to follow before a question occurred to him.

"But, Ms. Sasaki, why are you...?"

Ashiya immediately regretted this bit of indiscretion once he saw Chiho's face pointed at him.

"I know this is the right thing, but I'm still worried!"

"...Ah. My pardons."

Chiho and Ashiya clambered up the escalator, attempting to keep Maou in their sights.

He was due to meet with Emi at the ticket gate near Korakuen station's Marunouchi Line entrance.

Peering intently at the station map, Maou pulled the hand of Alas Ramus below as he began climbing a flight of stairs. He thought Alas Ramus might be tired out after walking all the way up from the Namboku Line turnstile, but instead she was running at full steam, prodding Maou to hurry up without even breaking a sweat.

Chiho, looking on afar, smiled a little bit to herself. The smile survived for only a moment.

"...!"

"Wh-what is it, Ms. Sasaki?"

Chiho gasped when they reached ground level.

She noticed a girl standing idly in front of the ticket gate, a watch bound tightly around her wrist.

She wore a soft, wide-brimmed hat, her usually straight hair tied back delicately, and the mules on her feet oozed chic. There was no mistaking her for anyone else but Emi.

Maou and Ashiya had yet to spot her because of how vastly different she looked from her normal self.

"Yusa... Wow. She's really trying hard today."

With her neck area mostly barren now that her hair was tied back, she had decided to put on a rather large necklace. It tied up the whole package neatly, enough so that even Chiho was impressed. It was a mature look, through and through.

"Mmh... That isn't Emilia, is it? Hmph! Not very practical battle wear. Does she not realize she is the Hero?"

Ashiya, finally following Chiho's gaze to its target, was focused on something completely different.

"What's Maou dressed in today, Ashiya...?"

"The same as always. No need for him to dress in such ostentatious frippery for Emilia's sake. And even before Alas Ramus, the presence of Urushihara has already made our budget a tragedy unfolding in slow motion. There was no money to purchase new clothing for the summer."

For a moment, Chiho's mind fell into competition with itself. On one side, she didn't want to see Maou being a perfect fashion match for Emi in her current state; on the other, the sight of him wearing slightly threadbare UniClo stuff alongside the Hero made her seriously question whether a fashion intervention would be in order before long.

Alas Ramus wound up spotting Emi before Maou did. Maou, dragged toward her by the girl, betrayed zero sense of disquiet as Chiho looked on from the rear.

Just as she expected, Emi beamed at the appreciative Alas Ramus, then returned to a sullen, glassy-eyed stare as she sized up Maou.

Chiho and Ashiya watched the whole thing unfold from behind a column.

"Hee-hee-hee-hee! What do you think? 'Cause I think Emi Yusa's got the perfect look going right now."

Suddenly, the two of them were grabbed by the shoulder. Shuddering, they turned around to face their assailant.

"Oh… You're Yusa's friend…"

"M-Ms. Suzuki?!"

Rika Suzuki stood there, still holding Chiho and Ashiya by their shoulders as she snickered softly.

The women of Earth had a remarkable, innate gift for sneaking up on demons.

"Wh-what are you doing here, though?"

Chiho shifted her glance from Rika to the faraway Emi.

"That's something I'd like to ask *you* guys if anything! Here I was, wondering what Chiho and Ashiya would be doing in the same place, and who do I spot you looking at but Emi and Maou, huh? So I figured, hey, we're all peas in a pod here, I'll just run up and say hi."

This rang a bell with Ashiya.

Emi and Maou were meeting up now because Emi had work during the morning. She couldn't have had any time to return home to Eifukucho after work, which meant that Emi must have reported to the office in that outfit.

"You wouldn't *believe* what a surprise it was to see her! I've *never* seen her show up dressed up like that. It's kinda hard to tell from this far, but she totally went to the salon yesterday. It's, like, totally obvious up close."

Rika brought a hand to her chin, brooding over her analysis, all but asking Chiho to give her opinion in response.

"R-really?!" Chiho squeaked.

"Oh, are you interested to hear more?"

"That, I, um, it, it's not that I, if I said no, I…"

Due in part to the heat, Chiho's cheeks were bright red. The reaction was even more intense than Rika imagined, making her relent a bit.

"Hee-hee! I'm sorry, I'm sorry. Didn't mean to pick on ya that much. You really don't have anything to worry about, Chiho. That's just Emi being all obstinate, you know?"

"…Huh?"

"Emi and Maou, you know, they generally don't get along too well, right? That's just her way of putting up a wall. So she doesn't get out-done by him. Y'know, though…"

Rika took her eyes off of them for just a moment, turning to Maou.

"It's funny how you can try really hard with something like that and totally miss the mark sometimes. Maou, meanwhile… He's totally natural. I'd say he won that battle."

Just then, Emi, Maou, and Alas Ramus began to walk toward the Tokyo Big-Egg stadium.

Turning around, Chiho found Alas Ramus flanked by her "mommy" and "daddy," holding hands with them both as she tottered along. The sight made a restless feeling churn in her stomach.

"Well, there they go."

Rika grinned mischievously.

"What're you two gonna do?"


The Tokyo Big-Egg Town was built in a large circle surrounding the Big-Egg stadium that served as the home field for the illustrious Tokyo Hulks, a professional baseball team.

Stretching from the Lagoon shopping complex next to Korakuen station to the Big-Egg Hotel by the stadium, the park offered a wide variety of attractions. If you wanted to visit a full-sized amusement park without taking the train out to the suburbs, this was it.

There was no real entrance gate separating the park from the outside world; instead you paid for access to each individual attraction, allowing passersby to make visits to particular rides or exhibits on impulse.

The mall across the street from Lagoon and the Korakuen station also boasted a wealth of shops that catered to the needs of young and old alike, making it a popular shopping spot for Tokyoites of all walks of life.

The live superhero shows held on weekends and holidays were another unique attraction for the complex.

While they weren't covered by the One-Day Passports that otherwise allowed unfettered access to all attractions, the shows—each featuring whatever live-action hero or heroes were currently lighting up TV sets nationwide—played to sellout crowds full of excited kids and bored parents nonetheless.

Yes, this was a theme park that'd put a smile on anybody's face. Anybody, that is, but the confused-looking and vaguely prune-like Emi and Maou as they let Alas Ramus drag them hither and yon.

At certain times of the day, the pond built on the second outdoor terrace of the Lagoon building would play home to a concert, with fountains of water swaying to and fro to the piped-in music. The trio happened to be just in time for the show as they passed by, the undulating streams of colored water making Alas Ramus exclaim "Oooooooooo…!" with mouth agape.

"Hey."

"Whaaat?"

Maou, enthusiasm already flagging in the summer heat, grunted dully at Emi as they watched Alas Ramus become enthralled.

"You put some sunblock on her, right? It's pretty sunny out."

"Ahh… Well, they said it'd be okay as long as a doctor prescribed it, but…"

Based on Urushihara's research, going with a doctor-prescribed infant sunscreen over the types sold in drugstores was the conventional wisdom on the Internet. Doing so would (allegedly) prevent future problems with the child's skin.

Maou's health insurance, however, didn't apply to Alas Ramus. And taking an uninsured, undocumented child to the doctor, in addition to whatever issues that presented within the rules of Japanese society, would almost certainly create problems with the current way of life over at Devil's Castle. Thus, Maou had failed to provide the appropriate sunscreen for his charge.

"Well, you could at least think about buying her a hat or something. There's clothing shops in Lagoon here, so let's go there first. If you're gonna step up and care for her, you really need to start looking out for what's best *for her*."

The way Emi so quickly adopted that lecturing-wife tone belied her previous position on another world. Maou didn't have much of a leg to stand on.

"Yeah... Sorry 'bout that. ...Whaddaya think, Alas Ramus? Having fun?"

"Oooooohhh... Aaaahhhh...!!"

"Absorbed in those fountains, huh? Well, great."

Watching from a terrace that overlooked the show, Ashiya, Chiho, and Rika focused on the trio below.

"Wow, what a happy li'l family, huh? That girl's sure taken a shining to Emi, hasn't she?"

"...She's so cute."

Chiho sighed at the sight of Alas Ramus, still hypnotized by the fountain show.

Ashiya, for his part, was keeping a keen lookout to ensure Maou remained safe, although he naturally hadn't forgotten another, almost more pressing task—ensuring his leader didn't splurge on anything.

Unaware of their pursuers' thoughts, not even aware there were any pursuers at all, the newly minted family watched the show to the end before walking hand in hand with Alas Ramus inside the Lagoon mall to search for a hat.

The other trio followed on, ensuring they stayed a discreet distance away.

"Hey, a UniClo."

Maou noticed a familiar logo on the information board near the entrance. Emi immediately stepped in to dismiss the idea.

"Forget it. Why are you so preoccupied with UniClo anyway?"

"What? It's cheap. Cheap and easy. Nothing I don't need."

"You could at least *try* going to another store sometime. I don't know what kind of picture you've got in your mind, but it's really not that much more expensive."

"Huh."

"Don't just go 'huh'! What happens if Alas Ramus winds up being as low-class as you are?"

"Nothing wrong with being frugal."

"...Let's go, Alas Ramus. We don't need this dead weight with us."

"Ded way?"

Pulled ahead by Emi, the girl timidly rode the escalator up to the clothing floor, filled with UniClo and a selection of other apparel shops.

"Hmm... These are still gonna be a little big for her."

Emi sighed to herself as she checked out a few children's selections and placed them above Alas Ramus's shoulders.

"She's gonna grow pretty quickly, though. I guess getting a bigger size isn't too bad, as long as she's not dragging it behind her. ...And I notice *you* aren't speaking up. You realize I'm still talking about several months down the line when I say 'quickly,' right?"

"If you're waiting for me to chime in every time you open your mouth, keep waiting. I'm not exactly interested in long conversations with you."

"Look, how long are you planning to keep this child anyway?"

Emi continued thumbing through children's accessories, draping them over Alas Ramus to gauge how she looked.

"...Who knows? Maybe her parents'll show up today. Maybe I'll be taking care of her until she gets married."

"Married...? I'm sorry if I keep asking this, but are you *sure* it wouldn't be better for everyone if you just stayed in Japan forever?"

"...Ooh, hey, this one looks pretty good. That'll cover her down to her shoulders, too."

Maou, oblivious to the conversation, plucked a straw hat off the clothing racks. It fit the little girl remarkably well.

"Maybe this isn't something I should ask, but don't you care about the generals you left behind on Ente Isla or anything?"

Emi was expecting a much less direct answer than Maou wound up giving.

"Them? Yeah, I've given up on those bastards."

"…Huh?"

"Hey, Alas Ramus, you can get this with a pink ribbon or a yellow one. Which one do you like?"

"Mmm, Market!"

Alas Ramus pointed at the hat with the yellow ribbon.

Emi found herself unable to respond to Maou's heartless, somewhat Devil King–like statement. Maou shrugged.

"Haven't you ever thought about why Emeralda and Albert and Olba and Suzuno just pop over here whenever, like, they're in the next city over?"

His eyes burst open wide as he glanced at the price tag on the straw hat Alas Ramus chose.

"…It's been over a year now. I kinda missed my window. Whatever part of the Ente Isla invasion force survived must've been stamped out ages ago. Otherwise, we wouldn't be having the most powerful fighters of the human world going on these grand tours of Earth all the time."

That much was logical enough. Officially speaking, all four of the Devil King's Great Demon Generals—Lucifer included—were defeated. The chain of command in the demon world had been slashed to pieces.

Emi had zero sympathy for Maou, something that came across pretty clearly by now.

"You… You think so? Well, jeez, *that* was easy. Guess that's the demon realm for you, huh? The big man at the top falls, and the rest just crumbles to dust."

"I couldn't have put it better. Without me, those guys are worthless. But even if I went back now, without any of my power, I'd be killed whenever the next would-be king decided to come around. That…"

Having resigned himself to the purchase, Maou turned his back to Emi and Alas Ramus as he took the hat to the register.

"…That, and even if I *did* regain my Devil King strength, no way I could conquer the world now."

"W-well, yeah. With the demons annihilated, there's not much point calling yourself Devil King anyway, huh?"

"Demons annihilated? What're you smoking, lady?"

Maou sneered at Emi in abject ridicule.

"When you humans fight a war, do every single one of you march down to the battlefield en masse?"

"Huh?"

It took Emi a moment to parse the question, but Maou proceeded on to the register, uninterested in continuing the discussion.

He had the cashier snip the price tag off before placing it squarely over Alas Ramus's head.

"Mph! Cute?"

Alas Ramus sidled up to the provided mirror as she glanced upward at Maou.

"Oh, yeah. Totally cute!"

A silly grin crossed Maou's face, the dark atmosphere of a moment ago tossed aside.

"Hey, can we worry about clothing her next time? It's right around lunchtime, so the attractions oughtta be pretty empty right now. Which one you wanna go on first, Alas Ramus?"

"There, Daddy! There!"

Alas Ramus pointed through a Lagoon window toward the Free Fall ride.

"Oooh, you're probably gonna be either too young or too short for that one, girl. How 'bout we wander around a little and check things out?"

Emi followed after the pair distractedly, still lost in a fog.

The trio following even farther behind exchanged glances between Maou and the clothing store.

"I've never seen two people look so depressed over buying a hat before."

"Yeah, who can say? Maybe it was really expensive or something."

Prompted by Rika and Chiho's chatter, Ashiya idly picked up a hat similar to the one Maou bought for Alas Ramus.

"Two...*thousand*, five hundred yen..."

He wheezed out the number, choking on each digit.

"He...he completely blew through the money we saved on that free pass..."

"Huh? Hey, Ashiya, you need something to drink? You don't look too good."

"Ha! Ha-ha-ha! No, uh, no worries! Onward, ha-ha-ha-ha!"

Hanging the hat back up with a strained, shrill chuckle, Ashiya beckoned Rika to leave the store with him. Chiho picked up a "New for Summer!" hat, peeked at the price tag, then wiped a tear away as she silently replaced it on the display.

"I gotta say, though, this is a lot more *normal* than I thought it was gonna be. Like, they're acting all mature and stuff, you know? I thought I'd step in if they started fighting or whatever, but I guess they're playing nice for the sake of the kid, huh?"

"Huh? What, so you weren't here just to gawk at them, Suzuki?"

Chiho couldn't resist asking an overly honest question.

"Oooh, Chiho, you shouldn't look down on your big sis like that!"

Rika gave a judgmental pinch on Chiho's cheek.

"Mmph, fthorry..."

"I'm not gonna deny that or anything, but, like, what else am I supposed to do with my time off, y'know? I just figured I've observe her and provide backup if need be."

"Ffraffup?"

"Sure. That girl's from Maou's family, right? If the girl likes Emi that much, she's gonna be awfully hurt once she goes away. At times like that, it helps a lot just to have someone to drink with you, right? Someone who knows what you're going through to some extent."

"Ffh... Right."

Her cheek finally released, Chiho rubbed her face with her hands.

"And *also*, I'm kinda interested in how Emi acts when she's out with a guy, y'know?"

"See? See? You're just gawking at her! You pinched me for nothing!"

"I'm not *gawking*, Chiho. It's kind of like being a voyeur, if anything."

"That's even worse!"

"Oh, are *you* one to talk, Chiho? You aren't even related to Maou. Why're *you* sneaking around him like that?"

"I-I-I'm not, that's…"

"Aw, c'mon. I'm not gonna tell anyone. Just go ahead and tell your big sis what's up."

"…I am glad *someone* is enjoying this, at least."

Ashiya began to grow weary of the two girls gossiping with each other to the rear.

"Aw, don't be such a party pooper!"

"Agh!"

Ashiya yelped as he was suddenly reeled in by the shoulder.

"And you, too, Ashiya… I know Emi's the indirect reason your company went out of business and all, but she's not your enemy any longer, is she? She's not gonna prey on you guys or anything, so why're you acting so serious about this?"

She *was* their enemy, from head to toe, and it wasn't that she'd prey upon them so much as she'd take their heads off and spit on their corpses, but there was no way he could say that to Rika.

"You know what, Ashiya? I think you should try reading some Natsume Soseki sometime."

"What? Why? Where'd that come from?"

"Oh, I just think it'd have a lot to teach someone like you. Like, how not to act so tough and formal all the time, y'know?"

Chiho and Ashiya found themselves at the mercy of this unassuming call-center girl, one with an uncanny knack for diving into the inner recesses of people's minds.

"Still…"

Rika continued at a whisper, away from Chiho and Ashiya as the pair blankly stared at each other.

"I do like that a lot more than taking the subtle approach, though."

Alas Ramus, holding a clutch of colorful balloons, was in paradise.

She had begged Maou multiple times along the way for them. Apparently anything done up in bright, flashy colors immediately attracted her notice.

"Ugh... I can just see it now. The doting daddy, unable to say no to his daughter."

Emi whined to herself as she drank some mineral water, using a paper fan passed out at Lagoon to keep cool.

Watching Alas Ramus shriek in delight on a small merry-go-round, Maou looking not so displeased himself atop a carousel horse behind her, Emi was plagued by an impulse to simply drop everything and return to Ente Isla right this minute.

Something Maou said a little while ago continued to ring in her ears.

Having the demon forces expelled by the armies of the human race filled her with nothing but pure, unadulterated happiness. It was, in her mind, the only conclusion to the battle she could ever accept.

Maou had a habit of hiding his true colors when it counted the most, so it was difficult to gauge his feelings for sure. But there was no sign of sadness or anger on his face as he theorized about how his former demon underlings were likely dead.

Something about his words, though, gave Emi the strangest sense that something she had taken for granted up to now shouldn't be. Something she had taken as much for granted as breathing, or drinking water...

"...mi? ...Hey, Emi?"

"...What? Oh, sorry. What is it?"

Lost in thought, she suddenly realized that Maou was off the merry-go-round and standing right next to her.

"Why're you spacing out on me, man? Is the heat frying your brain?"

"It—it is *not*! Stop sidling right up to me like that! What is it?!"

"I think Alas wants to check this out."

Maou pointed to a poster advertising the Tokyo Big-Egg hero show, arguably one of the park's trademark experiences, tacked onto an information board.

Emi recognized the show from the TV ad she saw earlier, but something else also caught her attention.

"...Did you buy a TV or something?"

The show was apparently a grandiose crossover event, with a team of five acrobatic heroes (each identified by the color of spandex they wore) uniting with a group of similarly colorful magical girls. It was running a brisk business, no doubt aided by the sunny Sunday weather, but Emi couldn't help but notice that these were all kids' TV characters.

"A TV? No. The antenna on the roof's still analog, even."

The response Maou gave was predictable enough.

"But, I dunno, Alas Ramus really seems to dig all these rainbow colors. I don't know if that rings a bell in her mind or something, but..."

Alas Ramus's attention was absorbed in the poster outside the stage, depicting the live-action spandex stars shaking hands with the anime-style magical girl heroines—a fairly surreal piece of art, from a grown-up's perspective.

"That's fine with me, but it's gonna cost you money apart from the Passport, right? Can you cover that?"

There was a fairly long pause before Maou could manage a response.

"............I can apologize to Ashiya later. I already bought that hat anyway."

Emi wondered why, despite being the Devil's Castle's sole breadwinner, Maou acted so cowed whenever the subject of his resident househusband reared its ugly head.

"...Well, whatever. I'll cover Alas Ramus's ticket, okay? You can find a way to cover yours."

"*Thank* you!"

It would have taken a mountain of motivation for the Devil King to ever bow gratefully to the Hero like this.

But, from Emi's perspective, the Devil King now owed a debt to her. That would be enough to cover what she owed Ashiya following the whole Suzuno thing. She even thought about claiming Maou's part of that debt as covered as well, but relented. It seemed a step too far.

She headed right over to the nearby ticket booth, but the clerk meekly bowed to her in response.

"The next show's sold out! It's gonna be two hours until the next one!"

Emi yelled the report back to Maou.

"Seriously? Well, how 'bout we get tickets for the next show and have some lunch for now?"

"All right! In that case, two adults and one child."

She went back to Maou.

"Here. One adult ticket. That's fifteen hundred yen."

"Got it."

The pair exchanged the ticket for some cash from Maou's wallet. Then, with Alas Ramus in Maou's hands, they glanced at the park map and walked off toward a nearby restaurant.

"Boy, they're getting really friendly with each other now, hmmmm?"

"……"

"……"

Rika, of course, was basking in the joy of getting Ashiya and Chiho to react to her commentary.

"One of those superhero shows, though, huh? I never went to any of those when I was a kid. Whaddaya think? Wanna go in?"

"That's…a tad much."

"I kinda doubt we'd get a lot out of it."

"No? Why not?"

Rika's brows furrowed in confusion at Chiho's and Ashiya's sudden lack of enthusiasm.

"Well, it's kind of for little kids, isn't it? It'd be sorta weird if the three of us went in by ourselves…"

"Wow, *somebody's* behind the times. This isn't just a father-son thing anymore."

"Huh?"

"Even grown-ups like watching this stuff these days. All by themselves, even. You used to hear about the ladies going crazy for the handsome heroes in kids' shows before they transformed into their fancy outfits. This is kinda their chance to see those characters in real life, you know? Or their prerecorded voices, at least."

"Huhhh?"

"And this anime here, with the girls..."

"...That's *Pretty and Pure*, right? I used to watch that when I was younger, but there's so many characters to keep track of nowadays..."

*Magical Girl Pretty and Pure* was a long-running animated series featuring a group of fetching, magic-wielding young women fighting evil, often wearing outfits resembling lighter, frillier versions of what you saw in the spandex-hero shows. It was the current stand-out anime hit for young girls, to the point where theatrical releases came out on a yearly basis.

"Some people dig that show because they're just anime fans, but a lot of the voice team have gone on to become successful actors, too, y'know? I saw a magazine article about how there's this huge mass of male fans who go nuts for it."

"Wow... So I guess it's got appeal for men and women, young and old, huh?"

"No, I, er, I would hesitate to go that far, but..."

Ashiya hesitantly attempted to stop Chiho from building too inaccurate a picture of *Pretty and Pure*'s audience in her mind. Just then, the noise from beyond the wall indicated the stage show was under way.

It wasn't visible from outside—not much reason to charge admission otherwise—but the cheers from the audience included a few deep, basso shouts that definitely were not prepubescent in nature.

Rika snickered as she noticed Chiho's face freeze.

"How 'bout we go eat some lunch, too?"

Rika pointed out an open-air Italian café poised directly in front of the stage-show entrance.

Two hours later, Maou and his family sat down on a bleacher row relatively close to the stage.

"We got a pretty good position, huh? Pretty amazing to think it's all advance tickets only. I mean, look at that stage. It's so tiny."

Sitting down on the long bench, Maou considered his surroundings. "I heard if they didn't assign seats, the kids in the back wouldn't be able to see the show."

"Huh? Why not?"

"Well, y'know, there're a lot of...folks out there, in the world."

Even with the assigned tickets, these were simple bleachers, not cup-holder-equipped stadium seating. It would be impossible to avoid rubbing elbows with their rowmates.

Alas Ramus was there, and their assorted purchases were also between them, but to Emi, Maou was still sitting far too close for comfort.

Even amid a crowd of onlookers, there was no way she could withstand such intimate contact with Maou over a long period of time.

The stage show was another sellout, and with the sun beating down on them, it felt a good four or five degrees warmer than outside. After a short wait, the loudspeakers suddenly blasted out a loud theme song as smoke and fireworks zipped across the stage. The show was set to begin with the spandex-hero segment first, although the loud explosions were already enough to send Alas Ramus reeling.

Every iteration of these hero shows seemed to have its own theme, its own special finisher moves, and its own giant robot all the heroes combined to form, all of which was helpfully outlined in the opening theme song. This time around, the heroes were modeled after ninjas, it seemed.

A large tree prop stood front and center onstage, about the height of a two-story building. Each of the five heroes dropped down from it, one by one, all with their own trademark pose.

"Wow, they're falling from pretty high up!"

"...Why are *you* so impressed? You're the Devil King!"

"Do ninjas really go around in those colors, though?"

"It's a kid's show. Relax!"

The hero team had a few ninjalike moves between the flash and flair, but Maou had his doubts over whether a ninja in fluorescent pastel colors would be much good at stealth.

The tree prop was apparently going to be recycled for the *Pretty and Pure* segment, where it'd provide the "Earth-mother strength" the girls needed to fight.

"Dang! Those guys can really move! They should, like, join Special Forces or something."

The enemies this remarkably conspicuous ninja team faced off against were, for some reason, a horde of space aliens.

A particularly loud cheer arose among the children in the audience once the aliens' boss entered the stage.

"Oooh, rock on! The villain's got a fan club!"

"They're not cheering *for* him. They're cheering about how he's gonna get his ass kicked in a sec."

"Oh, quit ruining the fun, man! Hey, Alas Ramus, which side are you—"

Trying to bring the girl into the conversation, Maou noticed something was off.

Alas Ramus, normally a bubbly, excitable girl who adored colorful objects, was staring glassy-eyed at the stage, her face totally expressionless.

"Uh…Alas Ramus?"

The tone of Maou's voice made Emi take notice.

"What's wrong?"

"I dunno, she's kind of spacing out. Hey, what's up, Alas Ramus? Your tummy hurt or something?"

"Se…pila."

"Huh?"

"Fall down…"

"What? What is it?"

The cheering from the crowd made it hard to discern Alas Ramus.

"Daddy, that's Sepila!"

"Huh? What's wrong?"

"All fall down from tree. Mommy took me and ran. Market's gone, too."

"Tree? Market? What do you… Agh!"

Maou was thrown into a panic.

He had no idea what triggered it, but out of the blue, there it was— the crescent moon mark, plain upon Alas Ramus's forehead.

The emblem was almost crystalline, bearing the same purple twinge found in the girl's eyes and that one little clutch of her hair.

"What…is that?"

Maou tilted her hat to cover it up, but not quickly enough to keep Emi unaware.

"…Didn't you notice it? That same mark showed up on her head the first time she showed up in my yard. It went away really quick, but… Hey, Alas Ramus, speak to me!"

"Whoa, don't shake her like that! We better get out of here. Um, pardon me! My child's not feeling very well…"

Not waiting for Maou's response, Emi picked up Alas Ramus, navigating the excited crowd as she shouldered her way outside the arena.

She considered calling for an attendant, but there was no explaining away the crescent moon on her forehead.

Tossing a glance behind her to ensure Maou was in tow with all their belongings, Emi carried away Alas Ramus, still staring into space and mumbling something to herself, as she searched for someplace cool and quiet to rest.

She tried touching her forehead, but she was neither warm nor sweating profusely. It wasn't a case of heat exhaustion, but Emi had no idea what the mark apparently causing all of this meant.

Jumping inside the Lagoon building in search of air-conditioning, she quickly spotted an empty bench. She sat down, then barked at Maou, who was lagging behind.

"Devil King! Buy me something for her to drink!"

"Uh, does this work?"

He showed her the bottle of oral rehydration formula.

"Give it!"

Emi snatched it from his hand and brought it to Alas Ramus's mouth.

"Get me something else cold, too! Not to drink, but to put on her head and stuff to cool down!"

"R-right!"

Even in his helter-skelter state, Maou faithfully followed Emi's orders, running off in search of a vending machine.

"Is she all right?"

Suddenly, someone called to Emi, Alas Ramus still in her hands.

Looking up, Emi saw a fetching young woman standing before her, clad in a long white dress and a broad-rimmed white hat.

Her eyes, which seemed to absorb everything they saw, fell upon Emi and Alas Ramus.

"Uh, yeah, she's fine. I don't think it's heat exhaustion, so she must have an upset stomach or something..."

"...Mommy?"

Suddenly, Alas Ramus—oblivious until now to Emi's voice—came back to attention.

Emi brightened up as she peered into her face.

"I'm right here. Are you okay?"

"Uh-huh..."

Her face didn't appear flushed, but the voice indicated she wasn't all quite there. Emi tried to hide her forehead, pretending to wipe her head clear of sweat.

"May I have a second?"

Then, the girl in white knelt down to eye level, bringing her hand above Alas Ramus's head.

"Wh-what're you doing?"

"Sshh. This will take just a moment."

There was nothing threatening to her voice, but Emi still fell silent as instructed. On the new girl's ring finger, there was a ring embedded with a small stone.

For a moment, Emi noticed that it seemed to shine purple in the sunlight. Then:

"...Oo...ooh?!"

Out of nowhere, Alas Ramus picked herself up.

"Ngh? Ooh? Huh? Daddy?"

Squirming as if waking up from a bad dream, Alas Ramus swiveled her head around to gauge her surroundings.

To Emi, the biggest surprise was that her forehead—exposed to the world after the sudden motion knocked the hat off her head—was back to normal, the moon mark wholly disappeared.

"Ah, Mommy—wpph!"

Moving quickly, Emi picked Alas Ramus up, keeping her safely to the rear as she rose to face the girl in white.

"There's no need to be so distrustful. I am not your enemy."

The girl, perfectly composed, brushed her skirt away and smiled.

"Nor am I the enemy of this child, either... You have done well to keep Alas Ramus safe."

"!!"

Emi never voiced the name in front of this girl.

"How did you know that...?"

The woman smiled serenely.

"How could I not? It is a very important name to me."

Emi's heart skipped a beat as she watched her.

The conversation with Emeralda three days ago flashed across her mind.

Obviously she was indicating that she knew Alas Ramus.

Was this woman...?

Emi felt a warmth quite different from the summer heat, but the smiling woman suddenly melted into a serious-minded glare.

"You need to be careful. They've probably noticed the Yesod fragment in that girl's forehead now. The enemy will make their appearance soon. The Heavenly Regiment in Gabriel's command are on the move."

"Yesod...fragment? Who's Gabriel...? Wait. Are you—"

"Hey! Emi! I got some stuff!"

The moment the enraptured Emi attempted to ask the fateful question, Maou thundered in, bearing a bottle of water and a can of juice.

Emi's attention was distracted for just a moment, when:

"Mommy..."

"‼"

The girl in white was gone.

It was completely without warning, like she had been talking to a daydream.

"Good thing there was a whole wall of vending machines nearby. Here... Huh? Oh, did Alas Ramus wake up?"

"Hi, Daddy!"

"Oh, uh, hey. Well, jeez, that wound up being a lot of nothing, huh? I mean, great, but... Hey, what happened, little lady?"

"Whaaa?"

"Um... Ah, never mind. But hey, Emi, what's—*urphh*!"

"Why can't you *ever* see what's going on? You never do! Never, never, *never*!"

"Wh-what?! What did I ever do?! Why'd you have to punch me like that?"

"Mommy's scaaaary!"

"Ooh! There he is! That's him over there!"

"Hee-hee! Good job, Chiho! There's the power of love, huh?"

"Aw, stop messing around like that!"

"Ughh... You must have a pretty wimpy stomach, Ashiya. Who ever heard of someone getting sick on olive oil? It took a long time finding you, you know."

"M-my apologies..."

Thanks to Ashiya's stomach proving overly sensitive to the olive oil from the Italian restaurant they dined at, Chiho and her friends had lost sight of Maou, Emi, and Alas Ramus.

Failing to spot them among the crowd leaving the stage show, they decided to walk around the park grounds for a little while. Soon, Chiho noticed Emi from behind, Alas Ramus in her hands, all but dragging Maou as she walked.

They were headed for the Tokyo Eye, the gigantic Ferris wheel that jutted high above the park.

"Are they going on the Ferris wheel? Emi looks like she's dead set on it, but..."

"It must get pretty hot on that thing this time of year."

"Oh, all the gondolas on that Ferris wheel are air-conditioned. As long as you've got sunscreen on, it's pretty comfy."

"H-how wastefully luxurious!"

Ashiya proved typically quick to criticize any AC usage that didn't involve his permission.

"But you have to wonder... Why's Emi so eager to drag Maou into an enclosed room suspended in the air, hmm?"

"Suzuki!!"

"Jeez, I'm just joking, Chiho! Boy, you can look really scary when you want to, huh?"

Knowing full well that Chiho was aware it was a joke, Rika was just being a bitch.

"Well, you wanna follow them? I doubt we'll see anything, but... Are you okay with that, Ashiya?"

"I think so..."

He nodded, arm raised upward, his face still a tad pale.

Given the intense heat and the sad state of his regular diet, eating a sumptuous Italian meal in an open-air café was enough to KO his stomach with one punch.

"Y'know, I don't know what drove the both of you to do this, but I don't think anything bad's really happening, huh?"

Rika's overly sunny observation, the result of her lacking a few pertinent points of knowledge, made Chiho and Ashiya exchange glances with each other.

"Hello there, and welcome to the Tokyo Eye Ferris...wheel...?"

The ticket attendant at the Ferris wheel entrance found herself groping for words at the sight of the young family before him, a cloud of black, ominous miasma hovering over their heads.

Perhaps *ominous* wasn't the right term. The husband appeared downright frightened at the seething anger demonstrated by his wife, their two-year-old daughter seemingly unsure which side to take up with.

"Three!"

The wife presented three passes like a boxer throwing a jab. The attendant vigorously nodded and pointed forward.

"Right! Good afternoon! We'll be glad to take a photo for you guys right over there! Then you can buy a print of your special day at that booth over there!! Feel free to take a look once you're done on the wheel!!"

Another attendant stood near the gondola entrance, a large digital camera in hand, ready to sell a photo to them for the usual amusement park ripoff rate.

"I…I don't really need one…"

"Oh, we'll be glad to delete it if you aren't happy with it, ma'am! If you could just stand over there… Good! Okay, if I could have Dad pick up that cute little girl and stand in the middle… Perfect! Oh, would you mind putting her balloons behind you a little?"

The attendant seemed oddly amped up for this dysfunctional family photo.

"Daddy, what's that?"

Alas Ramus's eyes set upon the camera in the employee's hands.

"Hmm? Oh, that's called a camera. They'll use it to take your photo."

"Photo?"

As gifted in the Japanese language as she was, she still had trouble with concepts that didn't exist on Ente Isla.

"Uhh, you know, a picture… It's a tool that can draw pictures with magic. Just stay still and look into that black, round thing the girl's carrying."

"Ohhh!"

Whether she understood that or not, Alas Ramus peered intently into the lens as her curiosity took over.

"Okay, can I have Mom look this way, please?"

"……"

Emi had been anxiously turned to the side up to this point. But, not wanting to act too contrarian around an innocent stranger, she made a token effort to readjust her pose.

"Greeeat! Okay, here we go! One, two, and...*cheese!* ...Super! That was a nice picture! Come on back down here if you'd like to make a purchase later!"

Sent off by the oddly intense attendant, the trio finally boarded their gondola.

"...Ooh. Chilly."

They were expecting a sauna inside the booth, but a blast of cold air emanated from behind the seats' backrests, accompanied by some peppy background music. The seats were hard and bleacher-like, but it was surprisingly comfortable inside.

"Be careful with those balloons, okay? It'll take about fifteen minutes to go around once. No smoking, eating, or drinking allowed inside the gondola. Have a great trip!"

The attendant quickly went over the basic rules before shutting the door.

"Ooh, they're already on!"

Outside of Emi's or Maou's notice, Chiho, Rika, and Ashiya had just made it to the Ferris wheel ticket office.

"They're gonna get away! Hurry!"

Pushed on by Rika, Ashiya and Chiho hurriedly threw some money into the ticket purchasing machine.

"Um, excuse me."

"Huh?"

Someone suddenly called out from Chiho's side.

Turning around, she found an older woman, a child young enough to be her grandson next to her, looking helplessly confused by the adjacent ticket machine.

"Do you have any idea how to work this machine?"

"Oh, sure. First, you put your money in here... This is a touch panel, so..."

Chiho was well aware by now that some of the older generation still had trouble following the concept of how a touch panel worked.

The money slot on this machine was a fair distance removed from the panel itself, and the screen offered little in the way of guidance, displaying nothing but a simple numeric keypad. User friendliness wasn't a priority in this design.

"I don't think there's a children's rate for this Ferris wheel, so they'll both cost this much. So just push the number for how many tickets you want..."

Chiho was all but forced to take the woman step-by-step through the purchasing process.

Thanking her profusely, the woman headed for the Ferris wheel.

"Dahh! Oh, no!"

Then it struck Chiho. All this fervent instruction was costing the three of them time.

"......Huh?"

Then it struck Chiho again. The ticket booth and gondola entrance weren't that large, and yet Ashiya and Rika were nowhere to be spotted.

"Huh? Huhhh?"

She stared upward in a daze, only to find her eyes meeting with Rika's as her friend stared through the gondola window, face frozen in an awkward smile.

"Huhhhhhhh?"


"All right. Can we talk now?"

Maou, caged inside the small gondola, found no escape from the glare of Emi's pinlike pupils. Her gaze, seeping between the helium balloons in Alas Ramus's hands, was nothing short of terrifying.

"I should've known from the start you were acting fishy. Why did you come out and say that you'd take this girl? You *hate* dealing with annoying crap like that."

"Oh, well, that..."

"And back when that moon thing appeared on her forehead, you acted like you knew what it was, didn't you? Out with it! Everything! Right now!"

"Mommy! What's that? That big thing?"

"Um... That's the Tokyo Skytree."

"Yeah. That's where all the digital TV transmitters are. Thanks to *that*, Daddy has to pay for some stupid set-top box if he wants…"

"Don't change the subject!"

The gondola swayed slightly at the shuddering impact of Emi's voice.

Two gondolas behind, Rika and Ashiya were alone.

"Dehh… If we were just a little faster, we could see what was going on inside…"

They had successfully clambered into a gondola, but the booths were hardly see-through, and getting a clear vantage point on the gondola two places ahead was easier said than done.

"…………"

Rika sat opposite from Ashiya, eyes fixed downward around her feet.

Chiho must have gotten caught up in something. Rika thought she was with them, but the next thing she knew, she was alone with Ashiya.

"Is there something wrong, Ms. Suzuki?"

"Agh! Huh?!"

Rika, as loud and gregarious as she was a moment ago, was suddenly as quiet as a clam. Even Ashiya took notice.

"Uh, I, um, she, I'm sorry that—that I left Chiho, is all…"

"We were certainly in a great hurry, yes…"

Rika's forced response was enough to put Ashiya's mind at rest. With a sigh, he sat heavily on his seat.

"……!!"

The gondolas on the Ferris wheel weren't exactly roomy by design. With someone as tall as Ashiya sitting down, it was unavoidable that they'd brush against each other with their knees or legs.

The sheer love for life Rika showed up to now was, in the end, something she could express mainly because Chiho was around to egg her on.

If a third party was there, touching bodies or being cramped in a tiny space was nothing that bothered her. But here, alone with a man in an enclosed area, was something she had never experienced before in her life.

Especially if the man was Ashiya.

When they met a week ago, in the midst of all the furor surrounding Emi and Suzuno, she didn't think of him as much more than kind of an off-kilter young man. In the past several hours of activity together, that impression only deepened.

"Are you all right? Your face is a little red. Did you get sunburned?" Ashiya asked.

"T-too close!"

"Hmm?"

"Oh! Um. No. It's fine, it's fine! I guess that sunscreen sure doesn't work as advertised, huh? Yep." Rika flailed her arms in response, pulling herself as far back as humanly possible.

Ashiya, paying this act no particular mind, began taking in the view outside.

The attendant said one ride around the wheel would take fifteen minutes, but to Rika, the sheer embarrassment was something she questioned how long she could withstand.

Meanwhile Chiho, seated on a bench at the gondola entrance, was brooding over a can of chilled green tea labeled "Yo! Tea!"

"So, what?! Are you talking? Are you not talking?! You want to die?!" Emi demanded.

"Give me some more *choices*, man! You're gonna be a bad influence on this kid!"

The we-have-ways-of-making-you-talk ultimatum continued in the lead gondola.

"I mean, c'mon, does it really matter? It's not like I *did* anything. I'm just fine with being Alas Ramus's dad, okay?"

"Maybe *you* are, but I'm not! Didn't you see her?! That girl in the white dress, standing right in front of me? She talked about the Heavenly Regiment or something! If you want to stay on my good side, you better spit out everything you know, start to finish, right now!"

"See her? See *who*?! And since when was I *ever* on your good side?!"

"I'm not talking about you! I'm talking about her!"

Emi's eyes descended upon Alas Ramus, staring out the gondola window.

As the two of them watched the girl from behind, the gondola gradually reached its highest point on the wheel.

"...Someone gave it to me a long time ago."

Maou sighed, resigned to his fate, his face a grimace.

"Back before I was Devil King... Really, I was just a snot-nosed little kid. Like, *maybe* I could've taken on a *goblin*."

Emi, realizing that Maou was finally in the mood to talk, lowered her guard and sat down to listen.

"Back then...and I'm talking way before you were ever born...the demon realm was a real pile of crap. There were all these different roving tribes, and all it took was eye contact for them to start ripping one another apart. I was part of one of the weaker tribes—you could've blown us away with the flick of a finger. And one of them did. This huge, musclebound demon with a peanut for a brain annihilated us all by himself. He couldn't cast any magic, but he didn't need it. The first and last memory I have of my parents is watching them breathe their last on the dirt."

The personal narrative began without warning. It was perhaps an even worse influence on Alas Ramus's upbringing than anything Maou had done before, but Emi sat silently, not wanting to break the mood.

"The survivors were all slaughtered in a battle against another rival tribe. I was tossed out like garbage with the rest of them. I was pretty close to dying. But one person cared enough about a dirty little brat like me to save my life."

Looking at some far-off point in the distance, Maou continued, his voice taking on a nostalgic twinge.

"That was the first time I ever met an angel. I'd never seen such pure white wings before."

"Daddy, what's that?"

"Hmm? Ooh, you got a good eye, Alas Ramus! That's called a blimp."

"Bliiimp?"

Alas Ramus stared up at the dirigible for a moment, mouth agape.

"Uh, where was I?"

"At the point where an angel saved your life..."

"Oh, right. Anyway, I was basically this goblin-level goon, so I tried taking her on, even though I was wounded. Looking back, she must've been a pretty high-level angel, but anyway, she didn't even bother paying attention to me. Not that she killed me or anything, though. I was still a demon, more or less, so I would've healed by myself, but that bastard kept checking in on me, talking to me about all kinds of different crap. I wasn't able to move much, so I was forced to listen to it all. She taught me about a lot of stuff I didn't know."

Emi was, if anything, surprised.

Given that he went around calling himself Satan the Devil King, she expected that he was born that way, part of a prestigious lineage of noble demons (assuming such a thing existed down there).

"So it took a pretty long time to heal, I think. I was pretty banged up, after all. And after a while, it finally dawned on me that this angel wasn't gonna kill me. She kept on talking to me, no matter how much I hated it, so I started to learn a lot. But the more I heard from her, the more I realized there was no way angels should be going around helping demons. So I asked her: 'Why are you helping me?' "

"...And?"

"...Don't laugh, okay? If you do, I'm not saying any more."

For reasons only he knew, Maou averted his eyes in embarrassment.

"She said it's because I was crying."

"Huh?"

"She said she never saw a demon crying before, so she just couldn't let me be."

It was hard for Emi to imagine a demon crying at all, for any reason. It made her realize for the first time how little she actually knew about the collection of species her human compatriots called "demons."

"What reason did you have for crying?"

Maou winced at the question. But, realizing she didn't mean to poke fun at him, he resignedly continued.

"Well, a bunch of things. Like I said, I didn't really care much about losing my parents or the people around me. If I had to put it in words… I guess I was just pissed. Pissed at how weak I was. Pissed at how unfair it was, just dying without even a whimper like that."

Maou's eyes were still averted from Emi's, a side effect of retelling these bitter memories.

"But anyway, this angel took care of me until I was healed, and taught me about a lot of stuff, too. That was the first time I learned there was such a thing as the human world."

"!!"

Maou had glossed past it, but to Emi, this was a shocking revelation.

Was an angel the root cause that ultimately led to the Devil King's invasion of Ente Isla?

There was no conclusive evidence behind anything Maou said, of course. But if he wasn't lying, this fact had the potential to shake the very core of what little peace Emi's world clung to.

"And this girl…or the crystal she used to be, at least… She left it with me the day she went away. It was this beautiful violet crystal, shaped like a crescent moon."

"No! I'm looking!"

Alas Ramus yelped in protest as Maou lifted her up.

Nothing was on her forehead at the moment, but that crescent-shaped mark must have been meant to symbolize her original crystal form.

"'If you want to learn more of the world, take this seed. Plant it, and allow it to grow. Then, you will go far, Satan, my Devil Overlord.'"

"What?"

"That's what she wrote in the note she left behind. Literacy, too— that was another gift she gave to me. A revolutionary way to convey information, one that didn't involve violence or crazed gibbering for a change. So I'll gloss over the next two hundred years of glorious conquest, when I took the demonic rabble and forged it into a proper civilization, but there's no way that ever would've happened without the knowledge she gave me. So that's why I planted that crescent-shaped seed. I thought it would benefit me, sooner or later, even if I didn't know exactly what it was. Then, when I planted this crystal on that angel's command—get this—it actually sprouted into a tree. Kind of a letdown, you know?"

Now Maou's eyes were focused upon a not-so-ancient point in his life. The Devil's Castle—the original one, the symbol of the transformation he had engineered in the demon realms, built on the ruins of Isla Centurum in the center of the Ente Isla lands.

The Devil King, upon setting foot on a world that was not his own for the first time, planted the moon-shaped purple crystal in its soil, anticipating it would bud into a harbinger of the future.

He cultivated it inside a pot placed deep inside his personal chamber, fully exposed to the sunlight, in an area nobody but himself was allowed access to.

"I mean, it's not like I was tutored and trained from birth to be Devil King. Back then, in the demon realms, you couldn't spit without hitting someone whose name was Satan. We were taught that it was the name of some great demonic overlord, one who lived in an era before legend, blah blah blah. It's really a miracle any kind of legends existed at all in that dump before I came around. I have no idea why that angel called me 'Devil Overlord,' but I guess that's where I got my start. With her."

Maou gave Alas Ramus a pat on the head, but the girl escaped from his hand, plastering herself against the gondola window.

"But, anyway, that sort of thing. In terms of the role I had in taking that purple crystal and making it into Alas Ramus, I guess you could make the case I'm her dad."

"So would that angel be her true…?"

"It'd make sense, wouldn't it? But it was just this plain old crystal when she gave it to me, so... I dunno if you'd really call that an embryo or whatever."

Emi, breaking out in a cold sweat as she felt her pulse rise and an ominous premonition loom over her mind, asked the obvious question.

"Who was it?"

Laila had disappeared from Emeralda's sight. The woman in white knew Alas Ramus's name. The crystal that produced Alas Ramus was gifted to the Devil King by an angel. That girl now saw Emi as her mother.

It couldn't be.

A superstorm of anticipation, premonition, and anxiousness raced through Emi's heart.

"Nobody you know."

The storm dissipated into a light drizzle.

"...You aren't trying to hide her from me, are you?"

"I'm not trying to, but I don't think she's anyone that famous. She didn't show up in any of the sacred Church tracts or anything. Hey, but can you tell me why Alas Ramus is back to normal now? You know something about that, right?"

Emi found Maou's sudden vagueness inscrutable. But she answered anyway, reasoning she had already learned enough about Maou's past for today.

"She was healed by this girl dressed entirely in white. She put her hand above her, and that was all it took."

"...Whoa, what's up with that? Some kind of New Age deal?"

Maou must not have seen the woman. Emi pressed on.

"No! She was there when you got back! Didn't you *see* her?! It was like, I think her ring glowed a little bit, and then Alas Ramus was right back awake! Like she was just having a dream or something!"

"I didn't see anybody! What kind of ring?"

"Just a plain old ring. I think it had a purple stone in it, but..."

"...That's definitely *not* plain *or* old."

These occasional mental lapses on Emi's part were enough to make Maou scream.

"Did you notice anything else?"

"Well, I didn't have that much time before some idiot came in shouting at me like a crazy man."

"C'mon."

"Oh, and she said something about the Heavenly Regiment, and something about a…Yesod fragment? I think that's what it—*ow*!"

Maou instinctively landed a karate chop on Emi's hat-adorned head.

"Wh-what'd you do *that* for?! I'm gonna kill you!"

Emi quickly grew eager to ratchet up the conflict. Maou stuck to his guns.

"Look, are you *really* a knight of the Church, or what? I swear! Young people these days are so stupid! At least *try* to learn something for a change!" Maou bellowed as he held his head in his hands, hunching over in mental anguish. "Yesod… Yesod?! Not *that*, dammit! Jeez, of all the things that bastard could've pushed on me… So that thing before, too…!"

"Wh-what? What're you going on about all of a sudden?"

"Man, when we get home, Suzuno is gonna call you *such* an idiot."

"Huhh?!"

"Look, doesn't the word *Yesod* mean anything to—"

"Whaaaat, Daddyyy?"

Alas Ramus, attention focused out the window up to now, suddenly reacted to Maou and his *Yesod* keyword.

"Uh?"

Emi paused, confused on the meaning of this. Maou stooped down to Alas Ramus's level, his face somewhere between conviction and desperation.

"Alas Ramus, listen…"

"Yeah, Daddy?"

"What's that?"

Maou pointed out a red balloon. The girl replied at once.

"Gebba."

"And that?"

He next pointed to a dark-yellow, almost orange balloon.

"Tiparuh."

"And how about this bright yellow one?"

"Market. I like him!"

"And the white one?"

"Ketter."

"Wh-what's she going on about...?"

Emi blinked in helpless confusion over the unfamiliar terms.

"Okay, how about this?"

Maou fished a purple balloon out from the bunch.

"Me! Yeffod."

"Oooh, good girl. You can say it and everything."

"Oooo! Hee-hee!"

The gondola was nearing the end of its journey. Emi squinted at the western sun illuminating the Big-Egg stadium.

"I don't really know why...but I got a feeling Alas Ramus is something way beyond a demon. Or an angel."

"Huh?"

"Gevurah, Hod, Malkuth, Keter, and then Yesod. They're each the names of the Sephirah, the world-forming jewels that grow on the tree of Sephirot. I think...Alas Ramus might be the personification of the Yesod Sephirah."

Chiho, waiting on the bench as Maou's and Ashiya's gondolas spun slowly around, was wallowing in self-loathing.

By herself, able to more calmly assess the situation, she now realized she was in no position to criticize Rika's rubbernecking habit.

She had pretended this was all for a just cause, offering to lend her cell phone to Ashiya in case anything happened to Maou. But, as she now admitted to herself, all she was doing was stewing in her jealousy over Maou's pseudo-married relationship with Emi.

"Maou said he believed in me and everything, too…"

Having that trust be shattered by Chiho herself was something she couldn't dare to face up to Maou or Emi about.

As she dwelled on the point, a deep, helpless sense of shame enveloped her.

"Maou… I'm sorry."

Taken in by waves of anxiety and jealousy, she did the one thing she should never have done. Chiho stood up and walked down the stairs, not bothering to wait for Ashiya and Rika.

Not long after she was gone, the gondola bearing Maou, Emi, and Alas Ramus came down.

"Whew… Sure is hot out, huh?"

"Mmmph!"

Maou and Alas Ramus winced at the blast of hot air awaiting them outside.

Emi, eerily silent, was the last to exit.

"Thank you very much! We have your photo here if you'd like!"

Turning toward the voice, Maou was greeted with a print of the photo they had reluctantly taken of themselves, complete with special commemorative mounting.

"Oooooooo!!"

"…Ugh, I look terrible."

Alas Ramus's eyes gleamed as she spotted herself in the photo. Emi, meanwhile, winced. Her face in the picture looked like she just swallowed a wasp.

"You can have this photo, along with a special mounting you can write a personalized message on, for one thousand yen. We can make copies, too!"

"Wait, it's not free?"

Maou blurted out his honest reaction. Emi slapped him on the back of the head.

"Hmm… A thousand, huh…?"

"Daddy! Daddy, look! Look!"

Alas Ramus clearly wanted the photo. But considering the cost of the photo paper, printer ink, and mounting, it was pretty clear which side of this exchange was profiting the most out of it.

"...We'll just take one, please."

To Maou's surprise, it was Emi who made the snap decision. Taking a thousand-yen bill from her wallet, she accepted the photo and passed it over to Alas Ramus.

"Yaaay!"

Opening the twofold mount, Alas Ramus exclaimed her joy upon seeing herself, the vaguely half-smiling Maou, and the outright sulking Emi inside.

"W-wait, are you sure?"

"It's just a thousand yen. You don't have to act so cheap all the time. This is her first photo, isn't it?"

"Well, I guess so, but..."

"And lemme just warn you! Next time Eme and Al get here, don't show that to them! It'd put my position with them at stake, all right?"

"Oh, so it's okay with Ashiya and Chi and Suzuno and so on?"

"It's kind of too late with them, okay? Don't you dare show Lucifer, though!"

"You are being *so* stupid."

Snickering over Emi's admittedly stupid demands, Maou crouched down to look at Alas Ramus.

"Okay, Alas Ramus, say 'thank you' to Mommy."

"'Ank you, Mommy!!"

Emi's face turned bright red at the childish squeal, loud enough to make everyone in the gondola loading area turn around.

"I...I'm just doing what any mother would do! It's not my fault her father's such a worthless bum!"

It was hard to tell what she was making excuses for. Perhaps she simply wanted to make it clear that her gesture for Alas Ramus had nothing to do with feeling sorry for Maou.

"C-Come on! Let's go!"

Maou and Alas Ramus walked behind Emi as she descended the stairs, face turned away. Then, he paused.

"Hold on, Emi. I got a phone call."

"Huh? ...Oh, me too. Wait here a second, okay, Alas Ramus?"

The pair both received a call at the same time—Urushihara to Maou, Suzuno to Emi.

"W-we lost them?!"

Ashiya was exasperated to find the gondola loading zone deserted. They were sitting only two gondolas behind, so they shouldn't have been separated by longer than a minute or two.

Running down the stairs, Ashiya scoped out the shopping area ahead of him. Maou and Emi were still nowhere to be seen.

"I...I wonder where Chiho could've gone, too."

Rika, despite spending the past fifteen minutes inside an air-conditioned gondola, was notably red in the face.

"Maybe Chiho decided to chase after them... What should we do, Ashiya?"

This was seriously bad news. If Chiho didn't find the errant couple soon, Rika would have to be together, with Ashiya, by herself, for even longer!

"I...am not sure what we can do. We have no way of contacting her."

"Huh?"

"I am afraid I don't have my own cell phone."

"What? Really?!"

Released from her air-conditioned prison, Rika was slowly returning to her normal self.

"I had planned to borrow Ms. Sasaki's phone if anything untoward happened...but now..."

It was approaching the evening hours, but the park was still fairly crowded, too much so to make searching for Maou and Emi a practical option.

"...Well, so be it. This is kind of pushing it more than I like, but..."

Rika took out her own cell phone and brought up Emi's number. "Uh, hey, Emi?"

Ashiya was about to scream in response to Rika's brazen act of recklessness, but fell silent as Rika put her index finger in front of his lips in a classic "shut up" pose.

"Hmm? Oh, no, nothing too important... I was just wondering if your date with Maou was going okay and all... Ha-ha-ha! Aw, sorry, sorry. I know, it's for the sake of the kid and all. I'm not calling at a bad time, am I? Are you about to eat or... Huh?"

Rika, attempting to ferret out Emi's location under the guise of her trivial banter, wasn't expecting the response Emi gave.

"You're going back home now?"

"What?"

This threw Ashiya. Rika attempted to hide her own surprise as best she could.

"Ohh, I gotcha. The kid's probably pooped by now, huh? Yeah. Well, at least she had a lot of fun today, right? Okay, sorry to interrupt you on the way to the station and all! Have a safe trip back!"

"...Well, that explains that."

Rika shut off her phone as she turned to Ashiya.

"They're gone... Ugghh! That's no fun."

"In that case, there is little point remaining here. Do you think Ms. Sasaki might have left as well?"

"I dunno about that, but I guess that was kinda mean, huh? Leaving her down there and all. Hey, next time you see her, do you mind telling her I'm sorry?"

"Oh, no, not at all. In that case, I had best hurry on myself. Thank you for your help today."

"Oh... Wh-whoa! Wait a second!"

Rika found herself stopping Ashiya, just as he was about to run off in search of Maou.

"Um... So, uh... Oh, right! Here..."

Fumbling around in her bag, Rika finally produced a notebook, ripping a page out of it and jotting something down before handing it to Ashiya.

"Is this...your phone number?"

"It's my...uh..."

"Your?"

Ashiya scrutinized the digits on the paper.

"Well, you know, the next time something comes up...I could, like, maybe help you guys out...or whatever?"

Not even Rika had a clear picture of what kind of something she was referring to. But if she didn't say something, there was no way she could withstand the oppressive atmosphere within her mind any longer.

"I see... Well, certainly, I may just be calling upon your services again sometime in the future."

"...Huh?"

Her request couldn't have been more awkward, but Ashiya nodded, completely convinced by it.

"As I mentioned, I have yet to purchase my own cell phone, so if I need something, I could use Maou's to..."

Ashiya stopped at that point, shaking his head as he recalled something. Maou's cell phone served as the chief link from Devil's Castle to the outside world, but he realized that giving his supreme master's digits to a semi-acquaintance he rode the Ferris wheel with might not be the best thing.

"Though...I feel, perhaps, that I have learned something from today. It may put an additional burden on our finances, yes, but perhaps the time has come for me to have my own cell phone. Have you any purchasing advice?"

Rika's face instantly flushed a bright crimson.

"I understand you work for the same phone company as Yusa. I cannot say whether I would buy a device from your company or not quite yet, but if you have the free time, I would greatly appreciate some guidance when I make my choice."

"Uh... Sure! Yeah, give me a call anytime!"

Rika nodded eagerly, all but standing on tiptoe to drive the point home.

"Thank you very much. In that case, I will be sure to contact you soon...from a public phone, I imagine."

"All right..."

"I'd best be off, then."

With a light bow, Ashiya turned and ran off toward the Korakuen rail station.

"No way... Oh, man, what am I doing...? This is totally nuts!"

Rika, meanwhile, remained rooted to the spot until Ashiya was no longer visible.

"What am I gonna do... What am I gonna do... What am I gonna do?!"

After a few more moments, she began to walk unsteadily in the opposite direction, toward Suidoubashi station.

THE
DEVIL
KING
FEELS
THE
PAIN
OF
LOSS

Amid the darkness of untwinkling stars, there was a great land, one bathed in red and blue.

This land, which shone a glistening azure, took the form of an enormous engraved cross, each branch teeming with life.

In one part of this great blue landscape, the stars were accompanied by a planet teeming with life. Therein lay a vast wilderness, one bereft of any sound. Not even a single breeze flowed through it.

A single vast tree, itself the same color as the azure land, loomed ominously in the wasteland.

This tree, standing in the vast, flat wilderness, lived for countless months and years. It brimmed with the force of countless souls, countless lives; but externally, it resembled little more than a withered husk.

There were no leaves to cover the heavens, no flowering buds to decorate the passing Springs, no fruit with which to celebrate this blue world's bounty. There was just the tree, standing there alone, as if it had committed a great sin it could do nothing to atone for.

Ten shrines were built around this vast tree, as if to surround it, each bearing a name carved upon its entrance.

The first shrine was Keter. The next was Chokhmah, then Binah, Chesed, Gevurah, Tifaret, Netzach, Hod, Yesod, and finally Malkuth.

These names belonged to someone. They must have. But no one could say where the people who could read and write these carved names could be now.

These shines were not stately buildings, no shining pillars or exquisite roofs adorning them. Instead, they were ten perfect spheres, like great stones dug up from the earth, spread out across the land like the enormous fruit the great tree must have borne at some distant time in the past.

One day, the blue wilderness was greeted with motion once more.

From the sphere carved with the word *Yesod*, a large figure appeared.

"Ah. Good. Found that one relatively quickly."

It sounded like a man's voice.

With that whisper, four pillars of light appeared around the large figure, each one soon taking the form of people themselves.

"After we received no response from the Central Continent, I was expecting to spend centuries searching...but it looks like we've lost nothing at all. The 'fragments' resonated with each other in a certain place."

The people within the pillars of light began to murmur.

"The place Sariel disappeared to recently. Him, and likely..."

The large man took in the full length of the nearly rotted-out blue tree.

"Yes. That girl who stole the Yesod Sephirah is there as well."

The large man raised his arms to the stars. The next moment, a great hole to another dimension opened up, filled with light and hovering in the air.

"Let us go. Go, and return the tree of Sephirot to its intended form."

Then the five figures disappeared into the Gate.

Soon, the light from the Gate was gone, and silence returned to the azure land.

The five figures that once stood by the great tree now beheld the land engraved with the cross of life—Ente Isla, the Land of the Holy Cross. The azure land stayed close to this land of life, lazily revolving around it, but never daring to stray near the crimson orb that lurked beyond them both.

✳

It was just a little bit before Maou and Emi disembarked from the Tokyo Big-Egg Ferris wheel.

"Yo! Bell! You around?!"

"Nrgh... Wh-what is it, Lucifer?"

Suzuno was surprised to find Urushihara outside of his closet fortress. She was even more surprised to find him visiting her room, in a state of panic.

She was enjoying a late lunch of boiled udon, causing her to almost choke on a mouthful when he burst through the door.

Urushihara noticed the heaping pile of chilled noodles in Suzuno's bowl. Suzuno nimbly followed his eyes.

"There is *none* for you."

"Yeah, I don't need any udon for a while. I ordered in some pizza just now, so... Wait! Dude, that doesn't matter!"

After making the confession, which would likely rile Ashiya back into his demonic form if he heard it, Urushihara asked Suzuno a question.

"Did you notice that just now?"

"Notice?"

Suzuno tilted her head in confusion.

"Guess not, huh? Hey, do you know how to contact Emilia? I'll call Maou myself. I think we better get 'em back here ASAP."

"Why? What do you mean?"

Suzuno frowned, noticing Urushihara acting sincere for a change.

"Just do it, dude. I don't know why, but this huge Gate just opened up somewhere in Tokyo. I think we got some trouble brewing."

With that, Urushihara zoomed back to his room and launched the SkyPhone app on his computer. Suzuno, finding it difficult to believe his behavior was just an act, picked up her phone and brought up Emi's number.

That was when five figures materialized in Villa Rosa Sasazuka's front yard.

"Whoa, whoa, you didn't say anything about visitors."

Maou flashed an easy smile, but still made sure to keep Alas Ramus behind him.

"So what happened first? The Gate, or this?"

"I apologize, Devil King... We were caught completely unawares."

"Yeah, I'll admit I didn't think they'd make a move *that* quick."

Suzuno grovelingly made the apology. Urushihara, meanwhile, demonstrated his usual lack of conscience.

"Ohh, there's no need to blame them, mm-kay? They were nice enough to give you two a buzz, after all!"

Maou and Emi, hurriedly returning to Villa Rosa Sasazuka, found themselves greeted by neither Urushihara nor Suzuno.

"Besides, we aren't doing anything *too* rough, ya know? It'd be a *huuuge* win-win for all of us if we can talk this out, so hopefully we can avoid any sticking points and stuff like that, mm-kay?"

The air inside Devil's Castle was stifling.

Chiefly this was because the population density inside was causing the room temperature to skyrocket.

There were, after all, ten people in a hundred-square-foot apartment. Though, in strict humanist-biological terms, Suzuno Kamazuki was the only "person" there.

"Gabriel?"

"Ooh, bingo! Right square on the head! You *must* tell me how you guessed! Have we met before?"

The giant, easygoing, weirdly intense man, one Maou would have loved to punch right now, seemed to be the leader of the uninvited guests.

He had blue hair, cut neatly at the shoulders, and his eyes held no apparent concern or anxiety over anything. His upper body was easily as long as Ashiya's, though, and the bulging muscles made him look like a professional wrestler. He wore a body-length toga, something that would've been stylish among the ancient Greeks, and it couldn't have looked less natural on him.

Besides the one Maou called "Gabriel," four other men were in Devil's Castle. One was holding a ridiculously ornate longsword to Suzuno's throat, while the other three stood guard around Urushi-hara as he sat cross-legged on the floor.

"Yeah, uh, I heard that one of the archangels up there was this huge freak that made your head hurt whenever you talked to him."

"Aww, that's just being mean! Hey, what kinda rumors are people spreading about me when my back's turned? I'm gonna have to bang some *heads* around, if you know what I mean!"

"That, and you're the guardian angel of the Sephirah known as Yesod, aren't you?"

"Ee-hee-hee! You *do* know how to flatter a man, don't you?"

"Can you knock that off? All right. Let's just cut the crap and get to the point. What do you want?"

"Well, that girl hiding behind you, for starters. And, ooh, if you don't mind my being totally greedy, Emilia's holy sword as well! Also, we ate all the pizza Lucifer ordered from Pizza Hat. Sorr-eeee!"

"You ordered that *now*? *Now*, of all friggin' times?!"

Not even Maou could retain his composure. Urushihara shuddered.

"Oh, stop getting your whiskers in a bunch! We'll pay for it later, mm-kay?"

"That's not what I'm worried about! ...Well, okay, I *am*, but still!"

Maou stopped himself midway. There was Ashiya's ire to worry about later as well.

"Oh, wait, wait, wait! How 'bout this: Give us the girl, or you'll never see your precious pizza money again!"

"What kind of parent would give up his daughter to a bunch of kidnappers to get out of a pizza tab?!"

Maou was screaming by now.

"Besides, aren't you guys kind of late? How many days d'you think she's *been* here with us?"

"Hey, now, maybe it was a few days to you, but we've been searching for centuries by this point. Centuries! So cut me a little slack if we were off a tad, mm-kay? I mean, when I picked up pulses from the Yesod fragment, I was just about beside myself! You wouldn't *believe* what a doggie downer it was when that girl's fragment was taken away from the Devil's Castle on Ente Isla. I was like, 'Oooh, not yet *more* centuries spent searching for that thing again...'—Oh!"

The man apparently named Gabriel stopped himself midspeech.

"Right! 'Cut the crap,' you said! Yes yes yes! Are you giving us the girl, or not? Which is it?"

He was nothing like what Maou expected—they never were, by his experience—but judging by his fixation on Emi's holy sword, these had to be servants of the heavens. Angels, in other words.

The large man didn't deny his name was Gabriel, either. Which meant, probably, that this was Alas Ramus's real parent, or guardian, or whatever.

"......"

But the look on Alas Ramus's face as she stared at Gabriel was clearly one of alarm. There was no way she bore any friendly feelings toward him.

"Hey, Alas Ramus? Do you know this big lummox here at all? 'Cause it sounds like he wants to take you with him."

"No!! I *haaaate* him!!!!"

"Nooooooooooooooo!!!"

Gabriel put on a Shakespearian performance of shock following Alas Ramus's instant response.

"Stop calling me 'big,' you! Words can hurt, mm-kay?"

*That* was what floored him? The men covering Suzuno and Urushihara stirred, silently attempting to hide their embarrassment.

"Market, 'n' Ketter, 'n' Binah, 'n' Cocama, all gone! I *haaate* him!!"

"Ooooh, twist the *knife*, why don't you?"

Alas Ramus's follow-up was enough to make Gabriel bring a hand to his head.

"...I don't really get what's going on here, but if Alas Ramus isn't up for it, then I don't care if you're her dad or not. She's not going anywhere."

"Awwww… Okay, how 'bout the holy sword…?"

"I'll pass, thanks. I don't care if the gods themselves beg me for it. I'm not handing it over to anyone until I fulfill my mission."

"…Ooooh, you are making this *awfully* difficult, you know that? What kind of Hero and Devil King is this? *So* difficult. I really don't want to get rough here, but now that I've found this girl, I'm kind of beholden to get her back, sooooo…"

"Like I care."

"The holy sword, I *suppose* I can do without. Even if Sariel screwed the pooch on *that* one, at least we know where it is, more or less. But I'm gonna have to put my foot down when it comes to the girl. So… please? Just give 'er back?"

"Nope."

"She was kind of mine firrrrrst…"

"And I'm her dad now."

"No matter what?"

"No matter what."

"Even if it means you versus everybody in heaven?"

"Sounds like a risk I'll take. I ain't gonna make this kid cry."

Gabriel muttered forlornly to himself.

"…*So* difficult. This *really* gets my goat, do you understand…*that*?!?!"

He released a jet-propelled blast of holy energy from his entire body, one strong enough to nearly crush everyone against the room's walls.

It all happened in the blink of an eye. It was enough to make Maou stagger.

"I really hate forcing people like this. If you wanna surrender anytime, don't be shy about sayin' it, mm-kay?"

Gabriel, still as intensely happy-go-lucky as always, was in front of Maou's eyes before he knew it.

"Whoa!"

From the edge of his eye, Maou noticed the holes Gabriel had bored into the tatami mat floor with his feet, as a result of the blast.

"Y'know, even if you had all your Devil King strength, I'd probably still win and all, right? So…maybe just give her back?"

There was a quiet, almost sanctified air to the room, one so oppressive that it seemed ready to crush everyone inside.

"…Damn, are you serious?"

Maou swallowed nervously. Against all the foes he had fought in his life, nobody had ever intimidated him so much before.

It wasn't because he was weaker now.

It was because he was fighting a guardian of Sephirot, an angel several degrees more powerful than anything he had ever experienced.

It was a surprise. But it didn't make him relent.

"Well, it's still no from me. I'm the lord of all demons. I love doing things humans and angels just *hate*. Once I conquer the world, I'm gonna raise this girl to be the heir to my throne."

"I'll try to go easy on you, mm-kay? It wouldn't be fair otherwise, what with your total lack of demonic force and all. …And don't forget about the surrender thing, too!"

That was the signal that negotiations had failed.

Gabriel's conditions seemed generous enough. It went without saying that Maou had no chance of winning this.

A simple brush of his hand against Maou's arm would have been enough to turn him into confetti.

But there was one thing in the room capable of stopping an archangel's holy light.

"Maou!!!!"

It was a simple shout. Not magic, not a sword slash, but a shout.

But the shout was enough to halt the archangel's attack.

Everyone turned toward the source of the scream.

"Maou…"

It was Chiho.

Sweaty and out of breath, Chiho was atop the stairway, looking inside the room.

"Chiho?! No! Get away!"

Emi rushed to warned Chiho away. But the girl only shook her head.

"…I thought that I needed to apologize for today…"

"For today?"

"And then...this happened... I know I can't really do anything, but I couldn't just sit there."

Maou still had no idea he had been subjected to a stakeout from Chiho and her companions.

Chiho had made it back to Sasazuka ahead of the pack, but then returned home, unable to take the regret of betraying Maou's trust in her. But stewing in her room provided no solace either, and now she was here again.

"...You must be from this world, huh? Well, this isn't anything *you'd* be familiar with. Calling the police isn't gonna help at all. I bet you won't believe me, but me and this Sadao Maou guy..."

"I know all that!"

Chiho's shout stopped Gabriel's lips cold.

"I live here in Japan, but I know all that. All about Maou—about *Satan*, and Emilia the Hero, and Ente Isla, too. That...and how you're probably an angel here to pick up Alas Ramus."

Gabriel shook his head in comic disbelief.

"Well! I was impressed enough that you've been interacting so naturally with visitors from another world, but you even spotted me right off as an angel! Heavens be! Do I really look that angelic to you?"

The archangel's descent back into trivial flamboyance shook Chiho for a moment.

"...Up to now, if anyone's done anything really bad to Maou or Yusa, it's been an angel, so..."

The response was almost too honest for its own good.

Maou, Emi, and Suzuno looked on in astonishment. Gabriel and his crew winced painfully. Urushihara, meanwhile, busted out in laughter.

"Well. No comment when it comes to Lucifer, let me tell *you*, but what'd Sariel ever do to you guys?"

Gabriel was clearly thrown. There was too much previous evidence to deny the truth any further.

"Yeah, I'll grant you that Sariel and me didn't exactly live up to the image people have of angels around here..."

"Welllll, then why don't you stop digging a hole for yourself, mm-kay? Image is important, you know."

"Oh, like *you're* one to talk about image. And what about these guys you dragged in with you? These are, like, first-level street punks in a yakuza film."

Urushihara glared at the four figures guarding himself and Suzuno. For some reason, they stepped back, as if scared of him.

Gabriel sighed in exasperation as Urushihara flashed a victorious smile.

"Well. Anyway. I'm sorry, but, uh, we're a bit occupied right now? In several ways? I'm trying to talk this out, but if you don't want to get hurt, I'd recommend getting out of here while you can, mm-kay?"

"Ooh, dude, I love it. That's total level-one-boss street-punk dialogue. I can just eat that crap up all day."

Nobody was lending an ear to Urushihara's chippy repartee. Their eyes were on someone else.

"Please. Don't take Alas Ramus away from us."

They were focused on Chiho, her head bent deeply downward toward Gabriel.

Even though she knew the move assuaged her ego more than anything else, even though she had no idea what would truly make Alas Ramus the happiest, everything that Chiho saw drove her to take action.

"Alas Ramus really loves Maou and Yusa. So…please."

A droplet fell to her feet.

"Chi…"

"Chiho…"

"Aw, sheesh, lady, cut that out! C'mon, put your head up for me…"

Then, to the surprise of everyone involved, Gabriel found himself deeply moved by the actions of a simple human, a mere wisp of a teenage girl.

"This is totally unfair, mm-kay? You're all making me out to be the mean ol' angel here! It's like I'm some kinda grifter in a TV show, brushing off the crying girl in the corner while I strong-armed some poor schlub for the money he owed me!"

"What the hell are you going on about?"

Maou, somewhat unversed in the world of TV crime drama, quizzically looked on.

"Please... I really mean it...please..."

"Dahhh!! Come *on* already! Stop crying! Really, cut me a break already! Sheesh, if I knew *this* was gonna happen, I would've taken someone flailing at me with a baseball bat any ol' day! Hey, c'mon, give an angel some slack here!"

Gabriel, now completely ignoring Maou and Emi, did his level best to assuage Chiho's nerves.

"Please...please..."

But Chiho refused to raise her head, repeating her appeal to Gabriel over and over again.

"Ugggghhh, all *right!*"

Gabriel waved his hands in surrender, his voice indignant.

"You have until tomorrow!!"

"Lord Gabriel?!"

"What are you saying?!"

The men around Urushihara and Suzuno turned to Gabriel, their faces betraying total disbelief.

Gabriel ignored them as he uncomfortably watched the teary-eyed Chiho stare up at him.

"I... Oooooh!! Look, we angels, we've got our own problems to deal with, too, mm-kay? So first thing in the morning tomorrow, we're hoppin' right on back here! Feel free to get your family photos taken or whatever in the meantime! But don't think you can escape or anything, mm-kay?"

"R-really?!"

Chiho's face brightened.

Gabriel, unable to look her in the face any longer, averted his eyes.

"J-just till tomorrow! I can't wait any longer than that, mm-kay? And you, Devil King! If you try fishing your demonic power out from behind the closet or whatever, you're gonna pay for that! And that's a fact, Jack!"

"Th-thank you very much!"

He intended to lay a final line in the sand, but this pure, unsullied expression of goodwill from Chiho stopped him in his tracks yet again.

"Let… Let's go, you bastards!"

The outburst of holy power from before was now a barely discernible mist as Gabriel stomped toward the door.

"…Oh, nice closing line, Gabriel! 'Let's go, you bastards!' I sound like *such* a street punk…" With that final self-effacing remark, Gabriel shook his shoulders angrily and trudged out the door with his entourage.

The minions followed him out in line, like ducklings following their mother, each one of them nudging Maou's shoulder on the way in classic mafioso fashion.

"Ow! Hey! *Hey!* Dammit!"

Maou glared sullenly at them as they left, knowing full well he was outpowered, just as Gabriel took the first step downstairs.

"Agh!"

The demons heard the sound of something heavy tumbling down the stairs with a tremendous clatter.

"Lord Gabriel!"

"Lord Gabriel!!"

Gabriel had taken the stairs via the express route. He wasn't alone.

"Ah!"

"Wah!'

"Whoa!"

"Nragh!"

Four shrill, cut-off screams, followed by four heavy objects exhausting their potential energies in rapid succession, were heard from outside.

"Oh, like I'm not having a bad *enough* day!!"

Gabriel was heard squabbling with his entourage for another minute or two before the voices faded away.

Then, as if on cue:

"I am back, my liege. Ah, this oppressive heat…"

Ashiya, swaggering in with almost too much carefree abandon, wiped his brow as he climbed the stairs. Wholly unaware of the past chain of events, his lips curled upward a bit once he saw Maou and Alas Ramus were safe.

"I noticed a group of people leaving. More people from the MHK begging for your broadcast license fee?"

"…Not a care in the world with you, huh? We kinda have an emergency here. Where the hell were you?"

"Huh? Whuh? What?"

Ashiya took that moment to notice the dark, frigid atmosphere that prevailed in Devil's Castle, despite the sweltering heat outside.

"Um… Ignoring the completely clueless Ashiya for a moment…"

Now that the immediate threat was gone, Urushihara chose this moment to break the ice.

"What're we gonna do now?"

✳

The curtain of night wrapped itself firmly around Devil's Castle.

"Ooghooo!"

Satan, lord of the castle, the Devil King who once plotted to conquer all Ente Isla and plunge it into unimaginable terror, sat face-to-face with Emilia Justina, the Hero who stood up to crush his vile ambitions.

"Daouuu!"

Anxiety and murderous rage filled every nook and cranny of Devil's Castle. A single provocation, no matter how slight, would be enough to trigger a bloodbath.

"Naaarrhh…"

A light breeze, a droplet of rain, even a pebble clinking against the roadside could provide the spark to engulf the room in the flames of battle.

"Mommeee, Mommeee…"

Just as the brutal waves of crashing fury and force reached their peak:

"Wapph!"

The girl jogging around the Hero and the Devil King stumbled, nearly striking her head against the table in the middle of the Castle's sole room.

"!!"

The Devil King and Hero both responded at once, extending a hand of support.

That saved the girl from danger, but putting their arms out at the same time caused the Devil King's hand to brush against the Hero's.

"D-don't touch me!"

"Ow! Jeez, don't scratch me..."

With a frenzied shout of dismay, the Hero slapped the Devil King's hand away, leaving a line of red, irritated skin on his hand. It was just a scratch, not enough to break skin.

"Look, can you tell me what your problem's been tonight?" he asked.

"You've been relying on other people for *everything* here! And you pick *this* moment to get involved?"

"Oh, like you've been the ideal mother yourself!"

"Daddy, no! No fighting!"

A figure much, much smaller than the Devil King or the Hero stepped in to end the duel between the two natural-born enemies.

"Oh, uh, no, Alas Ramus, we aren't fighting or anything."

"N-no! Not at all! So don't cry, okay?"

"...Really?"

Alas Ramus peered closely at the two of them. Something about their hurried defense smelled fishy to her. She needed further confirmation.

"R-really! Really really!"

"Yeah, totally!"

"Nee-hee-hee!"

The girl, placing her trust upon the Hero and Devil King as they fell over themselves to lie to her, smiled in relief as she grabbed Emi.

"You'll be here foreeeever, Mommy?"

"That...ummmm..."

"...! ...!"

Maou sent her an invisible signal. Emi ignored the white noise.

"What about you, Alas Ramus? Do you want me... Do you want Mommy to be here?"

"Yeah! Together with Mommy! Forever!"

"Ahhhhh..."

Emi attempted a smile to hide the hopelessness in her mind.

"And Daddy, too!"

"Ohhhhh..."

Maou had no way of dodging this second salvo, either.

Then, awkward silence fell again.

Alas Ramus, not picking up on this, began a bold quest to climb up Emi's back.

Thanks to Chiho barging in at just the right time, Maou and Emi managed to keep Alas Ramus safe without anyone getting hurt.

But it only seemed to be delaying the inevitable.

No matter how much Alas Ramus railed against it, Maou knew—and Suzuno, with all her theological training, certainly knew—that the Sephirah called Yesod was the property of the heavens.

And right now, none of the people involved with Alas Ramus had any ability to fend for themselves against Gabriel.

Emi and Suzuno retained some semblance of fighting power, barring something like Sariel's special holy energy–draining skill.

But—and this was something else they already knew—they had no motivation to actively risk their necks over this.

Once Gabriel left, it was naturally Chiho who first questioned the unfamiliar "Tree of Sephirot" term.

"The Tree of Sephirot is the tree in Heaven from which everything in the world sprang forth. Anyone who partakes of the fruit of Sephirot, it is said, shall gain immortality and the gifts of boundless knowledge. The first human beings created by the gods consumed one of these fruits, as the story goes, breaking a divine promise and causing the gods to cast them away from the paradise they lived in."

"Wow, that's pretty similar to what we have on Earth. Like, Adam and Eve in the Bible and so forth…"

Suzuno nodded at Chiho.

"The tree bore ten fruits, known as Sephirah, each one corresponding to a different aspect of the world, or life itself. Each has its own planets, colors, metals, precious stones, and so on associated with it… For example, the first Sephirah, Keter, is said to govern over the soul, human thought, and imagination; it corresponds to the number one, its jewel is the diamond, its color white, its planet that of the god of the underworld, and its guardian angel Metatron. The fourth Sephirah is known as Chesed, governing over divine love; its number is four, its metallic element tin, its color blue, its planet that of the god of thunder, and its guardian angel Zadkiel… and so on down the line. All ten Sephirah possess aspects that correspond with the elements of the world, and I imagine Alas Ramus is attracted to colorful objects because they remind her of the colors each Sephirah lays claim to. Yesod, by the way, is the ninth Sephirah; it governs over the astral planes and one's self-consciousness, its number is nine, its metallic element silver, its color purple, its planet that of the blue heavens, and its guardian angel Gabriel."

The room fell silent for several moments after Suzuno's quick rundown. Maou was the first to speak.

"…You actually memorized all of that crap?"

"These are the core tenets of our theology!"

"Can you just, like, give us the thirty-second recap, dude?"

"What right does a former archangel have to say that?!"

Suzuno bit back at Urushihara's blithe request.

"Now, now, now… That's just Urushihara being Urushihara, so…"

Chiho's comment was enough to quell Suzuno's anger, though she still remained dissatisfied at his lack of dedication to his heavenly origin. Next, Emi spoke up.

"So why did she call herself 'Alas Ramus' from the get-go? Why didn't she say 'Yesod' instead?"

"It may be because this child is simply a fragment of the Sephirah, or there may be some other, as-yet-unknown reason. It seems clear, at least, that Gabriel did not give her that name. He never once referred to her as Alas Ramus. But regardless, assuming we should take the old legends at face value, if Alas Ramus is truly a fragment...a segment of the Sephirah Yesod from the Tree of Sephirot, then everything Gabriel told us would make sense. In other words, the elements of the world governed by Yesod are facing imminent danger. A danger that could affect the whole world. And if Gabriel wants to protect the balance of the world, as is his job as its guardian angel, then he would need Alas Ramus."

"Oh...so..."

Chiho sadly raised her voice.

"So Alas Ramus needs to go after all, huh...?"

"Not necessarily."

Suzuno's sudden veer over to her side caught Chiho by surprise.

"The presence of the fruits of Sephirot as the core that forms the world, and the guardian angels managing them are really only something laid out by our holy scriptures and mythology. It is not something anyone has ever seen with their own eyes. There has been no confirmation of it."

"Confirmation...?"

"For example, the tenth Sephirah, Malkuth..."

Suzuno was stopped midsentence.

"Market!"

Alas Ramus immediately reacted to the term. Maou stepped in.

"...Come to think of it, she talked about being friends with 'Market' on the Ferris wheel. Do Malkuth and the other Sephirah have personalities like Alas Ramus?"

Suzuno shook her head despondently.

"I have never heard of anything like that...but I think the fact this is news even to me could lead to what I am trying to say."

"Oh, right, sorry to cut you off. Keep going."

"Yes. Malkuth is located at the bottom level of the tree of life, governing over the physical world. Its number is ten, its precious stone crystal. It is associated with multiple colors, including bright yellow and olive green, and its planet is the Land of Life, which is meant to symbolize Ente Isla. According to legend, at least, if Malkuth were to cease existing for some reason, that would put the existence of crystals, the color yellow, and even Ente Isla itself in danger."

Suzuno paused for a moment, glancing around her audience.

"But take a moment to consider this. Could you imagine all the crystals in the world disappearing all at once simply because some fruit fell off a tree in another world? What kind of phenomenon would it take for a single object to engineer such massive disasters across sea and land? Even the story in our scriptures about the 'first human beings' eating the forbidden fruit is subject to many inter-pretations. Is that fruit related to the Sephirah, or not? The Church has yet to reach a conclusive answer. As the Devil King just said, there may indeed be something to the Sephirah we could interpret as individual personalities. But, in the end, the idea that the Tree of Sephirot supports all in the world is simply something told in leg-end. There is no evidence of it. There are many of us who hold a con-nection with the heavens, but no human being has ever set foot in that divine realm. Thus, in my opinion, I doubt the world would be plunged into crisis due to Alas Ramus not being available."

"Dude, I'm sorry, is this college all of a sudden?"

"...That being *said*, there is no doubting the existence of heaven, or angels, and if they wish to have this fragment of Yesod back, we have no way of resisting them. It is a horribly cruel state of affairs."

The eyes of everyone were focused on Alas Ramus, held against Maou's knees.

"...Man, this is a *total* pain in the ass."

Maou blithely picked at his ear in response.

"Yo. Alas Ramus."

"Hiii, Daddy!"

"That guy just now wanted to bring you back to his home, but do you wanna go with him?"

"No!!"

The refusal was clear and intense.

"Okay."

Maou slapped one of his crossed legs.

"Right, end of discussion. If those guys tomorrow do anything Alas Ramus doesn't like, we're fighting to the end."

"Wh-whoa! Wait a second!!"

Emi was less than accepting.

"Don't you understand what kind of situation we're in?! Bell and I don't stand a chance taking on someone like Gabriel face-to-face, and Alciel and Lucifer don't even have any of their power back!"

"I know. If it comes to that, I'll take 'em on myself."

"Yourself? Are you crazy?! How can you say that?! You realize what kind of shape you're in?!"

"All *right*. Eesh, lay off a sec. Like me getting my ass beat by him is anything bad for *you* guys, right?"

"...I, wait, are you...?"

"This is what I *want*, okay? I don't want to give Alas Ramus back, because *she* doesn't want to *go* back. And to you humans, if I lose, then ding-dong, the Devil King's dead and the Yesod fragment's back where it should be in heaven, right? What's the problem?"

"But...but...!!"

"Devil King! Are you truly fine with that?!"

"Maou!"

Emi remained unconvinced, as Suzuno and Chiho found themselves similarly unable to remain silent. Maou rolled his eyes as they confronted him.

"Hey, Ashiya? Urushihara? A little help here?"

"...Y-your Demonic Highness, this is simply..."

"Uhh...well, not like I give a crap either way, but I'm really startin' to dig life inside this closet, so that would kinda harsh my buzz, y'know?"

"Oh, not you, too, guys..."

"And despite everything we say, you still fail to see?!"

Suzuno lashed out at Maou anew.

Alas Ramus, surprised at the suddenness of it, took a tumble off Maou's lap.

"No! Suzu-Sis, you're mean to Daddy!"

She stood strong, extending her little body as straight up as possible to protect Daddy from danger. Suzuno briskly pushed her aside as she moved to grab Maou by the collar.

"It matters little here whether you are Devil King or not! But all of us...even Lucifer, in his own way, finds the idea of Alas Ramus going someplace she dislikes as abhorrent! If Alas Ramus were to be taken away to a place like that...I would rather keep her in your hovel instead!"

"...I'm not exactly sure that's how a Church cleric is supposed to talk..."

"I may be a Church cleric, but I am also a politician! I know how to compromise for the greater good! Besides, look at the sheer arrogance of that man, acting like he's the sole steward of an object he let free for hundreds of years! The whole Tree of Sephirot is itself a pile of rubbish!!"

"So...is that what you're all saying?"

"What?!"

"Saying how?"

"...What do you mean?"

"Yes, my liege?"

"What..."

Maou let out a wry smile, baring his teeth to the crowd.

"You guys all really like Alas Ramus, don't you?"

"...!"

Suzuno gasped softly.

"...Well, thanks."

It was the one word no Devil King would ever say, but one he had been throwing around over and over as of late.

"But when it comes to picking a fight against somebody holy, the Devil King's kinda got a monopoly on that. This is too much for you guys. I've got something that belongs to the gods here, and I'm gonna keep it from them because I wanna. So if push comes to shove with Gabriel tomorrow, you don't have to step in, okay?"

Suzuno, bewildered, removed her hands from Maou's collar.

"And if it works out in the end, then great, right? Go hard or go home."

"Hey!"

"Wait!"

"Maou!"

"My liege!"

"...Dude."

"Guys, shut *up*!"

Maou waved his hands against the surround-sound wall of complaints.

"This isn't some kind of movie. All the 'tude in the world isn't gonna help me get past this guy. I'm a grown man, all right? Expect the best, but plan for the worst! Hey, Emi!"

"What?!"

"You're sleeping over here tonight!"

This was not the kind of risk management anyone had pictured.

"Whaaaaaaaaaaaa?!"

"How is this *possibly* risk management?!"

Emi glared at Maou, who still had Alas Ramus on his outstretched legs. She picked up the young girl, the toddler gleefully swinging her legs in the air in response.

"Hey, if I do wind up going at it with Gabriel, I figured that'd force you to get involved in the fight for me. You see? Always thinking two steps ahead! My mind's a steel trap!" Maou announced proudly.

"...Do you seriously mean that?"

"Well, more than I don't. I think I said this before, but it's about time *you* step up to handle something for a change, right?"

"Oh, me handling the Devil King's problems? Yeah, they'd be cheering my name back home if they heard *that* one."

"Yaaaayy!"

Alas Ramus's sudden cheer from within Emi's arms was likely a coincidence. It was still enough to make Maou and Emi feel ridiculous for a moment.

"Anyway. More than I don't, like I said, but I *am* trying to think about this logically a little. I'm not asking you to take up my side or anything, but if we *do* wind up throwing down, you could at least make sure Alas Ramus doesn't get hurt."

"Oh…well, if that's all you're asking for…but what do you mean, you're 'trying to think' about this?" Emi replied. "Do you have a plan, or are you just gonna enjoy your final night with this kid? 'Cause if you do, I'd like to hear it, or else I don't know what I can do here."

Maou wasn't speaking as if he intended to lose without a fight, but he betrayed no evidence of anything resembling a fighting chance. Apparently his stance was to make the most of what time they had so she'd have something pleasant to recall on the other side.

So here they were, all sleeping in the same room.

By and large, Alas Ramus had been a good little girl up to this point, except for the occasional fit she pitched about Mommy not being around. As a parent, it was only natural to want to sleep with Mommy for a change, even if just for a single night.

Chiho was wholeheartedly supportive, and Suzuno approved as well, although she did so with the most acerbic facial expression possible. Ashiya was dead set against it, but ultimately she agreed on the condition that he be stationed in Suzuno's room in case anything bad happened. Urushihara, meanwhile, could sleep anywhere as long as his laptop was nearby.

There was no guaranteeing anyone's safety tonight, so Emi, seeing no other option, agreed to spend the night in Devil's Castle so long as Chiho left early in the evening.

Ashiya accompanied Chiho back home, then invited himself into Suzuno's room alongside Urushihara. It was a very unlikely room share, given everyone's past history of being close confidants/mortal enemies.

Maou shot a glance at Emi, largely indifferent to her question.

"I'm just risking my life for a kid. Like any parent would. But, you know, I wouldn't worry much. If anything happens, it's probably not gonna be any big deal for you."

"…I wish I knew where that confidence of yours comes from."

"If you're expecting some basis for it, keep lookin'. But it's weird, you know? It's like, if it's for Alas Ramus's sake, I feel like I can do anything."

"Oh, so now the Devil King's playing the spunky against-all-odds movie hero again? Didn't you just say that a positive attitude isn't gonna help anyone here?"

"Yeah, and I'll probably be paying for that pretty soon. But, you know, all the guys who died against me and my demon forces…they probably kept going 'til the very end for their own kids, too. And if they can do that, why can't the Devil King, huh?"

Emi was fully prepared to crack back at Maou. But the serenity in his voice gave her pause.

"What… What's that… Stop acting like you're starting some glorious new chapter in your life."

In the end, that was all that came out. Even that was at a barely audible mutter as she averted her eyes, for Maou's sentiment reminded her of the face her father made as she was taken away from her village.

And just as he said, this was payback. Just desserts for the king of all demons, the monster who took countless lives, and separated her from her father.

And yet, oddly enough, Emi found herself dejected.

*The Devil King is facing the same torment, the same sadness I faced. So why is my chest in so much pain over it?*

"Mommy?"

Alas Ramus worriedly looked up at Emi.

Maou, watching the both of them, grinned a little. He turned toward the wall clock in an attempt to brighten the mood.

"Right! Better get some shut-eye, then!"

"Wh-what?! It's not even ten yet! That's way too early!"

"Too early for us grown-ups, but Alas Ramus needs to get to bed. Whether we stay up all night or not, Gabriel's still coming tomorrow."

"B-but…but…"

"Sleep together, Mommy! All sleep together!"

"Oooooh..."

The Devil's Castle lacked any fluffy beds or futons to sleep on. There were just a few medium-weight blankets to share. The effect wasn't nestling together as a big, happy family so much as three guys crashing on the floor with whatever was handy.

But to Emi, the idea of lying down in close proximity with Maou, whether Alas Ramus was between them or not, had to be tough to swallow. This, after all, was voluntary, far different from the last time she spent the night over.

And it was the same for Maou. He had trouble turning over to his side, the vision of Emi's hands upon Alas Ramus's throat the moment he fell asleep vivid in his mind.

But Alas Ramus was too eager to sleep together with Mommy and Daddy. Even now she was excitedly pulling the blankets out from the closet, spreading them out in any number of chaotic configurations.

"Whoa, whoa, don't trip again."

"Come here, Alas Ramus. That dumb ol' daddy of yours will take care of it."

Emi watched as Maou sluggishly helped set up their bed.

"...You better put on a light somewhere."

She said it out of something between caution and confirmation.

"Well, yeah. She gets scared when it's too dark."

That wasn't why she asked for it, but—oh, right, kids *did* use night-lights sometimes, right? Well, fine. That worked, too.

"Oh, does Alas Ramus have any nightclothes or anything?"

"You mean like pajamas? ...You know, that's actually all the clothes she has, I guess."

Maou glanced down at Alas Ramus's yellow dress as she set up three blankets on the floor.

"Uhh... You've been doing her laundry and stuff, right? Did you ever give her a bath?"

Emi was unable to hide her surprise at this new nugget of information. Apparently Alas Ramus had sported a single outfit since she showed up several days ago. In the dead of summer, no less.

"I did her laundry, okay? And I took her to the public bath. You don't have to treat me like an idiot. Her stuff dried really quick in the heat, and she just trotted around the room in her diaper otherwise."

"…I don't believe you."

Ignoring his sleeping partner's disaffected stare, Maou looked at Alas Ramus's straw hat hanging on the wall.

"Yeah, well, we haven't bought her anything besides that hat, so… I forget if the UniClo in Sasazuka sells children's clothes or not."

"Oonislow?"

"I really wish you'd stop treating UniClo as the solution to every single problem in your life. She's a girl, remember? Didn't you ever think about finding something cute for her to wear?"

"What do you want from me? I don't know where they sell that crap."

"Ugh… I should've expected that men like you wouldn't care about that."

"Well, look…"

Maou casually stood up, bringing his hand to the string hanging underneath the ceiling light.

"How 'bout we just worry about seeing this through, okay? So that I *would* have to care."

"Um…yeah. Sure."

Thrown off guard, Emi found herself nodding in agreement. Alas Ramus, having trouble following the conversation, groped upward.

"Mommy! Mommy, here!"

She patted her arm against the tatami-mat floor next to her.

"Okay, okay."

Keeping a wary eye on Maou, Emi uncomfortably laid herself flat on the floor.

Waiting for the moment she was down, Maou prodded Alas Ramus.

"Hey, better hug Mommy tight, okay? That way, she won't go away on you."

"Okay!"

"Agh...!"

Confused, Emi found herself slowly embracing the joyfully grinning toddler.

"Huh? Hey...what's that you've got there, Alas Ramus?"

Something thin and unbending made its presence felt between Emi and the girl.

"Picture!"

It was the mounted photo they purchased at the Ferris wheel.

"Wow, you must really like that... But it'll get all folded up and icky if you bring it to bed. Put it next to your pillow, okay?"

"Okey."

Emi gently took the photo and placed it bedside as Alas Ramus ruefully watched. Maou smiled a bit.

"Okay, I'm turning it off."

After a quick advance warning, Maou shut off the light, leaving a smaller night-light on to the side.

"Oof."

Emi, her eyes not used to the darkened room, felt goose bumps erupt across her body as she heard Maou grunt from far closer than she was expecting.

"G-get away!"

"I'm not gonna go hugging you, too, all right? I just can't get any farther away as long as Alas Ramus is like this, so..."

Looking aside in the darkness, Emi realized that the sleepyheaded child had somehow grabbed hold of both Emi's and Maou's shirts.

"...Pull anything weird and I'll kill you."

"You're *still* being a bad influence on her, you know."

"You're one to talk. You're like a walking, talking bad influence on society."

"And yet there's still someone out there who loves her daddy. Right, Alas Ramus?"

"Mm...Hee-hee!"

"I think she's denying it."

"Ah, she's just shy. She says it around other people."

"Daddyyy, tell me a story!"

Alas Ramus's voice was already heavy with fatigue.

"Hmm? A story? Don't want to hear a story from Mommy?"

"Mm…Mommy, tell a story tomorrow…"

"!…"

A dagger stabbed into Emi's chest as Alas Ramus revealed her future plans.

A pained smile crossed Maou's face as well, before he gave Alas Ramus a gentle pat on the stomach and looked upward in thought.

"Hmm, let's see… How 'bout we pick up the story from yesterday?"

"Okey."

"Great! Uhh, where did we get up to last time…"

"The traveler, and the angel."

"Oh, right, right. Boy, you have a good memory."

"Ee-hee!"

Emi, looking on curiously as Alas Ramus spoke to Maou, gasped a bit when Maou turned toward her.

"I started telling her stories 'cause it kept her from putting on a big scene or whining about being lonely at night. I had no idea her diaper was the cause that first night, though…"

"I wasn't asking."

Maou paid no mind to the gruff reply, slowly easing into his tale.

"Right…so the poor traveler, who was injured in the middle of his journey, was rescued by the angel."

The poor traveler, injured after an unfortunate run-in with a mean, nasty demon, was rescued by a kind, gentle angel.

The angel told the traveler all kinds of tales he had never heard before.

Tales of high, high mountains. Tales of wide, wide oceans. Tales of deep, deep forests. Tales of kings, and princesses, and stores, and gold. Tales about plants and fish. Tales about soldiers. Tales about gods, and the world of the stars…

The traveler was very excited at all this, and listened on as the angel kept speaking.

One day, the angel gave the traveler a special charm as a present. The traveler was overjoyed to receive it, and with the charm and everything the angel told him, he set off once more.

Thanks to everything he learned, the traveler eventually became a wise and just king, one who ruled for years and lived in great happiness.

"...*snrrrf*..."

"...And there you have it. Night."

It was hard to say when she fell asleep. But once Maou wrapped up his tale, he immediately turned over and away from Emi.

The only sound was the cry of the kingdom of summer insects outside.

"...Hey."

"...Yeah?"

Emi caressed the hair of the sleeping Alas Ramus.

"What happened to him after he became king?"

Maou turned his head back. Even in the dimness of the night-light, she could tell he was looking at her like a father escorting her drunken daughter away from her wedding reception.

"I just made that up to get her to sleep, man. How do I know? He lived happily ever after, the end, all right?"

"He didn't go back to his homeland or go searching for the angel or anything?"

"...Look."

"Oh, just tell me. I'm gonna need some material for my turn tomorrow."

"......"

Maou failed to understand what made Emi say "tomorrow." He flashed her a very deliberate look of scorn before turning away from her again.

"She's not gonna be able to follow some kind of epic backstory, you know. Just make up whatever you want. That'll be perfect."

As far as he was concerned, the subject was over. Emi bunched her eyebrows in dissatisfaction.

"Hey, can I ask—"

"Just go to sleep. If you start talking to me, we're gonna fight and Alas Ramus'll wake up."

"If the traveler became king and everything, why did he want to go to some other country? I thought he lived happily ever after."

"......"

"...No?"

It was now the softest of whispers.

"Well, getting to be king probably made him greedy."

"Eh?"

"...If Alas Ramus asks about it, I'll make something up for her."

Maou flew through the sentence in a hurry before breaking into a loud, contrived snore.

He wasn't Alas Ramus. There was no way he could fall asleep that quickly. It was just his way of expressing his lack of interest in answering any more questions.

As if called to action by the sound, Alas Ramus removed her hand from Emi's shirt and sidled up to Maou's side.

"......"

Watching on, Emi gave Alas Ramus another caress before bringing the blanket up to her shoulders and turning her back to the two of them.

She now faced the wall separating them from Room 202.

"...He's got *such* a twisted mind... I'm so worried, I don't know if I'd even dare leave this to him."

The thought whispered itself out of her mouth.

In Room 202 of the Villa Rosa Sasazuka apartments, Suzuno and Urushihara sat silently.

There was an old-fashioned mirror stand emblazoned with a cherry blossom design accompanied by a traditional round tea table. The paulownia-wood dresser to the side was brand-new.

While the room's furniture was strictly "old Japan," the refrigerator was full-sized and boasted all the latest energy-saving features, and the combination drum washer / dryer outside offered built-in disinfecting and a stand for ironing. The microwave, however, was as compact and simple as the one in Devil's Castle, likely due to amperage issues with Villa Rosa's ancient wiring.

The electric fan was the latest model from Tyson, one of those bladeless types where air seemed to magically flow from an empty oval frame. Urushihara stuck his hand in and out several times to entertain himself.

"...Nothing?"

Ashiya strode in through the front door.

"You did return Chiho safely, yes?" Suzuno inquired immediately.

"Of course. She was rife with concern for my liege until the moment we parted."

"Indeed. But we certainly cannot afford to bring her into this affair."

"Absolutely. If anything were to happen to Ms. Sasaki, we'd be unable to continue our current arrangement. I told her not to set foot near our Devil's Castle until some sort of closure has been reached."

"...Well. A wise decision, there."

Ashiya idly sat himself down in the center of the room.

"Alciel, I need to ask you something."

"What? If you're expecting rent, forget it."

"Who would ever dream of saying such miserly things? I am not *you*, after all. I wish to ask of you, and your demonic forces."

Suzuno lifted her head from resting on her folded legs.

"What drove you to attempt to conquer the world?"

It was an unusual question to lob at two young men who looked like they hailed from Anytown, Japan.

"Because I...have grown less and less able to understand why the thought even occurred to you to invade our land," she finished.

"...I have to say, I envy your refrigerator."

"Um?"

Ashiya's reply seemed completely unrelated. But, as he appraised the top-of-the-line, enviro-friendly fridge Suzuno had bought on Emi's recommendation the other day, his face was deadly serious, and so too his voice.

"Open the door, and I am sure you will find the meat, the milk, the vegetables you bought yesterday. Anything missing from today's menu, you can run to the store to purchase. You can make wonderful dishes, and eat them at your leisure. ...I, and His Demonic Highness, too, I imagine, invaded Ente Isla in search of such things."

"...?"

"I am not asking you to understand me. Regardless, it is my lot to work as hard as I can until the day we can return to Ente Isla... Do you understand me, Urushihara?"

"Hey, I'll work, dude. Once I can."

"Listen, you..."

In consideration for Room 201 and its current occupants, Ashiya and Urushihara's verbal scuffling proceeded at a hushed tone.

Suzuno, listening to them, placed her head back down toward her folded knees.

✳

"...oof..."

Emi rose, awoken by the one-two punch of the early morning sun and the rapidly rising temperature. She squinted at the cracks and blotches of an unfamiliar ceiling.

"...!! Uh...?"

The sudden recollection of a reluctant night spent in Devil's Castle flooded back to her mind, making her attempt to leap upward.

"...Whoops."

The attempt was foiled by Alas Ramus, sleeping peacefully as her body was straddled against Emi's.

She noticed just in time. If she had bolted upward as planned, she would've woken up Alas Ramus along the way.

With a sigh of relief, Emi craned her head upward to look at Maou on the other side.

He was looking less than graceful.

Apparently succumbing to the heat, he had tossed away his T-shirt, snoring loudly in the morning sun. Emi was almost expecting a snot bubble to blow in and out of his nose with each breath.

"Nnnnh…"

Slowly, Emi removed her arm so as not to disturb Alas Ramus. She thought any touch might wake her up, but she remained still, apparently deep in sleep.

The clock on the wall still hadn't passed five AM. It was easy to see how deeply into summer they were.

Thanks to sleeping on bare tatami with a blanket over her, she was sore from head to toe. Stretching out her head and shoulders, Emi yawned, thinking about how they needed to purchase at least a futon for the child.

Nothing could be heard from Suzuno's room. They must have been asleep. The main concern at the moment was whether Chiho had actually heeded her advice and stayed home.

Giving the adjacent Alas Ramus a light brush on her hair, Emi grabbed her bag, took out the bottle of 5-Holy Energy β she brought along, and chugged it in one swallow.

There was no telling when Gabriel would arrive, nor if he would (which hopefully he would not), but *if* it came to a fight, she needed all the force she could muster.

It was because Alas Ramus needed her protection. It was definitely *not* because the Devil King had smooth-talked her into it.

"This is for Alas Ramus…for Alas Ramus…"

She muttered the mantra to herself as she winced at the energy shot's medicinelike aftertaste.

"Better wash my face…"

Emi made a step toward the kitchen sink.

"Mornin', child!"

Until that moment, Emi had completely failed to notice the other presence in the room.

"Gnhhh!!!"

The man, in Emi's blind spot opposite the kitchen before now, placed a hand over Emi's lips before she could react.

"Now, now, no fussing! I'm not gonna do anything rough, mm-kay?"

"Mnh! Mrnngh!"

Emi tried to kick Maou awake. He was just barely out of range.

"Oh, stop! They're both livin' it up in dreamland...and they'll be stayin' in there awhile, too."

Emi glared back at the smarmy voice's owner, her entire consciousness focused upon him.

"Oop, look out."

Then, almost too easily, the man removed his hand from Emi's mouth and edged away.

Given the size of the apartment, however, there wasn't much edging away to do without going out a window. He would still be within easy range of Emi's holy sword.

"You angels sure have forgotten your manners, huh? Kidnapping people, putting bugging devices in people's bags, trespassing into people's apartments without permission..."

The man laughed heartily in his utterly nondivine, high-pitched voice.

"Aww, but this is the Devil's Castle! Hopefully I can get a pass on *that* at least, hmm? I mean, we're talking the bad guys' headquarters here!"

"You're here kind of early, aren't you? Or did you think it's okay to take this girl away just because the date on the calendar's changed?"

Emi's right hand was pointed squarely at Gabriel's throat.

In the blink of an eye, the Better Half sword appeared in her hand, its point aimed straight for his neck.

"Hang on, hang on! I mean, didn't I say I wanted to talk this out yesterday? Because you're kind of being *awful* judgmental with me right now!"

"Alas Ramus or not, you wanted my holy sword, didn't you? If someone's trying to prevent me from my goal, I won't hesitate to take him down."

"Oh, you are *such* a party pooper. Women these days are *soooo* self-minded, aren't they? No *wonder* so many people aren't getting married anymore. You girls are scary!"

Whether due to his off-kilter personality or the natural confidence that came from being an archangel, the holy sword wasn't enough to make Gabriel so much as flinch.

"Oh, and just so we're on the same page here, it's not like I cast a spell or put a barrier up to keep the Devil King and the folks next door from waking up, mm-kay?"

"…What do you mean?"

"Well, and I'm just guessing here, but you guys probably didn't get a lot of sleep last night, am I right? The folks next door were up all night keeping watch over you, I guess, but they all conked out about an hour ago. Plus which, you were totally conked out, too, yes? I mean, since I stepped in here, I heated up the bento box I bought at the convenience store, ate it, went to the john, and did a little morning constitutional around the front yard, but you people were sleeping like *logs*, I tell you. I mean, not like I expected a red carpet, but come *on!*"

"……"

Come to think of it, Maou worked until midnight the previous evening, only to be jostled awake by Alas Ramus early in the morning.

"And as someone who prides himself on being the most gentlemanly archangel in heaven, I'd *never* attack a family while they're asleep. So I figured I'd wait until you or the Devil King woke up. We could talk a little more, and maybe I could help you see the light this time, mm-kay? So, uh, could you put that blade away for a sec?"

With pleading eyes, Gabriel pinched the edge of the sword with two fingers, attempting to push it away. Emi held firm.

Neither this world nor the one above needed an archangel so willing to fall into mortal vices like microwave cooking and jogs around the block.

"Hey, look, unlike your pal Sariel, I don't have any natural defense against holy power, sooo…y'know, really, I'd like to settle this like grown-ups."

"…Like *you* have any right to say that."

"Uhm?"

"You probably have those goons from yesterday surrounding the apartment by now, don't you? The Heavenly Regiment or whatever?"

Emi's charged question visibly disquieted Gabriel.

"Now listen, lady, I have *no* interest in hurting anyone, mm-kay? I just want to get what I'm getting, then get *out*. But cut me a break! The Devil King was ready to duke it out right in the kitchen yesterday. So, all right, yeah, I have 'em on lookout. Ooh, but listen, we had to expend a ton of energy just gettin' *me* through a Gate, so they're all kinda pooped right now, y'know? And, whew, it's gonna be even *worse* once we have that girl with us on the way back. So, c'mon, be an angel and listen to one for a change, mm-kay?"

"…!"

"Aaaghh! You just poked my Adam's apple a bit with that thing on purpose, didn't you?! For a Hero, you're pretty darn good at terrorizing people, you know that? Oww!"

The point Emi silently thrust forward made contact with his neck. It didn't penetrate skin, but Gabriel at least acted like it threw him into panic.

The clamor was enough to finally make the rest of the room stir.

"…Ngh, stop making all that noise… Jeez, it's still only five… Hey, whoa, come *on*!!"

No matter how much sleep he had missed the previous night, this would be enough to wake up anybody.

Maou was greeted with the sight of Emi facing off with an unfamiliar man, Better Half at the ready, in his already cramped apartment.

"Ooohh… Daddyyy?"

Alas Ramus came-to soon afterward, as Maou struggled to get his head around these rather sudden events.

"Gabriel… You didn't have to come *this* early, you know…"

"Ooh, hey, sleepyhead! Sorry I had to call upon you like this, mm-kay? My schedule for today is just *packed*, let me tell you."

Maou picked up Alas Ramus, putting her off behind his shadow. But with so little demonic power remaining, and his foe already so close to him, the battle was virtually over before it began.

"Y-you shouldn't be brandishing a sword like that, y'know. Not around the little one! It'll be a bad influence! So just put it away, mm-kay?"

Gabriel, however, was his usual ebullient self.

The fact he was willing to weaken his own Heavenly Regiment in order to come here seemed to indicate supreme confidence. With a name like Gabriel backing him up, it seemed certain that this man was not the frivolous, scatter-brained ditz he acted like.

"It's not like I'm out here looking for a fight against heaven or the angels. But they just keep coming for me, you know? That's why I have to fight them."

"Yikes! …That's some mean logic to argue against."

Gabriel shrugged in despair, his face embittered.

"Okay, well, hopefully you don't mind if I talk first, then… Ooh, but try to make sure that point doesn't hit my hayoid again, mm-kay? …Y-y'know, if I could offer a compromise here, at the very least, if I can get home with either the holy sword or that girl, then I don't have a complaint in the world right now. I'll explain everything to you, and I mean it. But after that I'm giving you two choices. Hand it over, or no?"

Gabriel retained his composure as he spoke, his raised hands waving around to back up his point.

"I'm the guard of Yesod, a Sephirah from the Tree of Sephirot that forms the foundation of the world. And Yesod got stolen a long time ago, mm-kay? And as if *that* wasn't bad enough, the thief split the Yesod Sephirah into a bunch of fragments and tossed 'em all over the place. And you know, Emilia, the Better Half sword in your hand and that girl behind the Devil King were both born from those fragments. And…and, you know, having stuff like that outside of heaven for long is real, *real* bad news!"

"My sword…from a fragment of Yesod?"

Gabriel raised a finger in the air, breezily continuing on as if discussing something he read in the news that morning.

"You betcha, lady! You see that? The purple crystal embedded in it?"

He used his finger and his eyes to point out the handle of Emi's sword.

The Better Half's handle was emblazoned with a wing motif, the center of which was decorated with, yes, a jewel that shone purple. Emi had assumed it was just some nonessential piece of design work.

"That Better Half's one pretty dangerous dealie-o, you know? Pretty high-priority to get back for us. But then you, Satan—y'know, before you invaded Ente Isla, we had *no* idea where the heck you were! I've been going around for centuries, picking up a shard here, a fragment there, but I just had the worst time finding the fragments the girl and that sword came from, mm-kay? And, you know, I was trying to keep this search a secret 'cause I didn't want any of the grand pooh-bahs to know I messed up, if you know what I mean, but going off by myself all the time to look…well, let's just say that raised some eyebrows. Folks thought I was plotting against the gods, can you *believe* that? So Sariel figured out what I was *really* up to first. I almost got booted off the island, if you know what I'm gettin' at! Ha-ha-ha!"

Of *course* Gabriel was the sort of angel to laugh at his own jokes. The cold stares surrounding him were nothing he concerned himself about.

"What's so dangerous? We need the holy sword to defeat the Devil King. There's nothing *dangerous* about it."

"There kinda is to *me*…"

Maou was ignored.

"Well, that's what you humans say… I mean, that's what the Church said, anyway, way back when they got hold of those fragments. And if I told you *why* they're dangerous…well, all that time I spent looking for them would go to waste, y'know? I can't very well go around doing that!"

"What the Church said…?"

"That, and gee whiz, lady, use your head! Like, did you think you can just go to the big-box store and buy magical swords that *only* affect demons and Devil Kings? The Better Half's power is amplified by holy force, mm-kay? Just like the Light of Iron magic your Church knights use. The only difference is the form it takes! You can search the entire universe for all I care; there's no such thing as a special antidemon weapon!"

"But...but this sword brought me straight to the Devil King inside his fortress..."

The glowing of Emilia's holy sword had led her party of invaders down the correct path to the Devil King during their assault on his Ente Isla headquarters. That was what had allowed them to navigate the castle's labyrinthine corridors in such quick order.

"Lady, I don't think it was leading you to the Devil King. It was directing you to where that child was."

Gabriel's reply was nonplussed.

"The separate Yesod fragments were attracted to each other. That's all there was to it! And thanks to *that*, I had to waste a lot *more* time running around like a chicken with its head cut off searching, mm-kay?"

And after the fragments resonated with each other, the Hero dove into her final battle against the Devil King. A battle where she used her sword's holy force to bring the demons' leader to his knees.

"Y'see, you probably used up so much holy force during that fight, that child's fragment likely stopped reacting to anything else for a while. And then you took a little weekender over to Nowheresville, Japan, so *that* trail went cold on me, too, until I figured out where the heck you were. I had no idea the fragment had become part of the Devil King's gardening hobby, either!"

The last time Maou saw the tree that sprouted up from the crystal he was given, it had only begun to form two trunks snaking around each other. Only a few hardy leaves had budded on it, and it would be long before it would bear any flowers or fruit.

He had completely forgotten about it by that point. He wasn't expecting that crystal to amount to much in the first place. If anything, he was impressed that it had actually grown into *something*.

But then, as Maou recalled all of this, Gabriel suddenly grabbed hold of Emi's holy sword.

Surprised, Emi attempted to pull it back. The weapon refused to budge.

"Nuh-uh-uh! That hurt me on kind of a paper-cut level, but unless something really goofy happens, that holy sword isn't enough to beat me, as things stand."

He turned an easygoing eye toward Maou.

"So are we all working with the same playbook now? Great. Now let's just all act like adults here and listen to what I'm asking you, mm-kay?"

This was, in other words, his final notice. His aim was to show what he saw as the obvious result if Emi demonstrated any hostility toward Gabriel at this point.

Without any stockpile of demonic power backing him up, Maou had absolutely no chance of victory himself. And that conclusion wasn't about to change with the presence of Suzuno or the other demons.

Which meant that Maou had only one card up his sleeve.

Maou took a deep breath and faced up to Gabriel.

Emi and Gabriel tensed up for a moment, expecting Maou to make a suicidal lunge toward the archangel.

"...Huh?"

"Hey, hang on, what're you doing?!"

Their expectations were unfounded.

"Please."

Maou had prostrated himself on the floor.

The human personification of Satan, the Devil King who once stood at the apex of all demons and still publicly avowed his ambition to conquer the world, was now rubbing his forehead against the floor in front of an archangel.

"Please don't take Alas Ramus away."

The voice, and the physical act, were both sincere.

"Daddy...?"

Alas Ramus, unable to grasp the meaning behind Maou's behavior, swiveled her head between Maou and Gabriel.

"Um, look, if I have to remind you, I'm an angel, mm-kay? And you're the Devil King, last time I checked. If you think I'm gonna fold like I did with that girl yesterday, you've got another think coming, bucko."

There was a touch of irritation to Gabriel's reply. But Maou was expecting it.

"I'm not saying for free, okay? You let her stay, I'll let you have my head. That ain't a bad deal."

"What?!"

"Whoa, whoa, come on! Stop being stupid!"

This was enough to bewilder the both of them.

"You... *I'm* supposed to defeat you! You can't just toss your life away here!"

"Lay off. Tell all your pals back home that you teamed up with an archangel to do me in, for all I care. What's the big problem with that?"

"That's a *huge* problem! Who the hell would ever want to team up with *these* freaks?! I need to defeat you by my own hand, or else it's meaningless!"

"Why's it matter what *you* think about it?! We're supposed to be worried about Alas Ramus!"

"Uhm, would you folks mind not bickering like a married couple for a moment?"

"We're not married!"

"We're *not married*!!"

"Wowwww, way to give it to me in stereo..."

Gabriel was at least half impressed by the show.

"Mommy, Daddy, stop fighting!!"

For the first time in the past twenty-four hours, Gabriel and Alas Ramus agreed on something.

"Hey, uh, can I butt in with a question real quick? Why are you, the Devil King, being such a concerned hen over this girl? This girl you all but forgot about until a few days ago?!"

"Because I became 'king.' Because I got distracted by greed, just like *that* demon did. Because I forgot about the things I needed to cherish!"

His mind flashed back to that day, when the claws descended upon him, giving him a vision of death amid the red sky and parched land.

"This girl is a symbol of hope. A symbol I picked up after being snatched away from the edge of death. After getting a new lease on life. ...But somewhere along the line, on the way to becoming the leader of all demons, I forgot about that."

Sadao Maou, once a lowly demon hardly even worthy of the name Satan, rose up and slowly hugged Alas Ramus.

"Daddy...ow."

The girl squirmed a bit in Maou's tight embrace.

"You let this girl be for hundreds of years by now and nothing bad happened, right? So please...don't take her someplace she doesn't want to be. I'll stake my life on it."

"...Y'know, I can't say I like this assumption that I'm gonna do all these mean things to her, mm-kay? Like I've been trying to tell you, she belongs in heaven. She is a fragment of Yesod—"

"I know all about that! That, and the Devil Overlord Satan of the past!"

Emi noticed Gabriel's face harden the moment Maou said it.

The "Devil Overlord Satan of the past" must have been the one Maou was talking about last night. But what did that have to do with Gabriel?

"...That's why I can't let her go. I don't want to let her go. So please...just...!"

Maou fell to his knees, unable to finish.

"Sorr-ee. Change of plans!"

"Gah...nh..."

Maou writhed in pain on the floor. It was hard for Emi to tell, her sword still restrained by Gabriel's strength, but it seemed like he was unable to breathe.

"You know, I really had no intention of going this far, but that's kind of digging your own grave there, mm-kay? I try to be a good-natured angel when I can, but if *that's* what you're going to bring up, I'm kind of obliged to take action."

"Graaaaahhhhh!!!"

"D-Devil King?!"

Gabriel peered closer, as if to bring home the point. As he did, Maou's neck began to twist inward, enough that Emi could see it, as if being clasped by an invisible hand.

"My liege! My liege, what is it?!"

"Get back, Alciel! Let me crush him with my Light of Iron!"

Suddenly, the alarmed voices of Suzuno and Ashiya rang out from the outdoor corridor.

"Oooops! Got a little too loud for my own good, hmm? Well, not that it'll amount to anything. That barrier isn't gonna fall apart *that* easy!"

Gabriel remained unfazed. They could hear the sound of something heavy banging against the door, but despite being an original from the apartment's construction sixty years ago, it didn't so much as crack.

And even now, Urushihara was nowhere to be heard from. He was probably the lone resident who was still asleep.

"Emilia, the Hero... Just to make sure we don't regret anything later, I'll take care of the Devil King, mm-kay? I know you've got your own issues and stuff, but I'll be happy to pass along a revelation to the Church or whatever about you getting the blessings of an archangel, blah blah blah, like what the Devil King said. That sound good to you?"

The situation was desperate.

The demons in the apartment were powerless, the holy sword's power bound.

"That *does* sound good to you, doesn't it, Emilia?"

Gabriel's eyes remained on Maou as he spoke, his voice as free and guileless as if he was asking someone for extra sugar in his coffee. That was about as much as he cared about the human world.

"...No deal."

"Hmm?"

"It's my turn to tell this girl a story. If you take her away, I'll wind up breaking my promise."

"Whaaa? Aw, come on..."

His words belied disappointment, but his tone betrayed a singular lack of interest in Emi's declaration.

Emi's frustration mounted.

"I don't *care* about what all you stupid angels are dealing with! I am the only one who's gonna cut the Devil King Satan down! I'd *never* give anyone else the honor!!"

"Um...do you have anything less hackneyed you could say right now...?"

"Besides, what kind of so-called good guy would take a crying girl away from her own father?! Heavenly Flame Slash!"

"Oh? Whoa! Agh, ow, ow, ow, ow! Jeez, that's hot! What's up with *that*?"

Emi infused the blade of her holy sword with searing flame.

It had been enough to slash through the fallen angel Lucifer, but now it didn't so much as singe the palm of Gabriel's hand.

"Okay, maybe that didn't look like it hurt, but it did, mm-kay? Like, a lot! Y'know, I *really* didn't want any rough stuff with you, but why can't you see things *my* way here, hmm? I'm *supposed* to be the guardian of these fragments, y'know!"

"Who asked you?!"

"Well...nobody *asked* me, exactly, but this is my duty, and—"

"......"

"Gnh...haggh..."

"Who...was that just now?"

Even Gabriel, previously replying to Emi's question with a sullen tone, suddenly turned serious.

"We were playing. Having fun. That's all!"

A voice rose up from the feet of Emi, Gabriel, and Maou:

"Market told me. You were all big liars."

Her arms and legs were tiny, her eyes little buttons, but her will was strong enough to take over the room.

"He said you were liars, but you got to be gods anyway!"

Alas Ramus lightly brought her hand to Maou. That was all it took.

"...Gahaa!! *Koff*...egghh..."

"Huhhh?!"

Gabriel's hold on Maou loosened, letting him catch his breath as he broke into a cold sweat.

"I hate you! I hate all of you!"

"Truly?…"

Alas Ramus toddled toward Gabriel as she spoke.

"You took us all away, you kept us all alone…and…"

At that moment, the purple crescent-shaped mark formed across Alas Ramus's forehead as her yellow dress began to glow as brightly as the summer sun.

"…And now you're mean to Mommy and Daddy! That's *bad*!!!"

"Yagh!"

"Aaaahhh!!"

Then she emitted a bolt of golden light, sending Gabriel flying against the Devil's Castle wall.

The holy sword fell out of his hand, freeing Emi from his grasp.

"Alas…"

"Wait, Daddy!"

"Whoa! Hang—"

From the side of Maou, still unable to get up, the glowing Alas Ramus flew toward Gabriel's chest like a bullet.

"Grhhh!"

Squeaking like a toad caught under an eighteen-wheeler, his body was sent right through the wall with Alas Ramus, flying into the air.

"Whoa! Alas Ramus! …Heavenly Fleet Feet!!"

Leaving Maou behind, Emi focused her Cloth of the Dispeller upon her legs, giving her an instant blast of speed as she chased after them.

"Emilia!"

"Your Demonic Highness!!"

Gabriel's unexpected departure must have removed the barrier from the door, because Suzuno and Ashiya both suddenly barreled through it, taking the hinges off as they did.

Witnessing the disabled Maou and the giant hole in the wall, Ashiya's eyes burned with menacing rage.

"Currrrrrse youuuuu, Emilia! Such a heinous, despicable act of treachery!!"

Between the way Ashiya's mind worked and the scene he was presented with, no one could blame him for that conclusion.

"No... G-Gabriel...and Alas Ramus..."

"What?! He is here?!"

"Alas Ramus...she's fighting. Get...after her... *Kagff!*"

"Alas Ramus...?"

"Fighting?"

Ashiya and Suzuno, unable to grasp the situation, could do little more than glance at Maou and the wall.

"Suzuno, please, get...me up..."

Suzuno nodded at the groaning Maou. But:

"Halt, human! Stay where you are, Devil King Satan!!"

"Do not defy the will of Lord Gabriel!!"

Suddenly, the four lackeys that Gabriel had brought along the previous day flew upward, blocking the hole Alas Ramus had poked in the wall.

The Heavenly Regiment each bore a pair of white wings upon their backs.

"Ngh... Not you..."

Even if they wanted to fight, Suzuno was the only one with any capacity to do so. And no matter how weak Gabriel said they were, going one against four with a group calling themselves the Heavenly Regiment didn't seem to present the best of odds.

Not at first.

"Heh. Do you even know who you're talking to?"

A new voice suddenly made the four angels freeze in place.

"You think a bunch of Gabriel's hatchet men are in any position to tell *me* to stay here?"

"Uh...Urushihara?"

Urushihara, clearly just waking up, stared the four angels down as he leaned groggily against the front door.

"Get out of our way."

There was nothing special to the order.

"……"

But it was still enough to make the four angels meekly clear the way.

"Maou, Bell: You're good. Get going. I'll make sure they don't bother you."

"Wh-what is…?"

"Did you forget what kind of angel I used to be, Ashiya?" Urushihara whined, cranky.

Lucifer was one of the Great Demon Generals who commanded his lord's demonic forces. But in another life, one chronicled in the many legends and scriptures that retold his fall from grace, he was the strongest angel in heaven—one who grew so powerful that he attempted to usurp the heavenly throne for himself.

"Before I fell, I was the leader of the archangels. Remember? And maybe I couldn't get away with that in front of Gabriel, but a bunch of Heavenly Regiment foot-soldier lackeys aren't about to defy *me*."

It was difficult for the denizens of heaven to resist an upper-level angel, even a fallen one.

That may have been the case, but the sight of the Heavenly Regiment folding against a fallen angel who slept all day and tapped away at his computer all night brought the quality of the Regiment's recruits into serious question.

"Eesh. You have the worst habit of actually being useful sometimes."

"You don't have to add 'sometimes,' Maou. Just go, all right?"

"R-right! C'mon, Suzuno!"

"Very well. Climb on to the head of the hammer! Hang on tight!"

Through the hole the archangel made, Suzuno and Maou flew off into the early-morning sky.

"Alas Ramus?!"

Emi's eyes were focused high in the skies above Sasazuka.

Alas Ramus charged forward like a heat-seeking comet. Gabriel could do little but defend himself.

"Ow! Owwwww! Agh!"

"Gabriel! Get away from Alas Ramus!"

"I kind of would if I could, but I *can't*!"

Emi's distraction left Gabriel's face wide open—long enough for Alas Ramus to smash right into it.

The collision was almost too painful to watch. It sent Gabriel hurtling into the heavens like a bottle rocket.

"Alas Ramus! You okay?!"

Ignoring Gabriel as he zoomed upward, hand covering the edge of his nose, Emi took Alas Ramus into her arms in midair.

"That's not faaaaair! I'm *way* less all right than *her*, mm-kay?!"

Gabriel whined in pain as he spread his large wings to slow his ascent.

"Ugghhh. I'm not even that good at fighting, either!"

He rubbed the side of his head with his empty right hand for a moment. Then:

"Whoop! Ta-dah! 'I'll be back,' am I right?!"

Emi had trouble figuring out what kind of reference Gabriel was making, but either way, he was clearly ready to ratchet up the battle.

"You're taking a *sword* to that child?!"

"Now listen, lady! Did you think the animal trainers at the circus take on those lions and tigers bare-handed?! I can't be Mr. Nice Guardian all the time, mm-kay?!"

"Oh, so now you're comparing Alas Ramus to a wild animal? I *dare* you to say that again!"

"Come *onnn*! That was just an example! You don't have to start acting like a mama lion on me *now*!"

"Mommy, be careful! That sword's really strong!"

Alas Ramus stood between Emi and Gabriel, as if protecting her.

"Strong? Oh, you bet it's strong! Though, to put it another way, this is getting scary enough that I feel obliged to whip *this* out, y'know what I mean?"

The easygoing tone of voice hadn't disappeared, but even if Alas Ramus hadn't pointed it out, it was clear that the regular-looking longsword in Gabriel's hand was nothing regular at all.

"The sword of Gabriel... Durandal, right?"

"Bingo! You know, this sword... There's no special voodoo magic on it or anything, but it's built to last and it's capable of slicin' and dicin' through just about anything! No fuss, no muss! Probably your Better Half, too, even. Besides, what kind of guardian gets beaten by just one of those fragments? Though I *really* wish she'd surrender. Maybe she's really a Yesod fragment, but slashing up a little girl kinda leaves a bad aftertaste, mm-kay?"

"...And you think that'll make us surrender? You know a villain's about to die when he starts acting like it's in the bag for—"

Just then, a light breeze passed by Emi's side. She felt a small impact on her right hand.

"Well, hopefully we can avoid being *that* clichéd with the script here, mm-kay?"

Gabriel's voice was now behind her.

"...!!"

Suddenly, Emi felt all the holy strength within her drain alarmingly fast.

Her holy sword was now broken at the middle of the blade—not broken, actually, but sheared off.

The residual glow from the sword flickered like a firefly, creating a mirrorlike glow at the edge of the cut. Until it sunk in that it had been sliced in half by Gabriel, Emi found herself unable to even move.

"Mommy!!"

Alas Ramus had the same response, flying over to Emi's side. But the child's only real fighting move was a head-butt.

What was Durandal capable of against *her*...?

"Not that I really care what happens to that sword, y'know. As long as I get the Holy Silver core, the fragment of Yesod housed inside, everything's hunky-dory!"

Gabriel rested Durandal against a shoulder in a show of strength.

"...Ow! Shoot, I cut my shoulder!"

Putting the double-edged, finely honed sword against his shoulder was enough to cut right through his clothing and penetrate skin.

"Hey, Alas Ramus?"

"…Mommy?"

Emi paid no attention to the farce unfolding in Gabriel's direction.

"…Do you like 'Daddy'? Do you want to be with him forever?"

"Uh-huh!"

Alas Ramus reply was immediate and unwavering.

"Oh, but I like you, too, Mommy! I don't want to leave you, either!"

It was oddly touching, how she hurriedly tacked that on to the end.

"Well, good."

Emi nodded lightly.

"In that case, I'm not about to sit and watch a child who loves her daddy that much get separated from him."

Summoning her resolve, Emi funneled her holy force into her sword.

The broken blade gradually repaired itself, returning to its original, Phase One shape.

It was a bit thinner and less sturdy looking than before, but it was enough.

"If it'll make those I need to protect happy, I'll keep fighting all I want!"

"Geh… This is getting really complicated, you know that?"

Emi's show of force was enough to make Gabriel wish he was somewhere else.

"…Try not to see me as the bad guy here, mm-kay? 'Cause I know saying this is gonna make me sound kinda like one."

Gabriel struck a fighting pose, one that seemed to fly in the face of all known fencing styles. But with his speed, his strength, and the honing on his weapon, one hit was all he needed.

"You know that once you lay a hand on me, it's kind of my job to make a serious response to that, right? Just so you're aware of that beforehand?"

"If my choices are 'fight' or 'watch a child cry,' I'll fight anyone, anytime!"

"Look, I know she *looks* like a child, but she's the Yesod Sephirah inside, mm-kay…? Oh, now I'm sounding like *such* a villain…"

No longer willing to listen to Gabriel chide himself, Emi tried to work out a way to win this apparently hopeless battle.

Even when she'd been at full attention, she'd had her sword cleaved in two. A well-timed pattern of strikes wouldn't work here. She had to finish off Gabriel with a single strike…but how could she deal with that speed…?

"Moooove!!"

Just then, someone zoomed in behind Gabriel's back.

"D-Devil King!"

"Daddy!"

"Ngh!"

Maou, now up to lofty heights riding on Suzuno's war hammer, barreled right into Gabriel from behind.

Just as he leaped off of the hammer, Suzuno swung her Light of Iron at the angel.

"Searing Lightwave!"

The shock wave emitted from the head of Suzuno's hammer as she shouted made a direct hit on Gabriel's rear end as he attempted to dodge the hammer itself. Maou, for better or for worse, was still on his back.

"Whooaaahhh!!"

"Aaaaagh?!"

The blow was enough to send Gabriel, his center of gravity up high due to Maou riding piggyback, tumbling end over end in the air.

"Leeeeettt meeeee gooooo!"

"Nooottt haaaappeninnnnng!!"

As they spun like a top in midair, the archangel and Devil King engaged in…something. Whatever it was, as the Doppler effect made their shouting indistinct, it wasn't exactly an epic battle of good and evil.

"Eeeeemiiiii! Hurry uuuupppp! Take 'im down with meeeeee!"

Maou's yell as he and Gabriel continued to imitate a clothes dryer finally made Emi snap to.

"N-no! What are you, stupid? I can't kill you right in front of Alas Ramus!"

"Shuuutttt uuuuuppp!! This's the only chaaaaannce!"

"Hngh!"

"Agh!"

Not even Gabriel was willing to stand this for long.

With about as much effort as it takes to swat a fly, Gabriel peeled Maou off his back and tossed him into the air.

"Daaahh!!"

Maou, his momentum still spinning him around, hurtled away at subsonic speed. It took several seconds for him to begin falling.

"D-Devil King!!"

Suzuno chased after him in chagrin, but she was too slow and too far away to catch up.

"Mommy."

Emi, watching this helpless charade unfold, suddenly found herself under the full attention of Alas Ramus.

"...What is it, Alas Ramus?"

"Mommy, are you always gonna be with Daddy? Do you like Daddy?"

The child had a tendency to ask the most inopportune questions at the most inopportune times.

And after they had that massive argument in front of her, too. And even though she knew full well the difference between regular people and the Devil King.

This farce was enough to bring a smile to Emi's lips.

She didn't want to hurt a child. But she couldn't lie, either.

"I... Yeah. Yeah, we're always gonna be together."

"Really?!"

Emi answered the sweet, innocent smile on Alas Ramus's face with one of her own.

"Really. I mean it."

It, along with her smile, came directly from her heart.

"Until death do us part."

As long as Sadao Maou remained the Devil King.

"Yaaaaay!!"

Alas Ramus gave a sincere, childlike yelp of excitement. Then:

"?!"

Along with it came a shock wave, one that made it feel like an earthquake was rumbling across the air itself.

Suzuno, in pursuit of the falling Maou, was rocked by someone passing by at enormous speed, almost making her lose control of her own flight.

He would have hit the ground by the time she regained control. Or should have.

"Daddy."

But Maou was there, hovering in midair, just a few feet above his landing point.

Or, to be exact, he was stopped by the embrace of Alas Ramus and the ball of golden light around her.

"Alas Ramus... You..."

"Daddy, Daddy, Mommy said she'll always be with you!"

"Huh?"

Maou remained outstretched in the air, unable to parse Alas Ramus's report. He was floating maybe a yard or two above the Villa Rosa Sasazuka front yard, sure, but *this* was a lot more puzzling to him.

"So don't get all lonely, okey, Daddy?"

"Uh, what are you...?"

"I'm gonna be with you and Mommy forever, okey?"

"Uh?"

The simple, innocent words were spoken alongside another unexpected wave of light.

This one was softer, warm like a bunch of feathers, and it whited out Maou's surroundings in an instant.

"So bye-bye for a little bit, okey?"

By the time Maou fell to the ground, his support suddenly taken out from under him, the comet of golden light was already rapidly ascending to the heavens. He watched on from below, incapable of anything else.

He shouted loudly after it, not paying the alighting Suzuno any notice.

"Alas Raaaaaamuuuuuuuuuus!!"

* * *

As if responding to the roar, a burst of dazzling light unfurled itself from high above, soaking in the rays of the sun as it shone a bright silver.

"Gabriel... Sorry to disappoint you, but I'm going with choice number three."

Emilia was there, her silvery gauntlets and leg guards emitting a clear, bright light, like an evening street lit by the full moon.

The right hand bearing her holy sword featured a simple, fingerless gauntlet to prevent the hand armor from butting against the blade's handle. Her left hand featured a much heavier glove, the streamlined pattern on the shield it bore resembling the one on her metallic gaiters.

It was the partial corporeal form of the Cloth of the Dispeller, something that never physically existed before but had now materialized in a mere flash of light.

Outside of the gauntlets and leg guards, she still wore her standard Cloth. But the Better Half grasped by one hand was now whole once more, the edge lopped off by Durandal before now glowing silver.

"Aye yai yai... Ooh, yeah, I guess the Church didn't stop at giving you *one* piece of Holy Silver, did it? I kinda forgot."

Gabriel frowned, his Durandal at the ready.

"I don't see any shard forming the core of your Cloth, but, eesh, no *wonder* that girl was attracted to you. Well, this is just *great*. I wasn't expecting you to evolve it *that* way... We'd better get serious, mm-kay...?"

Gabriel's expression hardened as he prepared for battle, but his words were just as light and airy as always.

Just then, something passed by his side.

"Nagghh!!! Uh? Huh?! What the heck was *that*?!"

A sharp pain ran across Gabriel's back as he shouted.

He had never experienced this kind of pain in his life. To Gabriel— an archangel of heaven who had almost never had a human lay a scratch on him—it was a wholly novel sensation.

"Is…is…is that…?!"

A small, faint, extremely superficial cut was clearly visible on his left arm.

This was a completely unthinkable state of affairs for Gabriel. Just a moment ago, he was clenching his fingers around the Better Half like it was a French croissant.

"…Nice to see angels bleed just as red as we do."

Emi—or, to be more exact, the Hero, Emilia Justina—flicked a drop or two of blood off the tip of her Better Half before turning back toward her foe.

"Leave here at once, Gabriel. I have zero intention of meddling in the affairs of heaven. But even more than that, I don't want to see that girl cry."

Emilia averted her eyes in sadness.

"W-well, it kinda doesn't really *work* that way, mm-kay? …I'm not exactly in a position to just turn around and leave, y'know. How many hundreds of *years* do you think I've been looking for that Yesod fragment?"

"Oh, so you still want to fight me with *that* sword?"

"!!"

Finally, the look of breezy disaffection on Gabriel's face disappeared for good.

Just like what happened to the Better Half earlier, the top part of Durandal, the archangel's sword sung about in mythology, was sheared off.

Adding insult to injury, cracks ran down from the mirrorlike edge of the cut, all the way to Durandal's handle. The next moment, the blade fell to pieces, losing its shape entirely.

"…Well. Guess I just punched my ticket back home, didn't I?"

Gabriel's surrender came far more easily than expected.

"But this doesn't mean I gave up, mm-kay? And I doubt Sariel has, either. Someday, we're gonna bring all the fragments of Yesod back in one place. I'm just giving you a reprieve 'til then, got it?"

"Heh. Try not to sound like such a loser, loser. But I still got a question for you. Like the Devil King said, if you've really been searching for centuries and nothing bad's happened in the meantime, why are you so hell-bent on getting it back now?"

The question left Gabriel agape for a moment.

"...Well, *that's* a surprise. After all that's happened, *that's* what you're asking me?"

"?"

Emilia squinted her eyes in confusion.

"...Maybe it's time you think a bit about what you really are, lady. That, and why we had this little fight just now. You'll work it out sooner or later."

Then, without waiting for a reply to his enigmatic answer, Gabriel raised the hilt of his all-but-ruined Durandal higher into the heavens.

"And I'll hope, when that time comes, that you'll put the peace of the world first. For *real* this time."

Another blast of light emitted from his hand.

"Unless you want the scourge of Satan, the Devil Overlord, to return."

"Wh-what the hell?!"

Maou and Suzuno had to shield their faces against a particularly strong burst of light in the air.

It looked like a gigantic explosion at first sight, but as the light dissipated, they realized that something was falling out of the sky.

Planting a foot on the ground, Suzuno flew into the air, attempting to find a closer look.

"E...Emilia?!"

She quickly realized the falling object was human—and none other than Emi.

She was either wounded, or that previous burst of light had knocked her out. Either way, she was plummeting downward, unable to control her descent. Rolling directly under her, Suzuno managed to catch the limp body before it struck the ground.

"Emilia! Are you safe?!"

Emi seemed unconscious at first sight, but upon hearing Suzuno's voice, her eyes popped right open.

"Oh...Bell... Yeah, I'm fine. Also, Gabriel's gone."

"What?!"

Shocked, Suzuno turned up toward the quickly fading explosion above.

There, she saw just a faint, twinkling light in the air, the Sasazuka sky otherwise back to its normal self. No one could be seen, and Gabriel was clearly out of the picture.

But the sight did nothing to soothe Suzuno's mind.

There was nobody at all up there.

Suzuno and Emi were the only people in the sky.

"Hey! Emi!"

They couldn't see who was shouting from below, but the pained concern was clear in his voice.

"Where's Alas Ramus?"

"......"

Maou, watching Emi and Suzuno slowly descend, found his voice rising.

"What happened to Alas Ramus?!"

"......"

The sight of Emi averting her face to him made a painful sense of foreboding rush down his back.

"He... Gabriel didn't..."

Emi didn't reply. Instead she simply muttered to herself, as if complaining to some unknown presence.

"Ugh... What're we gonna do about *this*...?"

✳

"Yo, Chi."

Just as she was departing from her shift, Kisaki stopped Chiho from leaving.

"Oh, hi, Ms. Kisaki! I'm just about off."

"Sure thing. Good work today. Do you have a moment?"

"Oh, of course. What's up?"

It was nine in the evening. Chiho, beckoned by Kisaki's hand, had a fairly clear guess what the topic was.

"I was just wondering… That little girl you had with her, is she back with her family?"

Chiho resignedly nodded to herself inside.

"Oh, I guess you noticed, huh?"

"Well, you know, he was kinda shambling around out there like a zombie, so…"

She was referring to Maou.

At the dining area and behind the counter, Maou acted like the quintessential puppet with its strings cut. There was no strength to his voice, he made a litany of careless mistakes, and his overall work performance was a far cry from the typical Maou—enough to make Kisaki more concerned than angry.

"And I know we're just gonna have to wait for him to work through his feelings and everything, but that's just… I'm sorry to put this on you, Chi, but if this keeps up with him, can I count on you to maybe give him a little support on the work front?"

"Sure. No problem."

"I know I was just a little bit harsh with him today, but…well, I can't get *too* soft, so…"

"Oh, no, not at all, Ms. Kisaki. I'm sure Maou knows you're just saying all that for his sake. Anyway, see you tomorrow."

"You got it. Be safe."

After leaving Kisaki with a bow, Chiho checked the time and began walking toward Sasazuka station.

Alas Ramus had disappeared.

Maou, seeing Emi fly off with Gabriel and return by herself, was crushed. Heartbroken, was how Suzuno put it, and that was the only window Chiho had into the battle that took place in the wee hours of the morning.

She thought she had come to Villa Rosa Sasazuka early enough for a front-row seat before Gabriel's gang arrived. She hadn't. Instead, Suzuno had shocked her with the words:

"Alas Ramus is...gone away."

Suzuno, Ashiya, and Urushihara sat dejectedly on the stairs, their minds far off in another place. The massive hole in the upstairs wall told the story well enough for them.

Chiho was used enough to witnessing extraordinary events engineered by beings from other planets by this point to realize she was at the scene of a battle.

The fact this apparent early-morning furor wasn't enough to alarm the neighbors or summon the police bothered her a little, but there was no time to dwell on that.

"Um, Ashiya, is this...!"

"My liege is...unhurt. He is resting in Devil's Castle...but he wishes to be alone at the moment."

"What happened to...to Alas Ramus? Did that Gabriel guy do something to her?!"

A sudden rush of concern drove Chiho to bring up Gabriel's name. Urushihara was nonplussed.

"Dude, how should we know? Emilia's kind of off in her own little world, too, so... But it's kinda logical to assume that Gabriel took her and left."

"N-no!"

Chiho's voice was a mix of pain and sadness.

"There was no way to restore my liege's power this time. Not with the Heavenly Regiment guarding us. And I doubt Emilia could have fended for herself against an angel guarding the Tree of Sephirot. Neither of them are hurt, at least, but...as much as it pains me to say, chances are that Gabriel left with her."

"Well, not like *we* coulda done anything about it, right? I mean, that girl was a Yesod fragment, dude. It's kinda natural that Gabriel would want her back in heaven. Besides, it's not like we had any duty to—"

"Urushihara!!"

Chiho bellowed at Urushihara to find his silence.

"Don't *say* anything else! If you do, I...I'll make you regret it!"

"......Eesh."

Urushihara pouted for a moment, but still took the hint.

"...But what's wrong with Yusa?"

"Emilia has already returned home. Apparently she had to report to work. ...I understand that her clothing and belongings were ruined, but how could that girl be so heartless..."

Ashiya's reply was weak and droning.

"You had best go to school yourself, Ms. Sasaki. I'm afraid His Demonic Highness is..."

Ashiya paused to take a pensive look at the hole upstairs.

"...likely not in the mood for conversation."

Chiho followed his eyes upward. Just then, she felt some unknown sensation bubbling up into her chest, something strong enough to make tears well into her eyes.

"I-I'm sorry... I'd better..."

She briskly bowed at the trio, hiding this onrush of emotion, and left the apartment building behind her.

"Alas Ramus..."

She whispered the little apple girl's name on the way to school as another tear came to her eye.

They had only been together for a short while, and yet even Chiho was experiencing a profound sense of loss. She could only imagine how it was for the man Alas Ramus had loved as her father.

*And even at a time like this, I can't be by Maou's side.*

She clenched her teeth at her helplessness.

"...Ooh."

Noticing the phone in her bag vibrating, Chiho wiped away the tear and took it out.

"Yusa?"

It was a text from Emi. It invited Chiho to meet with her, whenever it was convenient.

Chiho replied that she had work after school, only to have Emi say that even late night would be fine, so could they meet up? If she was that insistent, there was no reason to say no.

And now, on the way home from her shift, Chiho spotted Emi inside Sasazuka station.

"Hey, Yusa! Sorry to make you wait!"

"Oh, hi, Chiho. I'm sorry to keep you out. You must be tired."

Emi looked far more tired than Chiho was.

The loss of Alas Ramus must have weighed upon her as well, in its own way.

"Oh, no, it's fine…but what's up?"

"Um… Well, how 'bout we chat inside that Tacoma's Best? There's a table free over in that corner. My treat?"

"Oh? Um, sure, but…"

Emi ordered a coffee blend at the Tacoma's Best coffee shop at the far end of the Sasazuka station mall. Chiho went for an iced soy-milk latte.

Scoping out a table in an isolated nook of the coffee shop, Emi plopped down on the cushioned seat and let out a long, deep sigh before diving straight into the topic at hand.

"So did you hear about this morning from anyone?"

So *that* was it. Chiho nodded solemnly.

"…I went over to the apartment."

"Oh…"

"Um…so, so did Alas Ramus really get taken away?"

"……"

Emi looked even more somber than Chiho, hanging her eyebrows low against her face.

That was what must have happened.

"…If I just had a little more power…"

"Oh, no, Yusa, this isn't your fault…"

"…If I had the power to fight against Gabriel by myself, this wouldn't have happened."

"No, you…you really don't have to torture yourself over this…"

"No. This all happened because I didn't have the strength to do it."

"Mommy, are you okay? You feel sick?"

"Yusa..."

"Chi-Sis! Mommy, are you hurt? Where's it hurt?"

"No, no, I'm fine. Just in the heart, a little. ...Huh?"

"Oo?"

Emi and Chiho stared down at their feet.

"Aaaaggghhhhhhhhh?!!"

Chiho instinctively tried to stand up, bumping her knees and almost toppling her soy-milk latte as she did.

"Ow!"

The blow was enough to send her tumbling to the floor.

"Chi-Sis! You okay?!"

A small, chubby hand patted Chiho's face.

"Alas Ramus!!"

Chiho, still kneeling on the floor, shouted out in surprise.

"What? Why? How?! Why are *you* here right now, Alas Ramus?!"

She looked up at Emi, back turned as she sat, her face clearly red as she rested an elbow on the table.

"Wow! You're okay! That's great!!"

Chiho let out a delighted cheer as she embraced the child.

"Wabpf!"

"B-but why?! Maou and Suzuno and Ashiya all thought that Alas Ramus was gone!"

She didn't mention Urushihara, who largely couldn't have cared less.

"...I never thought *this* was gonna happen, either."

Emi mumbled the response, back still turned.

The way she put it, Emi had felt something strange from her holy sword the moment she saw Alas Ramus emit a flash of bright light.

"Y'know what I did? I ate the sword."

"...Huh?"

Alas Ramus ate the holy sword.

Chiho's eyes nearly bugged out as she attempted to parse the sentence in her mind.

"It was like she just bunched it up like a wad of bread and popped it in her mouth. Could you imagine how much of a panic that put me in?"

"......"

There was no way she could formulate a reply to that, either.

"Anyway, I guess that was her way of 'fusing' it with the Yesod fragment she has. Gabriel and I were shocked. Neither of us knew what had happened."

"I'm with Mommy forever now!"

"So then, I guess those were two Yesod fragments brought together, and the sword is kind of part of my body, so I guess that kinda led to the next thing."

Emi put her hands above her head, attempting to keep Alas Ramus out of sight from the other cafégoers.

"Wah!"

Then, Alas Ramus disappeared into a swarm of light particles.

In the time it took for Chiho to blink in surprise, a beautiful knife had appeared in Emi's right hand.

It must have been Emi's holy sword, but it was wholly different from the one she had before, the purple globe of light around it glowing noticeably brighter.

Then a gauntlet of finely forged silver appeared over Emi's hand, something Chiho had never seen in battle before. Then:

"Mommy, you scared me!"

The sword talked.

"It...talks...? Whaaa?! Is that really..."

"Sure is."

"How do I look, Chi-Sis? Do I look cool?"

"...Alas Ramus became part of the holy sword. And the Cloth of the Dispeller."

Chiho's jaw fell to the floor.

"So...so you didn't tell Maou or anyone else? I mean, you should see how depressed he is right now. He's totally not himself at work."

"Oh, no? Well, huh. Must've really hurt him, I guess."

"Well, *yeah*! You saw how much he liked having her around..."

"Tee-hee... I'm sorry. But I figured I could get away with this much. Besides..."

In another moment, the dagger disappeared from Emi's right hand, and Alas Ramus came back into existence before Chiho's eyes.

"I thought it'd be best if he understood what it meant to lose something a little, too."

Once the glow accompanying the transformation dissipated, Emi gave Alas Ramus a reassuring caress on the head.

"Gabriel went home with his tail tucked between his legs. Not that he could do much. I mean, if Sariel's Evil Eye of the Fallen wasn't enough to pull the sword out of me, what *is*, you know? The last thing Bell and the Devil King saw was Gabriel whining like a schoolboy before diving back through his Gate... But anyway, that's not what I wanted to ask you about."

"...Um? Oh, uh, so what is it?"

Chiho's brain was having trouble keeping up with this conveyor belt of revelations. Emi continued to show her no mercy.

"...So as you can see, Alas Ramus fused herself with my holy sword, so now we're able to move around with a little more freedom."

"Right."

"But—and this is something she said before all of that happened— but apparently she's under the notion that me and her 'daddy' are gonna be together forever..."

There was brief silence. It was followed by a groan from Chiho's side of the table.

"Uhhngh?"

"I mean, the whole day through, all I heard in my mind was 'I want to see Daddy, where's Daddy,' and so on ad nauseam... But if I keep leaving this girl in Devil's Castle, what if something happens then? I won't have my holy sword on me."

"I don't know if I'd worry about *that* first—"

"And the *worst* part, you know, was that Rika was no help to me at all today. She was all freaking out about something, too."

"You mean Rika Suzuki?"

"All through our whole shift... Even afterward, too, she was acting all weird and fidgety, you know? And she kept checking her phone, too."

Emi gulped the remains of her lukewarm coffee blend and brought a hand to her head in despair.

"I can't do this! If this keeps up, I won't be able to work—at the call center, *or* as the Hero! I still have to slay the Devil King, but that would mean having Alas Ramus kill her own 'daddy,' and if I store her in my body in holy-sword form, she's whining and moaning in my mind and I can't focus on anything... I just don't know what to do..."

"Kind of a weird case of postpartum stress..."

Chiho could feel a headache forming as the Hero of the Holy Sword whined apace. None of this was helping her understand the situation at all.

In her mind, Emi owned one of the most envious positions in the world, one which she'd gladly trade places for in a heartbeat.

"I don't know if this is gonna be a solution or anything, but..."

"But what?!"

Chiho continued calmly as Emi nearly leaped off her seat.

"But, um, if you moved into an empty room in Maou's apartment building, that'd at least make Alas Ramus happy."

"Nuh-uh. *Not* happening. That'd make me feel like I lost to him, kind of."

"Yusa, *you* don't have to start acting like a child, too!"

"But, come on—"

"Whee! Moving to Daddy's house!"

Alas Ramus, the apple girl completely oblivious to Emi's anguish or the ways of the grown-up world, continued to pick up solely on the things that mattered to her.

✳

"You're lighting that campfire again?"

Emi and Chiho, visiting Villa Rosa Sasazuka together, stared on listlessly as Maou burned a bunch of *ogara* sticks. The wisp of smoke extended upward into the sky as the western sun just barely peeked above the horizon.

"This is called the *okuribi*, okay? Could you at least *try* to learn a little about Japan?"

"*Okuribi*? Huh. Great. ...So why're you doing that?"

"It's so I can guide the souls of the ancestors I called over here with the *mukaebi* back to their own world. Normally you'd do this at the end of the Obon holiday, but I don't think anyone's gonna care if I push it up a bit."

Maou let out a languid sigh.

Out of the corner of her eye, Emi noticed that Maou's listlessly dangling hand was holding the framed photo they took together with Alas Ramus.

"This is my way of getting Alas Ramus back up there, to...wherever, okay? ...And I guess I wasted my money on *that*, too. Didn't even use it once."

Maou's eyes were pointed at Dullahan II, its yellow plastic child's seat reflecting the white light of another summer sunset.

A light breeze entered the scene, taking up the wisp of smoke and dispersing it into the sky.

"I don't feel like talking to you today. Go away."

"Oh, thanks a lot. I'm here because I wanted to ask you something, okay? And I better get an answer."

"......"

Maou distractedly turned his grimace downward without a word.

"Lemme ask you about that charm the traveler got from the angel. What happened to that once he became king?"

"!..."

Maou let out a soft groan, face still turned downward.

"I just want to know for reference. If you had that planned out, can you tell me?"

"...So that's all? You're just here to screw around with me?"

"Sure. Fine. It's just me, coming over here to laugh at the Devil King while he's moping all by himself."

"You Heroes and angels are just the nastiest bastards, aren't you?"

"Not as much as you demons are."

Chiho silently watched the exchange unfold.

She thought Maou would erupt in rage, but after a few moments, he faintly spoke.

"...Once the traveler became king, he forgot all about the charm. Then a lot of stuff happened to him, and once he was back on the road as just another dusty wanderer, he came across it again. He swore he'd treat it better this time, but...maybe it was payback for what he did as king, who knows, but anyway, someone took it from him, probably."

"Hohhh. Innn-teresting. But he still remembered that it really meant something to him, huh?"

"...Look, what do you want?"

Maou glared at Emi, shooting daggers from his eyes.

But, for her own reasons, Emi was no longer ready to bully Maou around. Her face was a little red, her eyes removed from Maou's.

"...Huh?"

Seeing this made Maou even more suspicious.

"So I think he'll probably treat it really well next time. What do you think?"

"I agree."

Chiho spoke up for the first time.

"What is *with* you two today...?"

Even the normally slow-on-the-uptake Maou noticed they were hinting at something.

"Well, it's not like I know what kind of great treasure this was for the traveler, but if that's how you put it, it must've been really important, wasn't it?"

Emi raised her right hand. It emitted a dull glow.

"Do you know how it feels to lose something precious to you now? If you do, then you better treat it right this time."

Then, a small miracle suddenly unfolded before Maou's eyes.

"Daddy!!"

Maou was astonished to see the little girl appear, as if materializing from thin air in front of the *okuribi* fire. He froze, eyes wide open, like a deer scoping out an advancing minivan on the highway.

"Alas…Ramus…? What on, hang on, how did you…?"

Staggering to his feet, Maou accidentally dropped the photo he was holding.

Alas Ramus, the girl he thought gone forever, was unimpressed.

"Daddy, no! Don't drop it! You'll hurt it!"

She nimbly picked up the picture and held it against her chest.

"Is…? No way, is this for real? Are you really Alas Ramus?!"

Maou fell to his knees on the ground, patting the girl on the head, face, and shoulders as she held on to the photo.

"Eek! Daddy, that prickles!"

Alas Ramus laughed like a puppy in response, grabbing Maou's hand with her own.

"So…there you have it."

Maou paid no attention to Emi's words.

"Wow, so…so he didn't take you away…"

"I figured I'd let you stew in your own juices for a while longer. But Alas Ramus kept going on about seeing her daddy, and it struck me as kind of a 'demon' move overall, so I brought her over here. I hope you appreciate… Wait."

Emi's flurry of excuses was cut off by something that stunned her.

"Are you *crying*?"

"Uh? Huh? Buh?"

Maou brought a hand to his own face. There, for the first time since that day when he thought he'd lose his life, lay a single stream of tears.

"Wh-what kind of Devil King are you? *Crying* like that?! What are you, stupid? Quit it!"

Emi, flustered by Maou's reaction, couldn't decide what to do next. She opted with the safe choice of yelling at him.

"Daddy, are you hurt? Are you hurt?!"

Alas Ramus, also noticing the tears, looked up at Maou, looking about ready to cry herself.

"No, this is just, um, it's like, kind of an accident, and things."

The ex–Devil King tried his best to hide the tears. It didn't work.

"You must be really happy, Maou. I mean, Alas Ramus is back!"

It was Chiho's smile that did all the explaining for him.

"Everyone cries when they're happy like that, you know."

Maou blankly looked at Chiho.

"So, did you learn something new about this world?"

"Chi-Sis, is Daddy okay? He isn't hurt?"

Chiho patted the head of the tearful Alas Ramus.

"He's okay. Daddy's just really happy to see you, is all."

"I'm *not* crying!"

Suddenly, Maou indignantly stood up.

"Wh-who the hell's crying here?! Besides, I knew all that anyway! I'm the father of this girl! And I knew Gabriel and the Heavenly Regiment ran away, too!"

Not even a grade-schooler would put on a strongman act like that in this day and age.

"Wabpf!"

His point made, he then abruptly picked up Alas Ramus.

"We…we even made Alas Ramus's food for today! Yo! Ashiya! Suzuno! We're eating! It's time to eat!"

With that, he ran up the stairs, not even bothering to put out the *okuribi* fire.

"…I'm amazed he could keep the act going for that long. But are they really going to eat in there?"

"I think they'll be eating in Suzuno's place for the time being. They're still gonna sleep in their own room, though. It'd be cooler that way anyway, is how they put it."

"Yeah, that sure sounds like them."

With a wry smile, Emi looked at Villa Rosa Sasazuka's second floor.

Seeing this very Sadao Maou–like reaction, she was forced to admit that there was a sense of relief somewhere in her heart.

The mysteries behind her Better Half sword had only deepened, and she had no idea how the Devil Overlord Gabriel mentioned was involved.

Upstairs, she could already hear Ashiya and the gang exclaim their surprise.

"You know, though...you don't think anyone's gonna call the cops or anything, do you?"

"I was just thinking about that, actually, but...well, it's getting a lot of looks from people, but that place is kinda falling apart anyway, so... Besides, we wouldn't really want the police here anyway, right? All's well that ends well."

"True. And it's not like *I* have to worry about it. I'll need to have Alas Ramus over at my place for a while anyway."

"Mommy! Chi-Sis! C'mon! Let's eat!"

"Whoa, Alas Ramus! Watch out! You're gonna take a tumble like Mommy did!"

Alas Ramus was near the top of the stairs, calling for Emi and Chiho. Maou was just in time to grab her from the rear.

"Come on, join us. Suzuno made it all, so it's not gonna mess you up or anything."

"...What do you think?"

"Well, despite every intention I had, I'm her mother now, I guess. Better keep an eye on her diet."

Emi gingerly began to climb the stairs.

She thought she could feel Chiho snickering to herself as she followed behind. Apparently the act Emi put on was about as convincing as Maou's.

There was no telling what Gabriel meant by his parting words. But as a bona-fide Hero, there was no way she could proceed down the road to ruin. Not if she wanted to preserve the peace over dinner tonight.

For now, at least, she was able to think that to herself.

＊

Tokyo Big-Egg Town

"That child fused herself with Emilia's holy sword?!"

"Yes! Completely! And *boy*, I just couldn't believe it!"

"Goodness. It must have been terrible. But enough about that. I was thinking about finally asking out my goddess, but what do you think!"

"Dahh! Just *once*, I was hoping you'd think about someone besides yourself. Nice to see I'm wrong yet again!"

"Now, now. What do you expect from me anyway? My Evil Eye of the Fallen is useless against her. What could I do to help?"

"A lot less than I was *hoping*, apparently."

"That's, um, really bad news, though, isn't it? The Yesod they call Alas Ramus fusing with the Better Half?"

"That's why I *came* to you! That's why I'm practically having kittens right now, if you hadn't noticed! That's why I'm asking for some advice! Don't you see how much danger this is gonna put us all in?! This is no time to work on your game with the ladies, mm-kay? Ugh! Why did I give that girl even a *moment* of kindness back there?"

"Looks like the opposite sex is giving both of us a few problems, hmm? I'm starting to empathize with you a little."

"Oooooh, I could just *punch* you right now!"

"Ahh, don't get in such a tizzy. What do you think, though? Isn't she beautiful? They used her in one of the paper placemat ads, you know. Those things're going for fifteen hundred yen on ReLay right now!"

"You asked for it!"

"Gah!"

"I *said*, try to act a little concerned, mm-kay?!"

"You don't see any value to this? Pft. Philistine. But Emilia didn't know what she was doing, right? She didn't mean to fuse Alas Ramus with the Better Half?"

"No! Probably not! Why?!"

Late at night, upstairs at the Sentucky Fried Chicken in front of Hatagaya rail station, the archangel Sariel gnawed at a chicken wing and some cold potato wedges as he addressed Gabriel.

"Then perhaps we could avoid the worst-case scenario if we corralled the other 'half.' The second wing, apart from the Better Half."

"...We could. But who can say where that even is—"

"Pfft! I shouldn't have expected you to understand at all. *Someone* has a lot to learn about love between a man and a woman."

"......"

"Hey! Don't just sit there shaking your fist at me! Just think about it for a second!"

"Who?! Sorry I'm so stupid, but I don't know, man! Also, I don't exactly remember hearing about *you* ever successfully finding a girl in your life!"

"Hee-hee-hee! Ah, but all of my experiences come down to right now, this very moment, when I finally bag my goddess... Oww!!"

Without warning, Gabriel slapped Sariel in the face.

"*You* try being the archangel who had to handle all the sexual-harassment complaints filed against you, mm-kay?"

"A-all right! I'm sorry, I'm sorry! Just stop hitting me! I need to put my best face forward for work tomorrow!"

"If *that's* your best face, hon, you got problems. Think about where I'm coming from! I'm the one who couldn't get that sword back, so I'm the one who's gonna have to answer for it. But what if *they* knew that it's all because you're playing demigod Casanova with some human girl, huh? You wanna wind up like *he* did?"

Sariel rubbed his swollen cheek as he ejected a whiff of laughter at the exasperated Gabriel.

"I will do anything—even make the gods, make the whole world, my enemy—to consummate my love!"

"I wish you had a sign or something you could put up to show when you're not being sarcastic with me... So, what? Who is it? Who's this guy with the other half, whom I'd surely know the identity of if only I was such a hot stud like you?"

"Well, who made off with the Yesod Sephirah in the first place? Think about *that* stumper, and the answer should be obvious."

Sariel grinned salaciously as he kept his face guarded.

"One of the wings was granted to his daughter. Who got the other one? Well, who else could?"

Sariel waved a chicken bone in the air to drive his point home.

"Nordo Justina. Emilia's father."

# THE AUTHOR, THE AFTERWORD, AND YOU!

It's surprisingly roomy up there, when you ride a Ferris wheel by yourself.

They took my photograph solo, too, but gave me this picture of some strange man at the end. Who's this guy? Oh, it's the author? Am I obliged to accept that?

If you ever go on a certain Ferris wheel in the city of Tokyo and you catch sight of a school of tuna fish jumping around wearing red glasses, that's just the afterimage of my presence. Enjoy the ride.

The Devil King and Hero hijinks in this volume mainly rotate around the theme of child rearing.

Along those lines, I have a notice and a request for everyone who's been nice enough to read this.

As I wrote this novel, I read through a number of books about Your New Baby, interviewed a few people involved with research into child raising, and even browsed around a few of the "mommy Q&A"-type Web forums.

One thing I learned along the way was that between generations, and even between individual parents, there are huge differences between what people see as right and wrong in child care.

Whether it's what kind of diet to give, what type of baby equipment to use, or what sort of medications are safe for them, there are all kinds of stances people take depending on age, region, or just who they are. Maybe some weird man with no child-rearing experience who enjoys riding Ferris wheels by himself is in no position to say this. But my take-home from my research was that when it comes to child care, there might be such a thing as *better*, but there's no such thing as *best*.

So I'd like to note that the scenes in this book involving young children are just one of the likely infinite number of approaches to child care taken all around the world.

I sincerely doubt that anyone would dare use this novel as their personal alternative to Dr. Spock. But to anyone currently raising young children, I strongly encourage you to take whatever steps *you* see as appropriate, especially when it comes to food and drink.

Also, there's a scene in the book that portrays purchasing sunscreen for children at a drug store in a negative light. Again, though, that's just one take. People are free to take a pharmacist's recommendations along those lines as well. Do it *your* way.

That, and heat exhaustion. Sometimes, that's not something an amateur can take care of with the basic kind of first aid you saw here.

When it comes to keeping your own child healthy in heart and mind, I encourage you to use suitable medical treatment and engage in whatever action is most recommended for your own child's situation.

Also, this volume depicts a group of people with zero experience or even interest in child raising doing their absolute best, occasionally burning out, then doing their best all over again.

Thanks to the earnest support of my readers, as well as the combined efforts of everyone involved with this publication, volume three of *The Devil Is a Part-Timer!* is finally in your hands.

For once, the characters haven't said anything too extremely inappropriate this time. I have no one to apologize to, which is a stroke of luck.

In fact, I've even received an offer to make a comic version of the story, even though I've only been at this for three volumes and just about a year's worth of authorship. It goes without saying that I'm elated by this.

I hope you'll all provide your warmest support to the Devil King, the Hero, and everyone else as their lives grow ever more frugal in the world of manga.

With that, I bid you farewell until the next volume.

THREE VOLUMES INTO *THE DEVIL IS A PART-TIMER!*, AND I'VE FINALLY
BEEN GIVEN THE SPACE TO WRITE MY OWN AFTERWORD PAGE. MY
NAME IS 029, WHICH IS PRONOUNCED "ONIKU" IN JAPANESE. OR
CAN BE.

AS MENTIONED IN THE PREVIOUS AFTERWORD, THE DEVIL KING'S
FINALLY GOING TO BE MADE INTO A MANGA VERSION. WHEN I
HEARD ABOUT IT FROM MY EDITOR, I REMEMBER HOW SURPRISED,
BUT ALSO HOW HAPPY, I WAS. HAVING SOMEONE ELSE BREATHE
LIFE INTO THESE CHARACTERS I'VE WORKED ON... I'M SO EXCITED
ABOUT IT, I'M PRACTICALLY BESIDE MYSELF! I CAN'T WAIT TO HEAR
MORE ABOUT IT. [VOLUMES 1–3 ARE OUT IN ENGLISH NOW FROM
YEN PRESS! —ED.]

BY THE WAY, WE'RE STARTING TO SEE A LOT OF NEW CHARACTERS
SHOW UP, BUT THE LANDLADY JUST DOESN'T WANT TO COME
HOME, DOES SHE? I BETTER CORNER WAGAHARA SOMETIME
SOON AND GET TO THE BOTTOM OF THAT!
(LAUGH)

ANYWAY, I HOPE I SEE YOU ALL IN VOLUME 4.

# ONIKU

THE DEVIL IS A PART-TIMER! 3
SPECIAL END-OF-BOOK BONUS

RÉSUMÉ
COLLECTION

# RÉSUMÉ

Maou, when was this?! —Chiho

**NAME**

## ALAS RAMUS (WRITTEN BY MAOU)

| DATE OF BIRTH | AGE | GENDER |
|---|---|---|

↑A little bit over a year —Chiho (ghostwritten)

**ADDRESS**
VILLA ROSA SASAZUKA #201
SASAZUKA X–X–X,
SHIBUYA-KU, TOKYO

**TELEPHONE NUMBER** Perhaps we should buy her a children's phone shortly. —Ashiya

| PAST EXPERIENCE | |
|---|---|
| | TOKYO UNIVERSITY OR BUST! —MAou |
| | ↑It's hard to tell if you're aiming high or waaaay low with her. —Emi |
| | *You think that's her daddy and mommy? —Chiho →* |
| | ↑No, apparently it was Alciel and Lucifer. —Suzuno |
| | ↑ ?!! —Chiho |
| | ↑NOT THAT I CARE OR ANYTHING. —MAou |
| | ↑Nobody asked you! —Emi |

**QUALIFICATIONS/CERTIFICATIONS**
Everybody loves babies! —Chiho ←That's a qualification...? —Suzuno

**SKILLS/HOBBIES**
being cute —Chiho

**REASON FOR APPLICATION**
in search of her father —Suzuno ←SWING AND A MISS... —MAou

**PERSONAL GOALS**
a happy, healthy family —Suzuno

| COMMUTE TIME together with me —Urushihara | FAMILY/DEPENDENTS | NAME OF GUARDIAN Sadao Maou, Emi Yusa —Suzuno |
|---|---|---|
| ↑And this doesn't give you pause at all? —Ashiya | . | ↑Oooooh, I like it. —Chiho |

↑Come on... —Emi

**NAME**
ALAS RAMUS (WRITTEN BY MAOU)

**DATE OF BIRTH**

**AGE**

**GENDER**

**ADDRESS**

**TELEPHONE NUMBER**

**PAST EXPERIENCE**

**QUALIFICATIONS/CERTIFICATIONS**

**SKILLS/HOBBIES**

**REASON FOR APPLICATION**

**PERSONAL GOALS**

**COMMUTE TIME**

**FAMILY/DEPENDENTS**

**NAME OF GUARDIAN**

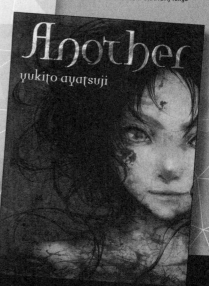